ARE WE THE KLINGONS

R. N. CHEVALIER

Are We the Klingons
Copyright © 2022 R. N. Chevalier

Produced and printed by Stillwater River Publications.
All rights reserved. Written and produced in the
United States of America. This book may not be reproduced
or sold in any form without the expressed, written
permission of the author and publisher.

Visit our website at
www.StillwaterPress.com
for more information.

Originally published in 2015 by Page Publishing, inc.
First Stillwater River Publications Edition.

ISBN: 978-1-958217-70-2

Library of Congress Control Number: [TBD]

1 2 3 4 5 6 7 8 9 10
Written by R. N. Chevalier.
Interior book design by Matthew St. Jean.
Published by Stillwater River Publications,
Pawtucket, RI, USA.

*The views and opinions expressed
in this book are solely those of the author
and do not necessarily reflect the views
and opinions of the publisher.*

For my wife, Donna, and daughter, Jazzy,
my inspirations and motivation.

PREFACE

This is not a *Star Trek* novel. I didn't mean to be misleading in the title. I used the name *Klingon* to show how inbred violence in that society of the future is parallel to the human race of the present. Being a huge fan of the entire Star Trek franchise as are millions of people around the world, I've taken the basic *layout* of the shows to give you, the reader, a mental image to use as a foundation of your imagination in visualizing what you are reading. Even people who are not fans of the shows know what *transporters* and *warp drive* do. These people also know what *phasers* and *tricorders* and *communicators* are used for as well.

I mean only to honor the shows' creator, Gene Roddenberry. Without his vision and persistence, the world would be a much darker place. I mean also to honor the thousands of men and women responsible for making the shows as great as they are. Their tireless efforts have given us some of the most entertaining video in the history of television. This novel also blends two other aspects of our world culture: Roman Catholic religion and Greek mythology. Unfortunately, some of the recorded histories of these two aspects have to be misrepresented, such as timelines and biological lineage. This novel is only to entertain and raise questions and should not be used as a point of historical reference.

So…

Sit back…get in the mood…and enjoy.

1

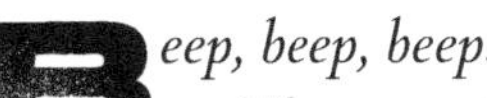eep, beep, beep.

The sound broke the silence, broke the darkness.

A shadowy figure rolled over under the blankets on the bed. The man, his head fogged with sleep and his voice covered in anger, began to wake.

"Open channel!" a voice from the bed rang through the darkness. A dim light started shining brighter from the computer monitor on the desk beside the bed.

"This had better be good!" The man was in no mood to be fucked with, and that was the most evident part of his statement. The face on the monitor took a deep breath and began.

"Bridge here, Captain. We're receiving an incoming message directly from the alliance high council. Ambassador Jacorrian, pro-consul to alliance president J'Darc. Encoded Priority Alpha One."

An alpha one priority message is used in times of total planetary disaster, and this struck the man in bed as odd. To his knowledge, there is nothing going on within the alliance to account for an alpha one priority message. He sat up.

Pipe it through, Lieutenant," the captain said in a more awakened voice.

"Aye, sir," the lieutenant on the monitor responded as his hands slid across the bottom of the monitor and tapped a button on the console.

"Hello, Captain," the new face on the monitor said with a fragment of a forced smile and a voice that almost sounded sincere.

"AtTionne, what is it? What's going on?"

"I'm sorry to wake you," Jacorrian said. The slight smile he showed now faded. "God have I got a mission for you." His tone more serious.

That's when the captain noticed the odd look on the fat sisarcian's face. Odd, even for him. Seeing that look brought the captain's curiosity to attention. "Do go on," the captain said, glaring into his screen.

Captain's log: Stardate 8708.10. My ship has just completed two and a half weeks of external refits and four days of phase-one testing of the new spacefold drive. All preliminary data shows very promising results. We are postponing phase-2 testing until we arrive at a remote star system just inside the neutral zone. Once there, we are to proceed with phase-2 testing and await further orders from Star Command. I am led to believe that the outcome of this mission will directly affect all life on H'Too Bar'kla, the home port of our ship and 95 percent of our crew, and one of the founding members of the alliance.

The door to the turbolift opened on the bridge. From the turbolift, one can see the captain's chair; the science station, where the first officer sat; the helm station, directly in front of the captain's chair; and the right half of the main view screen. The star pattern on the screen was static, showing the ship was traveling on impulse power. The captain stepped off the turbolift and headed for his seat in the center of the room, where the first officer is sitting.

From the corner of his eye, the first officer saw the captain approaching. He turned his head and acknowledged his CO's arrival. He rose from the center seat and moved to his seat on the right side of the captain at the science station.

"Good morning, Captain."

"Good morning?" His voice was thick with puzzlement. "Is it, Lucifer?"

The commander looked back at his captain with an expression of bewilderment on his face.

"What could be so important that Star Command would contact you at two in the morning?"

The captain's finger went up as to let his first officer know that he will respond.

"Helm, set course for Alpha N'barrie six. Warp factor nine."

"The Neutral Zone?" Lucifer asked the captain with a hint of confusion in his voice and an odd look in his eyes.

"Well, number one, all I can say at the moment is that when we arrive at Alpha N'barrie six, we are to await another message from Star Command, and if this mission continues, I'll brief everyone. Until then, I can't say another word…Star Command orders."

"Star Command orders," Lucifer said with a hint of surprise in his voice. "Must be an important mission."

"This mission could have repercussions so severe as to rock the very core of the alliance," the captain volunteered in a lifelessly dull tone that left everyone on the bridge unable to think straight let alone speak.

After an hour's long pause of a few seconds, seconds that could have passed for an eternity, the silence was broken.

"Helm. Engage."

"Aye, sir, we will arrive at Alpha N'barrie six in twenty-two hours, fifteen minutes."

"Number one, you have the bridge. I'll be in my ready room," the captain said as he stood and started walking toward the door at the left side of the main view screen. Lucifer noted that the captain seemed more lost in thought than he did just minutes before. He noted it but kept his opinion to himself.

The night-duty helmsman, Lieutenant Merah, keyed in a command sequence on his control console and the view on the view screen made a drastic turn. The stars that were static on the screen suddenly exploded into multicolored streaks of light flashing across the screen. The inertial dampening field generator on the ship produced a power field that made it possible for the crew to feel no change in the feel of the ship's movement as it increased to a speed of about six trillion miles per second in a heartbeat.

At five decks in height, two hundred and ten feet long, and eighty feet wide (one hundred and thirty feet if one includes the warp nacelles), the ship isn't the largest in the star fleet, but it is the most technologically advanced. It is the only commissioned vessel in the star fleet that is equipped with the new spacefold drive, giving it an unmatched edge in the galaxy.

Captain's log: Stardate 8746.60. The Heaven *has been in orbit around Alpha N'barrie six for sixteen hours. All phase-2 testing of the spacefold drive are proceeding as planned, and the preliminary results are better than we expected. There is an uneasiness aboard my ship, not from the tests, but from the silence of Star Command in response to our request to speak to Ambassador Jacorrian.*

The yellow alert Klaxon screeched through the whole of the ship, waking the captain up from a nap that seemed like it lasted for a nanosecond. "Shit!" the captain said as he jumped up from his bed. "Computer, lights." The lights came on as the captain got dressed with a fluidity of motion that surprised even him. He shook the cobwebs from his brain and took a deep breath. "Bridge. What's going on up there?"

Lucifer answered the captain's hail, a slight nervousness in his voice, "Captain, long-range sensors have detected a ship heading this way. They refused to answer our hails. They're not transmitting a transponder code, and they're masking their warp signature."

"I'm on my way."

The captain exited his quarters still adjusting his uniform. Not watching where he was going, he plowed into a passing crewman, knocking her to the floor. "I'm sorry, Captain," the crewman, an engineer's mate, said from the floor.

"No, Ensign, I'm sorry. I should have been paying attention to where I was going," the captain said apologetically as he held out his hand to help her up.

"Are you all right?"

"Yes, Captain. Fine," the ensign said as she came to her feet. "Again, I'm sorry, Ensign. Carry on."

The captain headed toward the turbolift before the ensign could respond. The door opened just a split second before the captain would have walked into it. It closed behind him just as fast.

The turbolift door opened to the view of the bridge that the captain found so hauntingly familiar. He rushed off the turbolift and headed straight to his chair. Lucifer, seeing him step off the turbolift when the door opened, was already in his proper seat.

"Unidentified vessel at five hundred thousand kilometers and closing," the day duty helmsman, Lieutenant Levi, said quickly with a slight raise in his voice.

"Raise shields," Lucifer said, half-shouting, "and lock phasers."

"Belay that order, Lieutenant," the captain interjected. "Open hailing frequencies."

"Channel open," came from the communications officer, seated behind the captain.

"This is the U.S.S *Heaven* to Proconsul Jacorrian."

The bridge crew looked at their captain in bewilderment. "Hello, Captain," the fat face on the view screen said. "I'll beam over in thirty minutes. Assemble your staff in the conference room then."

"Yes, sir. My first officer will meet you in transporter roo—"

"That won't be necessary," Jacorrian cut the captain off. "We'll beam directly there. You understand?"

"Yes, sir," the captain responded. "*Heaven* out." The captain turned to his bridge crew. "I was under orders not to say a word…I thought you all should know. I'll brief everyone after the meeting with Jacorrian."

The crew resumed their duties, no one saying a word. After twenty minutes, the silence was broken.

"Senior staff, report to the conference room in five minutes," the man in the center seat said over the intercom system. He rose and headed for the door at the back of the bridge, on the opposite side of the turbolift, the door that led to the conference room, a few doors down the hall. Lucifer followed. The door closed behind them.

In the conference room, the captain and the first officer were already sitting down when the rest of the senior staff started coming in. Dr. Anak was the first to arrive, followed almost immediately by Lieutenant Commander Benjamin, the chief engineer. Lieutenant Abaddon, The security chief, came in a few minutes later with Lieutenant Commander Asher, the spacefold drive technical chief.

The captain looked over his department heads wondering how they would take the news. His thoughts were interrupted by the high-pitched sound of a transporter beam.

In the air over the open floor space in front of the wall-mounted viewscreen, blue sparkles started to form out of nothingness. They quickly formed into silhouettes of three humanoids. In a matter of a second, the blue sparkles became three men, standing where just a heartbeat ago was an empty space. The man in the middle is Ambassador Jacorrian. The other two are strangers.

Jehovah and Lucifer stood to greet their guests.

"Welcome aboard, Ambassador," Jehovah said as he reached out to shake hands with the fat sisarcian. Their hands met.

"Hello, Captain," Jacorrian said as they shook. He turned to Lucifer and offered his hand. "Hello, Commander," he said. When their hands separated, he said, "This is Professor Uranus"—he gestured to the man on his right—"of the Alliance Medical Research Complex on Brantax Three, and this is Professor Cronus of th—"

"Of the Alpha Proxima Biological Research Facility," Dr. Anak interrupted as she started to stand and extend her right hand.

"So you know each other?" Jacorrian asked with a huge smile. "Only by reputation," the doctor started. "I'm Dr. Anak. Chief medical officer." They shook.

"It's an honor," Cronus responded. "A pleasure." He smiled as their hands met.

Uranus and Cronus sat in the empty seats at the end of the table while Jacorrian stayed standing in the open area where they beamed down. He stood quietly.

"What's this all about, AtTionne?" Jehovah asked, still informally. "What I'm about to tell you cannot leave this room until you're en route to your destination," Jacorrian began. He had everyone's undivided attention. He took a deep breath as he pulled a padd out of a pocket on his jacket, near the waist. He keyed in a sequence of commands on the padd, and the viewscreen started coming to life. The images were that of war, a distant war, by the looks of it.

"During the third world war on the planet H'Too Bar'kla, the National Libertarian Organization released a neurotoxin into the atmosphere in an attempt to wipe out the other side."

"But the toxin didn't work and the NLO was defeated within six months," Lucifer interjected. He then asked, "What do we need a history lesson for?" AtTionne smiled slightly.

"The only thing that didn't work, Commander, was the antitoxin that the NLO thought would make them immune from the neurotoxin…The toxin didn't do what it was intended to." Jacorrian continued, "What no one ever thought to look for was a different effect."

Everyone looked puzzled.

"The toxin was supposed to kill the population within seven to nine days. When that didn't happen, everyone thought the toxin was a failure, took a sigh of relief and went about life. Well, my friends, here comes the kicker. We discovered that the toxin caused a slight differential in the DNA code of the population of the planet. The generation being born right now is the last generation of the people of H'Too Bar'kla."

Everyone in the room was too stunned to speak. All the room wore the same blank expression of disbelief.

"The entire population of the planet?" Lucifer asked.

"If it were only that simple," Jacorrian said to answer Lucifer's question.

"What could possibly be worse?" Lucifer asked again.

"Since this happened before the discovery of warp drive and contact with other races," Jacorrian replied, "this toxin infected everyone on the planet. Not knowing they were infected, people left the planet. This genetic flaw is predominate in everyone who has ancestry on H'Too Bar'kla."

"Just how many people are we talking about?" Anak asked. "Our best guess…" Jacorrian paused for a second, "approximately one hundred and twenty to one hundred and forty trillion beings spread halfway across the galaxy…and one year to solve the problem."

"What do you mean 'one year to solve the problem'?" Jehovah asked quickly in a moderately harsh voice. The voice of authority. The voice of command.

"I must let Professor Uranus answer that one." Jacorrian motioned to Uranus, sitting at the far end of the conference table. The tall, slim man rose and walked to where the ambassador was standing. Jacorrian moved to sit down where Uranus had once been. Uranus keyed a quick command in the padd he was holding, and the view screen changed from the combat footage to a DNA strand, a gene sequence flashing in red across the strand.

"In one year, this genetic flaw will become prevalent and irreversible," Uranus answered. "At the Alliance Medical Center, I've been working on a new procedure called electrodinucleic transposition. It's been theoretical, until now…We're ready to try it."

"What exactly is electrodinucleic transposition?" Asher asked. "I've read about it," Dr. Anak interjected. "But it is highly specialized, and quite frankly, I was lost for a while in the biotechnical aspects."

"Quite simply, the procedure allows me to transpose a DNA strand from one species to another, changing the second species into the first." He noticed the confused faces in the room.

"As an example," he started, looking at the doctor, "I could take a strand of, oh, let's see…Ambassador Jacorrian and splice it into your genetic makeup. After several treatments of a broadband combination of seventeen different types of thermolytic radiation, your physical blood-and-guts body would become sisarcian. Your mental faculties, your soul if you will, would remain unchanged. Now, during the transposition, the genetic flaw would be isolated and corrected. You would then be transposed back to Bar'klaan, and while you were converting back, we would correct the damage in the DNA, and you would be cured.

"Amazing," the chief medical officer muttered as she began to fully comprehend the significance of this procedure.

After a few moments of silence the captain spoke, "What does this have to do with us?" He was looking at Jacorrian.

"Yours is the only commissioned ship in the star fleet that has spacefold technology," Jacorrian replied. "How are the tests going, by the way?"

Jehovah replied, "Better than we anticipated."

"Nine years ago," Jacorrian explained, "we sent out specially equipped probes. These probes carried the most advanced sensors we had. These probes could scan for anything. They had specialized communications arrays. They were designed to travel and warp nine point six, five for ten years before exhausting their fuel. They were sent out to scan for new lifeforms."

"The Outreach Program," Asher cut in. "I was part of the probe design team. My first assignment right out of the academy."

"Eight months ago, we discovered a planet on the far side of the galaxy at the tip of a spiral arm, that has just what we're looking for," Jacorrian stated.

"And what is it we're looking for?" Lucifer asked sarcastically. "A planet with an indigenous life-form that we can genetically manipulate to suit our needs," answered Jacorrian. "Unfortunately," he continued, "it would take close to eight years at warp nine to reach it. With the new spacefold technology, it will take about a minute."

"So what's your plan, AtTionne?" the captain asked.

"We are going to send two teams of geneticists and two teams of biologists to the planet that the probe landed on. We've named that planet 'Terra.' There will also be an eight-man monitoring team set up on the fourth planet, named Mars, for security purposes."

"Security for whom?" Benjamin asked. "Just what are you planning on doing? Steal their DNA?" Everyone was getting upset now.

"Whoa, whoa. You're getting the wrong idea. If you'll let me finish explaining, everything will become clear," Jacorrian said. It took a minute, but everyone in the room calmed down, and he continued, "The Outreach probes had very narrow scanner beams for a more detailed picture rather than incomplete data of a larger area. We don't know if there are going to be any other inhabited systems around. If a ship approaches, we want you to have warning. As for how we obtain the genetic samples…Let me finish, and that one will be answered."

"I'm sorry," Benjamin said apologetically. "I didn't mean to jump to the wrong conclusion."

"Let's try not to let it happen again, shall we?" Jacorrian countered.

Everyone eased up and were humbled quickly.

The ambassador sighed. "The scans from the probe," Jacorrian began again, more calmed this time, "indicate the life-forms to be a primitive species, very near primate. Maybe even simian. The research teams, under the direction of Professor Uranus and Professor Cronus here, will work scientific miracles of magic and bring back a large enough supply of uncontaminated DNA to save the future of H'Too Bar'kla."

"Can't we just get a DNA supply from one of the known races around here, alliance or otherwise?" Security Chief Abaddon asked. "Unfortunately not. There is a unique combination of reno-amino-clades in the Bar'klaan DNA that no other race in the known galaxy has, save one."

"The ones on Terra," Lucifer answered himself.

"The ones on Terra," Jacorrian reiterates. "It is by a miracle that the probe crashed, and one of those beings got so close we could do a DNA scan. Because they have the same combination of reno-aminoclades, the Bar'klaan race at least has a fighting chance."

"And what happens to these…Terrans because of what we do?" Abaddon asked quickly.

"Theoretically…" Cronus cut in to explain, "they will lack a higher reasoning ability, and they'll have an increased tendency toward extreme violence. They will also have improved creativity, and their evolutionary processes will be increased by ten times. These factors will make them very free-spirited and independent. They will be impossible to contend with in the future."

"That's 'theoretic'?" Asher commented aloud. Everyone laughed. Everyone except Lucifer whose facial expression was showing disgust. "Who the hell do we think we are? Who are we to manipulate the evolution of these beings?" he asked with astonishment and utter contempt. All eyes were on him. "I mean…what gives us the right to play god with these beings?"

"Certain concessions need to be made in order for our race to continue," the captain interceded. "Can you sit back and let your race become extinct and not do anything about it."

"Not at expense of another race. We did this to ourselves," Lucifer said, anger slight in his voice. "Why should they suffer?"

"Why do you think they would suffer, Commander?" Asher asked. "We would be advancing their evolution. Think of it…a million years of evolution in the span of a thousand."

"Would the change be exactly as it would if we didn't interfere?" No one answered. "Then answer me this, Doctor, how do you plan to manipulate the DNA to be usable for us?"

"In vitro fertilization," Cronus answered. "We'll use sperm from our men and the eggs from the female protohumans, and they will carry the babies to term. With each new generation, there will be advances in the evolutionary processes. The percentage of change from generation to generation will determine how long this will take."

"According to Ambassador Jacorrian," Anak stated, "we only have one year to complete the mission." Cronus nodded in agreement. "And it would seem to me," Anak continued, "that for a project of this nature, you can't use a female egg until the being reaches puberty."

"And your point is?" Cronus asked Anak, and he made it. "Last I heard, it takes slightly more than one year for a female to reach puberty. Has there been a breakthrough in growth acceleration that I am unaware of?"

"I haven't gotten to that part yet," Jacorrian interceded. "Exactly how much more is there, AtTionne?" the captain inquired. "I think this is it," Jacorrian responded. "We don't know how long the gestation cycle is for these protohumans, so that factor will be part of this larger one. The planet orbits around its sun every sixty point zero eight minutes, and the planet rotates once every nine point eight seconds. So…"

"For every minute that passes for us will equal about six days for them," Asher said, somewhat stunned by his own words.

"Exactly," Jacorrian said. "For every hour that you are there, they will have a full year pass. And for each year, the protohumans will age eight thousand, seven hundred, and sixty years."

"And what happens when we land on the planet?" Abaddon inquired. "Will we get caught in their temporal realm?" Everyone except the proconsul looked at him strangely.

"Very good, Lieutenant," AtTionne said. "Not many people comprehend temporal mechanics. And yes is your answer." He looked around the room and continued, "When the probe entered the outer orbital path of the eleventh planet, it passed through a temporal barrier. It was like increasing the speed of a movie right in the middle. If you pass through the barrier, you will fall into the same temporal realm. Part of the inventory you'll be picking up at starbase two, six, nine is a supply of temporal discriminators. One will be made available to everyone, and there will be one for the ship as well as surface structures. With these discriminators, you will be able to interact with the inhabitants, in their time frame, while staying in your own. To them, you will be immortal. Technologically, you will seem like gods."

"This still is not right," Lucifer cut in when he could. "With all due respect, sirs, we don't have the moral or ethical right to do this!" He was getting angry now.

Jacorrian stared at Lucifer coldly and started, "The morality and ethics issues are not for us to debate. That is better left to those who are skilled in those areas. We are here to carry out a mission. Ordered by your superiors. I'm sorry if this conflicts with your beliefs, but I need to know if you can handle this…If not, I'll have you replaced and reassigned. Nothing more will ever be said of it, and there will be no notation in your permanent record." He looked around the room. "That goes for everyone here…and on the ship."

After a second or two, Lucifer said, "That won't be necessary, sir. I'll deal with my beliefs on my own. They won't interfere with the mission."

"That's good enough for me, Commander," Jacorrian responded. "Shall we continue?" He turned and faced the captain as a smile grew. "When this meeting is over, this ship will make her way to starbase two, six, nine." He handed the captain the padd he's been holding since he arrived. "Here are the names of the passengers you will be taking on and the cargo manifest. You will then spacefold to within two solar days of the Terran system, just in case there is anyone there, we don't want to give them spacefold technology. When you get there, set up the monitoring station on Mars, then head to Terra and begin. Professor Uranus will have command of the mission aspect, but you, Captain, will have overall command.

"It's a simple enough plan, but so much can still go wrong. Godspeed to you all. We'll see you tomorrow at starbase two, six, nine, Captain. We really must be going now."

Everyone rose as the three men who beamed over moved to the spots where they beamed aboard. The proconsul flipped open his communicator and said, "Jacorrian here, three to beam over."

The three men started to turn into the familiar blue sparkles as the annoying high-pitched hum that accompanied the transporter beam resonated through everyone's ears. In a second, the three men were gone as was the annoying hum and the blue sparkles.

"Let's get under way to starbase two, six, nine. Maximum warp." The captain said as he headed for the bridge. The rest of the staff headed back to their departments.

As soon as the transporter completed its cycle, Jacorrian quickly headed for the control console. He hit the communication controls. "Jacorrian to bridge. Get me the Atlantis. On a secure line."

"Yes, sir" came from the console speaker.

In about a minute, another sound came from the speaker. "Atlantis here. Go ahead, AtTionne."

"Captain, you are to leave at once for the Terran system. We might have problems with some of the crew. If there should happen to be any problems, you are to secure the samples and eliminate everything. Like it never existed."

"Understood" came from the speaker. "We're on our way. Out."

CHAPTER 2

Captain's log: Stardate 8777.60. After nearly ten hours, we are finished loading cargo for our yearlong mission. All forty-one research team members are on board. There is a feeling of nervousness as we make final preparations for departure. The nature of this mission, the importance of our efforts, leaves each crewman bewildered. We can only do our best to ensure the greatest chance for success.

The communications and tactical consoles on the bridge of the USS *Heaven* were abound with activity. Departments were checking in as loading was being completed. Mission checklist reports were being made, and the mission specialists were checking in. Lucifer seemed to be on top of everything in the captain's absence. "Starbase two, six, nine to USS *Heaven*. All systems checked and confirmed. You are cleared for departure" came a voice over the ship's intercom system.

"Acknowledged, starbase two, six, nine. *Heaven* cleared for departure," replied lieutenant Kohath, the *Heaven*'s day-watch communications officer. "All stations show green. Confirmed. See ya next year."

The doors of the turbolift opened.

"Are we prepared to begin this little adventure, number one?" the captain asked as he made his way toward his seat in the middle of the bridge.

"We just received departure clearance from starbase two, six, nine, sir," Lucifer responded.

"Very good," the captain replied as he sat in the big chair. "Helm. Ahead, full impulse."

"Aye, sir," responded Lieutenant Levi, the helmsman of the watch, as he pressed a series of buttons on his console. "Heading away from starbase two, six, nine at full impulse."

"Hold our position at two million kilometers." The captain hit the intercom control on the armrest of his chair. "Spacefold control room. Set coordinates for Terran system."

"Coordinates set and confirmed" came the voice from the space-fold drive control room located at the aft section of deck one, about midway aft of the hull, in front of the spacefold drive manifold.

"Stand by." It took about a minute and a half, then he said, "We are two million kilometers from the base, sir."

"Engage spacefold drive," he said into the intercom. "Spacefold drive…engaged," Lieutenant Commander Asher said from the control room.

Suddenly, the main view screen showed a scene of visual intensity and psychological awe. Within a nanosecond of the spacefold drive activation, the static star pattern on the screen started to fold horizontally in seven equal sections, reversing every other fold, so as to give the appearance of four screen-wide tunnels connected bottom to top, bottom to top. Then, in an instant of an instant, the folds collapsed onto themselves, as all of space seemed to become two-dimensional, horizontal to the ship, leaving white streaks from where the stars were to where the stars are.

Then in another instant of an instant, the horizontal string of stars rushed to and engulfed the *Heaven*. Again, white streaks appeared from where the stars were to a place very far away from the ship. The color shift in the star streaks caused nausea in those who could see them because the change was so fast that the optic nerve could not translate the data to the brain fast enough.

From the spacefold drive control room, the view was somewhat different. Looking out of the control room, one see the spacefold drive manifold and all of space behind the starship. Because it faced aft, the streaks of stars lasted a heartbeat longer. The large window facing aft gave an unobstructed view of the manifold, and the airlock to the starboard side of the window gave direct access to the hull and manifold.

A technician monitored the spacefold drive unit from the control room while Asher controlled it from the secondary control system on the bridge. Since this was the first activation of the spacefold drive, Asher decided to engage from the primary control console in the control room.

From the control room, the spacefold drive unit seemed to glow an eerie blue-green light. This light slowly engulfed the ship like a light fog rolling over grassy plains. Then as the power level increased to the point of being capable of folding space, a ring of bright white light emanated from the spacefold drive manifold, staying a meter or so above the manifold in a horizontal position. Ensign Urania, one of the spacefold drive technicians working in the control room, saw the light ring she commented to Asher that it looked like a halo over the unit.

The color shifts were more prevalent from this aft view. Since the stars were shooting off in that direction, one could see them for a split second longer than the people on the bridge. The sickness was also more prevalent from this view for the same reason.

In what seemed forever but was, in fact, just twenty seconds, the streaks of light became stars again for a nanosecond, and the whole spacefold effect reversed itself.

The stars shot forward into a horizontal line of light. Then the stars unfolded themselves into equal sections across the screen. The sections unfolded, and on the view screen were stars in an alien tapestry laid out before them. The captain found it nearly incomprehensible that in twenty seconds, they traveled nine thousand light-years. It would take nearly ten years at maximum warp to get home.

"Set course for the Terran system. Warp factor three," Jehovah said after a few seconds.

"Course laid in, Captain," Levi said after keying in the command on his console. "ETA is forty-two hours, fifteen minutes."

"Very good. Engage."

The static star pattern on the view screen suddenly became the familiar streaks of blue and red blurs that were associated with warp drive. The rest of this trip should be uneventful.

"You have the bridge, number one," Jehovah said as he rose from his chair and headed toward the turbolift. Lucifer nodded without saying anything and stood to assume the seat, now unoccupied. The turbolift door opened just as the captain reached it. He stepped inside and the door closed.

Zero, eight hundred hours brought the regular bridge rotation in. Only fourteen hours until the ship arrives in the Terran star system. Jehovah stepped onto the bridge after the turbolift door opened.

"Report."

"All stations report normal. Nothing out of the ordinary," Lucifer said from his science station.

"Excellent" was the captain's response as he sat down. "Lieutenant Kohath," he continued, "open a channel to Professor Uranus."

"Aye, sir," the communications officer said as he manipulated the proper controls on his console.

"Uranus here" came a voice over the intercom system. "Professor. Jehovah here. We're fourteen hours away from the Terran system. Have your people started separating the equipment going to Mars so it will be ready when we arrive?"

"Yes, Captain. We just started. We'll be ready long before we get there. I'll contact you when we are finished."

"Very good, professor," Jehovah confirmed. "Be advised, professor. I'm going to make the announcement."

"Understood, Captain…Out." Uranus said, and the intercom went silent.

"Put me on shipwide intercom, Kohath."

"Aye, sir," Kohath replied and manipulated the proper controls. "All set, Captain."

Jehovah sat up a little straighter, a little more formal. "All hands, this is the captain. May I have your attention, please?" he began. After a slight pause, he took a breath and continued. "I am now authorized to fill everyone in on the mission ahead. We have traveled these nine thousand light-years from all we know to save the future of H'Too Bar'kla. Our history tells us that toward the end of the third world war, the NLO released a neurotoxin into the atmosphere, and because it didn't work, they lost the war. Well, that's not entirely true. "Recent data, discovered quite by accident and authenticated, shows the toxin did work, just not the way they planned. What didn't work was the antitoxin they developed for themselves. The toxin changed the genetic makeup of every person on the planet. No one escaped contamination. Now that change has taken its toll. Every child of Bar'klaan decent, no matter where in the galaxy they are, will be the last generation. The toxin manipulated the DNA and caused sterility. Unfortunately, no treatment for this sterility can be implemented. If a treatment did exist, we wouldn't be here right now. In three years, this manipulation will be irreversible, and the Bar'klaans will extinct as a race.

"We are here because the accidental crash of a probe revealed that the third planet of the system ahead is home of a protohuman race with DNA similar enough for us to use. Taking the DNA from a race we know is not possible for reasons that are beyond me. We must go to the planet Terra, genetically alter the evolution of the protohumans until we can harvest enough DNA to save everyone afflicted. All one hundred and twenty trillion.

"The planet we are going to has a solar orbit of sixty point zero eight minutes and a planetary rotation of nine point eight seconds. This means that for every minute that passes for us is equal to six days on the planet surface, and for every hour that passes for us equals one full year for the planet's inhabitants. There is a temporal barrier that's encompassing this system. We will need to wear temporal discriminators while within the system.

"Star Command didn't want a panic, so I was ordered not to tell anyone until after we folded space. Don't let the scope of the mission overwhelm you. Just do your duties the way you were trained, and I've no doubt we'll have a successful mission. Out."

The rest of the day went by uneventful. At about eighteen hundred hours, a message came in from cargo bay three.

"We're just completing the last of the equipment transfers into cargo bay three. Everything going to Mars will be ready in about thirty minutes."

"Very good, professor. We should be arriving at the Terran system in approximately four hours. Just relax for a while."

"Understood. Uranus out."

In cargo bay three, ensigns Erato and Clotho, two crewmen on the Mars monitoring team, were securing the last of the equipment for the team. They were nearly finished the inventory.

"Ya know," Clotho started as she checked a crate to the inventory list on the padd in her hand, "this really bugs the shit out of me."

"What's that?" asked Erato as she did the same thing.

"Us going to this planet and fucking with the evolution of those beings."

"Don't you understand the situation?"

"Oh yes. I do understand. But why should we mess with them? They didn't do anything to us. It's just not right."

"Yeah, well, I still believe in the greater good."

In the mess hall, Dr. Zeus and Dr. Hera were having coffee. Both doctors are heads of the teams of geneticists under Professor Cronus. The conversation they were having had familiar overtones.

"What do you think about this?" asked Zeus as he rose the cup of coffee to his lips.

"I think this is the greatest challenge of the ages," Hera said. "I can't wait to get this mission started. I'm so excited I can hardly contain myself." She smiled as she squirmed a little in her chair.

"I feel exactly the same way. This is such an awesome mission," Zeus added as he stroked the white hair of his beard. As he did this, Ensign Chanani, a ship-assigned biologist, was passing by. He stopped and looked at Zeus.

"How can you say that?" Chanani asked, his face showing a look of disgust. "How are you going to be able to live with yourselves? If I had known what this was about before we left, I would have asked for a transfer."

"Why?" Hera asked, an inquisitive look on her face. The biologist sat with the two geneticists.

"We are about to genetically alter this race. Change them forever. What gives us the right to do this? We're not gods."

"To them, we will be," Zeus said with a smile forming on his face.

"That's one of the things that makes this mission so exciting," Hera said with a gleam in her eye that could not be hidden. Her face was covered with a huge smile.

"That's not the point," Chanani continued. "We have no idea what kind of psychological trauma this is going to cause. What if it drives the entire species insane? What if they suffer irreversible cellular damage?"

"Oh well," replied Hera. "They're not like us. They're barely human. They only live a few months by our standards. If that's true, then their life cycle is so inconsequential that they could never be a benefit to the galaxy."

"What are you saying, Hera?" Chanani's tone getting a bit more serious.

"I think what she's trying to say," Zeus interjected, "is that these Terrans aren't worth a flying fuck!" His tone was rising as his smile grew. He snickered as his hand lifted to his mouth. He took a long sip of his drink.

"Fuck you!" Chanani said to Zeus, loud enough for everyone in the mess hall to hear. "And fuck you too!" he said to Hera as he got up and walked away. Zeus and Hera started laughing, for a long while.

The captain hit the intercom control on his computer console. "Bridge, here," Lucifer's voice echoed through Jehovah's quarters. "I need to speak with you, Lucifer. Would you come to my quarters?"

"I'm on my way, Captain."

It was a matter of about seven minutes.

Beep, beep, beep. The doorbell caught the captain's attention at the second chime.

"Enter." The door opened, and Lucifer stepped inside. "You wanted to see me, Captain?"

"Come in, Commander. Have a seat." He motioned for the man to sit with a sway of his right hand. "As I was coming to my quarters, I inadvertently overheard three crewmen discussing something. I was reminded of our meeting with the ambassador."

"And what would that be?"

"You brought to light certain issues you had about this mission. How are you with those issues now?"

"I still don't like what we're about to do, but I will do my duty then follow protocol when we get back. I won't jeopardize the outcome of this mission. I know the importance."

"I'm glad to hear that," The captain said. Then he continued, "And that's what I heard the crewmen discussing. And they weren't the only ones. In your estimation, could people's negative feelings for what we're about to do put this mission at risk?"

"That's hard to say, but it is possible," Lucifer offered. "To be on the safe side, I think it would be prudent to keep an extra eye out for a while."

"I'm afraid I have to agree, number one. We need to come up with a plan in case anything should happen."

"I'll come up with a rough draft as soon as possible. We'll iron out the details later," Lucifer said as he rose and headed for the door. With less than thirty minutes until the *Heaven* reaches the Terran star system, everything was proceeding as planned. The first officer's contingency plan was approved by the captain and implemented. Only the two highest-ranking officers on the ship and the ship's security team knew what that plan is. The captain ordered the issuance of the temporal discriminators to all on board, and each person was assigned their unit.

The ship flew through space now at six hundred million kilometers per second, much slower than the spacefold drive that brought them to this place.

CHAPTER

Captain's log: Stardate 8824.85. Just over forty-seven hours ago, we folded space to this location and are now in scanner range of our target: the Terran system. The anticipation is building, as is the discontent some members of our crews are having, over the upcoming hours. Now…the mission begins.

"Long range sensors detecting ten primary planets orbiting a medium yellow star. Six planets have satellites orbiting them," Lucifer said out loud from his science station on the bridge.

"I'm only interested in data on the star, the third planet and the fourth planet. Store data on the other seven planets in the database," the captain replied.

"Aye, Captain," Lucifer responded. "Switching secondary scanners to the two innermost and the five outermost planets," he said as he set the controls. "Primary sensor readings of the star are coming in," Lucifer stated. "The diameter of the star is one million three hundred and ninety thousand kilometers at the equator. The mass is one thousand nine hundred and eighty-nine to the thirtieth power kilograms. The core temperature is fifteen million degrees Celsius.

The surface temperature is six thousand degrees Celsius. The composition is as follows…ninety-two percent hydrogen, seven point eight percent helium, and less than one percent of the following…oxygen, carbon, nitrogen and neon."

"Helm, set standard approach vector to bring us into orbit around the fourth planet."

"Aye, sir. Vector set," Levi responded. "We are one point five million kilometers from the outer planet. ETA is seven point two five minutes."

The captain keyed the intercom button on his chair. "Professor Uranus and Dr. Cronus, please report to the bridge," he said into the speaker.

"Cronus here, Captain" came a voice over the speaker. "I'm on my way."

Then another voice sounded through the intercom speaker, "Uranus here. I'll be there in a minute."

"Lucifer." The captain turned to his science officer. "Activate the ship's temporal discriminator."

"Discriminator engaged, Captain" came the reply.

In less than three minutes, the turbolift door opened, and the two men called to the bridge stepped out.

"Ah, gentlemen," Jehovah said with a smile, "I thought the two of you would like to be up here when we enter the Terran star system."

"Yes…thank you," both men said nearly simultaneously as they loosened up just a bit.

"We will be entering the system in four, three, two—" Levi started but was interrupted. The bridge was bathed in a red glow, and a siren started blearing. "Sensors showing a barrier of chroniton waves. We're entering it." The whole ship vibrated. "Now," Levi finished.

"Thank you, Lieutenant. Slow to one-half impulse." The captain said.

Levi replied, "One-half impulse, aye. We are now in the Terran star system. We will enter Mars orbit in eight minutes."

The eight minutes seemed like eight hours to the people on the bridge. All eyes were on the main view screen as a small blue dot came into view in the center of the screen. Even from the distance they were at, the bridge crew could see lush vegetation and blue oceans. From space, it looked like paradise.

Lucifer started with his analysis aloud, "Planet diameter is six thousand seven hundred and ninety-four kilometers at the equator with a mass of six thousand four hundred and twenty-one to the twenty-third power kilograms. It orbits the star at two hundred twenty-seven million nine hundred and forty thousand kilometers, and the orbit takes twenty-eight hours our time.

"The mantle is composed of silicate rock as is the core. The core temperature is three thousand five hundred degrees Celsius. The planet has an oxygen-nitrogen atmosphere, suitable for breathing. Gravity is one point one of Bar'kla. Scans show rich mineral deposits and an abundance of sea life, but no surface life. There is a high concentration of radiation in the atmosphere."

"What's the cause of the radiation?" Jehovah asked.

And Lucifer continued, "Planet-wide nuclear Armageddon."

"That could explain the lack of humanoid life," added Dr. Cronus.

"It's already come and gone. The planet healed, the humanoid life didn't. What a waste."

"Destruction always is, Doctor," Jehovah said. "Continue, Lucifer."

"The closest satellite has a diameter of twenty-two kilometers with a mass of one point eight to the sixteenth power. Orbital distance is nine thousand kilometers and orbits every twelve seconds.

"The furthest satellite is twelve kilometers in diameter and has a mass of one point eight zero to the fifteenth power kilograms. It orbits at a distance of two thousand three hundred kilometers with an orbital time of seventeen seconds. Both moons are barren rocks with absolutely no value whatsoever."

"Tactical…report," Jehovah said without removing his eyes from the planet on the view screen.

"Sensors show no other ships in the area," Lieutenant Simeon, the day-watch tactical officer, said as she continued translating the data that flashed on her monitor. "The closest star system is four point three light-years away. There are no residual warp signatures, no abnormal neutrino emissions, no residual graviton waves, absolutely no sign of a space-capable civilization anywhere within sensor range. No sign there ever was."

Lucifer started again, "After analyzing the orbital path of the two planets. Data shows, a small section of the fourth planet is constantly facing the third planet. That would be the ideal location for the communications array."

"Any objections, gentlemen?" Jehovah asked the two men standing beside him with the smile of a politician.

"No. Not at all" came from Cronus.

"As good a place as any, I guess," Uranus responded.

Lucifer stepped in quickly with a voice filled with sarcasm and said, "Correction, Professor Uranus. It is the best place on the planet." Everyone on the bridge smiled. Most had to stop from laughing.

"Let it be known," Uranus came back with the same sarcasm and slight smile. Now everyone on the bridge was laughing. That lasted slightly more than a few minutes.

The captain, first officer, Professor Uranus, and Dr. Cronus all stepped onto the turbolift together, still laughing. Before the door closed, the captain said to Lieutenant Kohath, "Have Dr. Anak meet us in transporter room two. Then contact transporter room one and have them beam down the cargo and personnel for the Mars monitoring station to the coordinates locked into Commander Lucifer's console…Lieutenant Levi, you have the comm."

"Aye, sir," slipped through Levi's mouth as the turbolift door closed, and the unit sped off. Levi locked the ship into a geosynchronous orbit above the coordinates that will be home of the monitoring station and took the center seat.

In transporter room two, the landing party was getting the gear they would need on this away mission. Each man was assigned a type one phaser except for the two security officers, Lieutenants Gabriel and Michaels, who received type-two phasers, a communicator and a tricorder.

Everyone was in the transporter room adjusting their gear on their belts when Anak came in. He grabbed his gear from the top of the transporter control console and secured it to his belt as he stepped onto the transporter pad.

"Sorry I'm late. Had a slight emergency."

"Oh?" the captain resounded with sarcasm in his voice.

"Hey, I had to piss. What the fuck." Both men smiled as the landing party dissolved into glittering blue sparkles then faded into nothingness.

After the transport was complete, Lieutenant Commander Benjamin, the ship's chief engineer, who was also the one responsible for beaming the landing party to the surface, shut down the transporter control and quietly went back to engineering. He knew it would be some time before anyone would want to come back up. The sparkling effect began waist high in the middle of a sundrenched glade by a glistening blue lake. The blue lights quickly became the seven men of the away team. Just minutes later, crates and building supplies began to materialize ten meters away.

The seven men on the surface began to fan out with their tricorders in hand, scanning the alien landscape that lay before them. The men stopped to form a circle roughly fifty meters in diameter, and in the center of their circle is a pile of supplies and people that is growing with each transport cycle.

"Sensors showing nominal radiation," Cronus reported. "I'm reading the same thing," Uranus volunteered. "Marginal reading over here, Captain," Anak shouted.

"Good," Jehovah said as he raised his eyes from his tricorder and looked around. "Very good…I'm showing low readings as well." By the time the men finished with the sensor scans, all eight members of the monitoring team were on the surface starting to set up the foundations for the buildings that will be their homes for a while. Now the members of the research station were beaming down to assist.

The captain, first officer, and the doctor started walking south, away from the encampment toward the lake. In a matter of minutes, the three men seemed to be alone.

"This is a beautiful planet," Jehovah said admiringly.

"Yes," Anak agreed. "It's hard to believe this place was devastated by a nuclear holocaust."

"Doctor," Lucifer interjected, "the war that devastated this planet occurred more than a millennia ago."

"Well," the doctor answered back, "it's still a beautiful planet." Two hours later, the three men of the *Heaven* approached the glade where they beamed down. Instead of a peaceful glade, they found a small community already standing. The crew quarters were up as were the mess hall, medical facility, and monitoring station itself. All the buildings were cube-shaped and were connected by short enclosed walkways.

"I guess the burdens of space travel took more of a toll than we estimated. I'd swear we weren't gone for more than twenty minutes." The captain noticed.

"Welcome back, gentlemen," Uranus said as he approached the men. We were getting ready to send out a search party." He continued jokingly, "Did you enjoy your two-hour vacation?"

"Where are all your people, professor?" asked the captain. "Most are setting up equipment in the buildings, and a few are setting up the communications array just over that rise." He pointed to a small mound of dirt about two meters tall, looking almost like a grassy dune. "The rest of the complex should be ready in a few hours, then it'll be beamed down. We'll need a few more hours to get those sections secured and operational. We should be done by morning. Has the orbital sensor platform been deployed yet?"

"Excellent, professor," Jehovah said as his hand reached around to his back, and he brought it back to the front holding his communicator. "And yes. The platform was deployed when we finished with your supplies. We're going back to the ship. Contact us when you're ready to power up your energy matrix."

"We'll be ready in about thirty minutes."

"We'll be standing by." Jehovah flipped the lid of his communicator open, raised the black box to his lips, and spoke, "Jehovah to *Heaven*. Three to beam up."

"Acknowledged" came Kohath's voice through the speaker.

The captain closed the antenna grid and started to place the device back on his belt where he got it. Before he could secure it in its proper location, the three men started to sparkle and slowly fade away in a shower of glistening blue light.

Uranus turned and walked toward the laboratory section of the habitat wincing from the annoying high-pitched whine that accompanied a transport.

Entering the corridor from the transporter room, the doctor turned right and headed toward sick bay. The captain and the first officer took a left toward the front of the ship, and the turbolift.

"I'll see ya after duty," Jehovah said to Anak.

"See ya later," Anak echoed back.

Rounding the turn to the right at the end of the hall, the two walked the few meters to the turbolift entryway. A lift was waiting to take the two men to the bridge. It took less than five seconds to get to the bridge, and when the door opened, the men stepped out and assumed their duty stations.

Jehovah tapped some controls on the armrest of his chair. He started reading through the information that came up on the small screen above the controls. It took a few minutes, but he wasn't in any hurry.

When Lucifer arrived at his station, he began analyzing data in the raised view screen on his console. He channeled the data to the science lab where, during day watch, Lieutenant Phinehas, along with Ensigns Ahijah and Malcham, would analyze, categorize, and catalogue all the incoming data. They would then store it in the appropriate locations in the ship's library computer for easy access by the departments that need it.

"Incoming message from the planet, sir." Kohath's voice broke the silence of the last twenty minutes.

"Patch it through," he responded. "Uranus to *Heaven*. Come in, please."

"Go ahead, professor."

"Ah, Captain…we're ready for power initialization down here."

"All right, professor. Just a few seconds." The captain turned to the tactical officer, Lieutenant Simeon. "Initialize a focused, low-level tetryon beam. Channel it through the main deflector dish and send it to the power matrix on the surface."

"Yes, sir," she said and began keying in the proper sequence of commands. "One more second and…" She keyed the final sequence, and a white beam jetted out of the navigational deflector dish, located in the nose of the ship, and headed toward the planet.

On the planet, a white beam pierced the clouds and made contact with the circular-shaped plasma collector five meters from the monitor room. Every room with a window that faced the energy matrix glowed in an eerie incandescence that everyone noticed.

The lights on the control consoles started blinking to life. In seconds, the lights stayed on and the humming sounds of functioning circuits filled the room. The lights came on in every room. The air circulation kicked in. Gauges on the consoles started showing data.

"Energy level at thirty-seven percent and climbing," Ensign Hygeia said as she monitored the power indicator on the matrix control console.

"Excellent," Uranus said with some enthusiasm. "Excellent." A smile started to form on his face.

"Levels now at eighty-five percent," Hygeia informed the room.

Five seconds passed. "Levels now at one hundred percent. Ten seconds more will do it."

"Captain Jehovah," Uranus said into the station's long-range communications console.

"Yes, professor. What is it?" echoed through the complex. "Please discontinue tetryon beam in three, two, one."

On the count of one, the white beam ended as abruptly as it had arrived.

"Cronus here, Captain. Our power is holding at one hundred percent. Thanks for the assist."

"Our pleasure, Doctor. Notify us when you are ready to beam up."

"We'll need about thirty minutes to assist in the calibration of the sensors. We'll contact you then."

"Very good. We'll be standing by. *Heaven* out."

"The transporter room reports Professors Uranus and Cronus are aboard, sir," Kohath said to the first officer, who was in command in the captain's absence.

"Thank you, Lieutenant," Lucifer said while watching the planet on the view screen. "Helm, set a course for Terra, one-half impulse."

"Course plotted," Levi said as he pressed a series of buttons on the lower right side of his console. He shifted position, keyed in a few more commands, and said, "One-half impulse puts us at Terra in twenty-five minutes."

"Good, good…Engage."

"Aye, sir." Levi hit a final button, and the ship slowly and smoothly lurched forward, escaping the gravitational pull of Mars.

Fifteen minutes into the journey, the turbolift door opened, and the captain stepped onto the bridge. Lucifer seemed surprised.

"What are you doing here, sir?"

"Couldn't sleep…Uranus and Cronus will be here momentarily…I've in—" The sound of the turbolift door opening cut the captain off midway. Uranus and Cronus stepped onto the bridge. "I've invited them for the first look at Terra," Jehovah finished.

"Hello, Captain," The two men said nearly in sync with each other. "Approaching planet Terra in seven minutes. Lucifer said from his duty station. "Data should be coming in momentarily."

On the main view screen, a blue dot appeared near the center of the screen. As it grew bigger, everyone could see the white mist of the clouds in the upper atmosphere as well as the green of the lush jungles and the yellow of scattered desserts. The ocean's blue still dominated the planet. The planet has a large portion of ice covering its southern pole, but a small amount of ice at its northern pole. Spread out across the continents are rows of gray mountains.

"Data coming in now," Lucifer began. "Planet is twelve thousand seven hundred and fifty-six kilometers in diameter at the equator. Mass is five point nine seven six to the twenty-fourth power kilograms. Distance from the sun is one hundred and forty-nine million six hundred thousand kilometers.

"Crust is composed of silicate rock. Planet has molten outer core of nickel and iron and a solid inner core of the same material. Core temperature is four thousand degrees Celsius. Surface temperature is on average of sixteen degrees Celsius.

"The atmosphere is composed of seventy-eight-percent nitrogen, twenty-one-percent oxygen, and one-percent argon. There is also carbon dioxide present as well as trace gases.

"There is one satellite in orbit at two hundred thirty-nine thousand miles. Its diameter is two thousand one hundred and sixty miles at the equator. Its mass is eighty to the tenth power kilograms. It's composed of inert matter, essentially a great rock in space though sensors show that at some point in the distant past, this rock supported an atmosphere. Destruction seems to have been caused by meteor impact…There is one curious fact."

"What's that?" Uranus was the first to ask.

"The satellite has no rotation," Lucifer responded. "And that means?" Cronus asked this time.

"That means from the planet surface, the inhabitants will only see one side of the satellite as long as the orbit doesn't change."

As the planet rotated on its axis, the two scientists on the bridge were looking for a place to begin the great experiment. Then they saw it.

In the northern sector of the continent is a moderate size ocean. Several hundred miles to the south is a long skinny ocean. In between are two rivers. The rivers form a delta at their southern end, on the northern shore of the long skinny ocean. Approximately fifteen kilometers to the east is a mountain range, and to the west about twenty-five kilometers is a much larger river, several thousand kilometers long. At the southern edge of this river is another mountain range. Upon closer inspection, the entire region is within a large crater with the eastern and southern ranges showing more predominately than the northern and western, but they are there.

"Look there," Cronus said with a shout of excitement. He was pointing to a spot between the two rivers. "In the delta region…see? Just to the west of the mountains."

"I see it. It looks like the Tigris, Euphrates River valley, where life began, on H'Too Bar'kla."

"The delta would be the perfect location for a controlled testing ground. We could establish our laboratories in the mountain range, away from the indigenous life-forms. We couldn't ask for a better location," Uranus said.

"I agree," Cronus replied.

"Lucifer, scan the delta for life-forms. Helm, put us in a geosynchronous orbit above the target area."

"Aye, sir" came from Levi as he did what he was ordered to do. "Scans show approximately forty humanoids in the delta. Sensors are reading encampments. Two of them. All forty are stationary in the region. There are also approximately sixty other biological signs in the area. Sensors make them out to be quadruped. An altogether different species. That's it."

"Well," Jehovah responded. "We have about forty humanoids in the delta region. That's one hell of a start. We just saved months of reckon work."

"The gods must be smiling down on us," Cronus said softly. "Scan the mountains along the region of the delta for a suitable location for the lab complex," after a few seconds Lucifer answered.

"There is a plateau a thousand meters up. It faces the delta. It is right here." He hit a button on his console, and the image on the main view screen changed. A white outline surrounded a section of the mountain range fifty kilometers north of the mountain's southern end, at the beginning of the delta. The area within the square outline suddenly grew larger, and its magnified image covered the entire screen. The image showed a barren snow-covered plateau beneath a forest of rain driven by harsh winds, surrounded on three sides by shear drops and the fourth side, the side opposite the delta, is a mountain still rising into the clouds. "No need to worry about unwanted guests," Cronus commented.

"The plateau is one point five kilometers deep by seven point three eight kilometers long. The mountain on the back side continues up for six kilometers, and the drop on the three sides is slightly over half a kilometer straight down. Or up, depending how you look at it. Nevertheless, it is quite impenetrable." After a few more seconds, Lucifer continued, "It is the only plateau in the target area… There will be one problem."

"What would a mission be without problems?" Lieutenant Simeon joked.

"What is it?" The captain asked with a giggle in his voice. He found the tactical officer's statement amusing.

"The composition of iron and nickel in the mountain will make communications to the Mars monitoring station impossible."

"Why is that?" Uranus asked.

"Because the mountain extends upward for six kilometers, the iron and nickel will absorb the energy of the subspace signal. By the time the beam cleared the mountain, it would be too weak to escape the gravity well, and it would bounce off the ionosphere and hit the ground again."

"Any suggestions?" Jehovah asked, looking at Lucifer.

It took a minute, then Lucifer said, "Aim the signal from the plateau to a ground-based relay. From there, beam it to Mars." Everyone shook their heads in agreement.

"Put me on ship-wide intercom, Kohath," Jehovah said. "Ready, sir," Kohath replied.

"All hands, this is the captain. We are now in a geosynchronous orbit over the plateau that will house Olympus Station. All team members under the command of Dr. Zeus and Dr. Hera, report to transporter room two. All team members under the command of Dr. Hermes report to transporter room one, and all team members under the command of Dr. Poseidon and the rest of the support teams report to cargo bay three. Captain out."

In cargo bay three, Dr. Poseidon and his team, along with the rest of the support teams, such as the cooks and maintenance crews were gathered. Professor Cronus came in.

"Ladies and gentlemen, thank you for getting here so quickly. In a few minutes, components of the complex are going to be beaming in. It is our job to assemble these complex units and beam them into location on the plateau so other teams can get them operational. The environmental control room will be the first, we'll get ready. Then we'll do the command module and energy matrix module, then crew's quarters. Dr. Poseidon, will you man the transporter controls, and the rest of us will get building?"

Everyone started moving around, and Dr. Poseidon went to the transporter control unit in the far left corner of the room.

"Why are we assembling the structures here?" asked Ensign Nemesis, one of the station's computer technicians.

"Oh yes. I'm sorry," Cronus said. "The plateau is about half a kilometer up, and we don't have enough environmental suits on board…One of those little things we didn't think of."

"And how many more little things are there going to be?" She was a little nervous now thinking this was the beginning of the end. "Don't you worry about things you can't do anything about.

This is not some big crisis or conspiracy. Just do your job, and everything will be all right." As she walked away to help with the unit assemblies, Cronus said under his breath, "Fucking melodramatic bitch."

Poseidon slid his fingers over the controls, and a floor panel materialized in the center of the room. Within seconds, there were two more. All three were in a row separated by a centimeter. Dr. Apollo and Ensign Hygeia walked over to where two of the panels met. They both held up a square body laser rifle. Standing across from each other, they both took aim at the same spot at one end and fired. A blue beam fired from the barrels of both rifles and met in the centimeter gap between the two panels. The two moved the beams toward the opposite end of the panel. The seam left behind from the beams was nearly invisible.

No matter what job you end up doing in the Star Command, every cadet learns how to use a gamma welder in the academy.

Dr. Hestia and Ensign Notus did the same thing at the other panel. When all four people were finished welding the seams, Poseidon activated the transporter, and a wall appeared directly over the seam that was just welded. Ensigns Eros and Iris took hold of the wall to prevent it from falling over.

When the transport was complete, Poseidon activated it again, and a second wall appeared over the other seam. Ensign Fama and Lieutenant Morpheus held this one. The four people with gamma welders stepped onto the floor panels, each standing on the different sides of the two walls. They fired simultaneously and fired from one side to the other.

This same procedure went on for the outer walls as well as the roof. Team members were rotating the welding tasks, so everyone did a fair share. Once the structure was welded airtight, internal components were beamed into place. Several team members secured and connected the life support equipment in the center room. Other members were setting up computer equipment in the command module to the left while the remaining members were setting up the energy matrix in the right module. Work was steadily and smoothly going along.

An hour and a quarter later, the three-module unit was assembled inside and out. All that was needed was a power charge to the matrix, and the unit will be self-contained. Poseidon beams the unit to the plateau on the surface. Another unit was under construction within seconds. This one housed the kitchen, briefing room, and the commander's office. That went down in nearly the same amount of time.

Once the two units were side by side on the surface, three men in environmental suits beamed into the energy matrix module. They were Dr. Hermes along with Dr. Demeter and Ensign Eris. The doctor and the ensign were carrying gamma welders, and Hermes had with him a portable power unit. As the doctor and the ensign welded the two units together, the professor went to the energy matrix and connected the portable power unit to the matrix.

It took several minutes before enough energy could be absorbed into the matrix. As soon as the light in the room came on, he left the portable power unit connected to the matrix and left the module. He went into the life support module and activated all the equipment.

The air processor kicked on first, and the hiss of air flowed through the vents into all six modules. The heating unit came on next, and the flow of warm air could be heard. The pressurization unit came on last. In four minutes, an indicator on the control panel indicated the modules were ready to be lived in. The professor deactivated his environmental suit and slipped it off. He adjusted his uniform, then headed to the command module.

Once in the command module, he activated the computer systems. They hummed to life in seconds. He tapped the commands on the communications console and spoke, "Hermes to *Heaven*. Olympus Station activated."

Eris and Demeter entered the room, environmental suits left behind. They could hear the cheers of the bridge crew over the station's intercom system. The three smiled.

The hum of the transporter could be heard coming from the energy matrix module. Dr. Athena and Ensign Hecate entered the command module. "Hey there," Athena said happily.

"Hello, Athena, Hecate. Did you two come down alone?" Hermes asked.

"No," Athena answered. "Lieutenant Morpheus came with us to get the kitchen ready. Ensigns Hecate and Eris are outside gamma-welding the third unit in place. Ensign Notus is activating the rest of the computers throughout the nine modules."

"Excellent," the professor said. "This is going along much smoother than I ever thought it could." In the time it took to get the three units secured and operational, another unit was beamed down, and the work progressed. Professor Oceanus, the lead researcher of the biology division, and Professor Coeus, the lead researcher of the genetics division, beamed directly to the commander's office to begin ironing out the details of the mission ahead.

In transporter room, two doctors, Zeus and Hera, were awaiting instructions with their team members. Professor Uranus came in.

"Thanks for being patient everyone."

"What's going on, professor?" Zeus asked.

Everyone else mumbled in agreement with Zeus, wanting to know what's happening.

"Settle down and I'll explain. We've been given the tough job.

We get to go to the delta region and get it ready."

"Is that all?" Hera interjected, smiling.

"Well," Cronus stated, "just consider that on the plateau, it is cold, windy, and barren. In the delta, it is a warm fifteen degrees Celsius and sunny. All we need to do is set up force field units along the northern tree line, set up the station, and do some preliminary surveying."

"Well, what are we waiting for? Let's go," Hera replied.

Professor Cronus, Dr. Hera, and Dr. Zeus stepped onto the transporter pads, along with Dr. Hephaestus, Dr. Artemis, and Ensign Hades, all members of Dr. Zeus's team. The transporter operator slips his hands over the proper controls, and the six faded into glowing blue sparkles.

The sparkles became people in seconds. They stand facing a line of trees in front of them at thirty meters or so. They stepped forward fifteen steps, took out their tricorders, and began taking scans of the area. The next group materialized where the six were standing. Before the cycle was complete, everyone reported.

"I'm reading seven life-forms…humanoid…Twenty meters beyond the tree line," Ensign Hades informed the now twelve people on the surface.

"My scans are picking up three humanoids and two quadrupeds. One of the animals' heart rate is nearly stopped…Now it has stopped. The humanoids must be hunting for food. They are fifteen meters beyond the tree line," Dr. Artemis reported.

The six team members who just beamed down spread out to enjoy the scenic beauty of the delta region. They started scanning the area for everything from electromagnetic radiation to geological formations. The last five team members beamed down within seconds followed by the equipment needed to set up the Eden camp.

Force field arrays and generators are among the cargo being sent down, as were sensor and scanner equipment and a portable cloaking device for the field labs.

The field labs were beamed down fully assembled, thanks to Dr. Poseidon and his research team in cargo bay three. Since the units for Olympus Station were complete, they decided to assemble the Eden camp lab units.

The four segments came down one at a time, and thanks to

Lieutenant Commander Benjamin's expert transporter techniques, they were all beamed down in place. Ensigns Zephyr and Boreas of Dr. Hera's team secured the four segments with gamma welders.

As the two men welded the structures together, Dr. Aphrodite led a team of four, including herself, to the tree line with the force field arrays. The doctor and Ensign Dionysus went to the west end while Ensigns Aeolus and Polydeukes went to the east end, a span of twenty-six kilometers.

When Aphrodite and Dionysus arrived at the Euphrates River's edge, they set the force field array up a meter off shore. Aeolus and Polydeukes did the same at the shore of the Tigris River. The field generators and power supplies were hidden in the water just behind the arrays.

"Aphrodite to Aeolus," she said into her communicator as she stepped onto the shore from the river.

"Aeolus here. Go ahead" came from the speaker in the little black box.

"Are you all set to go?"

"Affirmative. Ready to engage power supply."

"Understood…Out." She closed the antenna lid and placed the communicator on her belt. She nodded to Dionysus who was still in the water, and she leaned over and flipped a switch on the field generator. A low-level hum came from the array as it started glowing blue. The same was going on at the other end after Aeolus flipped the switch at his end.

"Aaarrrggghhh!"

The sound could be heard from every direction. It echoed loudly everywhere. Back at the lab, everyone stopped when they heard the scream. After a few milliseconds, Professor Uranus pulled out his tricorder and aimed it in the direction of the scream.

"It came from the tree line," he said and started running in that direction. Several of the team members followed. When they arrived at the tree line, they saw it lying on the ground, obviously injured.

The humanoid was about a meter and a half tall and looked to weigh about fifty kilograms. Its entire body is covered with hair which more closely resembled fur. The protohuman's head is larger than the people standing over it. It has a protruding lower jaw with very large teeth. No team member could determine whether the creature was a male or a female. In its state of unconsciousness, it made grunting noises that didn't help in determining the sex of the creature.

"What happened?" Professor Hera asked when she arrived. "Readings show it apparently got caught in the force field when it was activated," Uranus said, looking up from the tricorder.

Dr. Hephaestus went into her medical kit and took out a hypospray. She keyed in a sequence using the three tiny buttons on the top of the unit. She put the nozzle on the neck of the humanoid and pressed the larger button under the three little ones. The hissing sound, denoting the injection, could be heard by everyone. Almost instantaneously, the protohuman's eyes opened wide. It sat up and started screaming wildly. All those standing there jumped back in surprise.

Dr. Hephaestus keyed in another sequence using the small buttons on the hypospray. She injected the humanoid in the neck, and it instantaneously passed out. The Star Command personnel relaxed. "This creature has no permanent injuries. It'll wake up soon with a nasty headache, but that's all," Uranus said after another scan with the medical tricorder he was holding.

"Hera to Olympus Station," she said into her communicator. "Go ahead, Doctor," replied a voice through the speaker.

"We have an unconscious humanoid here. Beam it directly to the sick bay. Leave it unconscious and begin detailed medical scans. Under no circumstances are you to allow it to regain consciousness. Got it?"

"Got it, professor."

In an instant, the hairy humanoid vanished in a mist of blue sparkles.

"By the time we get to Olympus Station, we should have a total workup of the protohuman and have a good idea on how to proceed with the mission," Hera said to Uranus.

"Good idea, professor," he told her as the group started walking back toward the laboratory complex half a kilometer to the north.

By the time the group returned, the four who went to set up the force field units had also returned.

"Where have the group of yours been?" Aphrodite asked. "And did you hear that horrible scream?"

"We went to investigate that horrible scream," Uranus told her. "What was it?" Aeolus asked before anyone else.

"It was one of the protohumans…It seems it was right in the path of a force field beam and was pretty badly stunned," Hera slipped in the answer.

"Did you get to see it?" Aphrodite asked in amazement.

"See it?" Hera stated. "We got it. It's at Olympus Station now."

"When will we get to see it?" Aeolus asked with obvious eagerness and anticipation. The other three had the same look.

"When the Eden station is completed and the communications relay is built, we will go to Olympus to begin the preliminary studies of the creature," Uranus told them.

"All we have left to do here is power up the systems, and Eden will be ready," Ensign Zephyr, who remained behind to complete the station setup when the others went to investigate the scream, informed them.

"Very good," Uranus said as he pulled his communicator out from behind his back. "Uranus to *Heaven*," he said into his little black box.

"Go ahead, professor," Lieutenant Rueben, the night-watch communications officer, said from the orbiting starship.

"I'm ready to beam up and meet with the captain, and Eden is ready for power," he informed the lieutenant.

"Understood," was the reply.

As the glowing white beam broke through the clouds, Professor

Uranus faded into the nothingness of blue sparkles. When the transporter cycle was complete, the professor heard Dr. Zeus inform the captain that the station was powered up to 100 percent. The message was broadcast over the ship's internal PA system so everyone would know how the mission was progressing.

Uranus met with the captain in the observation lounge, located at the rear of the ship, directly above the hangar bay. The two were standing in front of the wall-size window at the far end of the room generally used to watch ships arrive and depart from the starship. From this window, the area of the planet that the crews were working on was visible.

"I've been thinking about our problem with the communications relay, and I have a pretty far-out solution."

The captain stood silent.

"I figure our primary problem would be what would happen if the humanoids found the relay," he continued. "Take a look at the river to the west of the delta. We could establish the relay on the opposite side of the river so in the event any of these protohumans escape from the control area, they may not find it."

"And what if they should cross the river?" Jehovah asked.

"I've been thinking about that as well," Uranus went on. "Housing the transceiver in a deutronium casing would prevent any kind of scan. In fact, scans would show nothing but a solid mass. We would also construct a huge statue of a Pentarrian lion in a guarding stance over it."

There was a brief pause.

"I'm talking about a statue so big that when the first protohumans see it, after we leave, they will be struck with such awe and terror that they'll never go near it, never mind try to figure out what it's for. I know it sounds a little off the wall, but I think it'll work."

"You're right," The captain started. "It is off the wall. Way off the wall, but it just might be strange enough to work. Grab a few laser cutters and some antigravity cargo haulers and get it done. The transceiver is in cargo bay four, and you can take some of Dr. Poseidon's team to assist in the construction. They are off duty now. I think some may be in the forward lounge."

"If we could have access to a portable transporter unit, we could be done within forty-eight hours," Uranus said, but also half-asked.

"You'll find the portable unit in cargo bay one."

"Thank you, Captain. We'll be finished as soon as possible." He left the room quickly, full of energy and enthusiasm.

"Hey, Poseidon," Uranus shouted from across the lounge. Poseidon raised his glass in acknowledgement of Uranus's shout. He walked to the table where Poseidon is sitting and joined him.

It took about fifteen minutes for Uranus to lay out the plan to Poseidon. He took a few minutes to think about what was just presented to him then agreed to help. He went to the communications console mounted on the wall by the door.

"Poseidon to all off-duty team members and support staff, report to transporter room two on the double." he said into the microphone. The two men left the forward lounge and headed for transporter room two.

It took less than five minutes to assemble everyone in the transporter room. Poseidon and Uranus walked into a full room. When the men walked in, all the attention was shifted to them, and everyone got quiet. Uranus positioned himself in the middle of the twelve others.

"There is one more thing to be done before we can begin our mission. Olympus cannot maintain its communications array because of the composition of the mountain range."

"We constructed the array and beamed it down to Olympus several hours ago," Dr. Apollo informed Uranus. Everyone looked confused.

"We are going to construct a communications relay station away from the mountains," he told them.

"Where are we going to put it?" Ensign Nemesis, a research assistant, asked.

"We're going to the opposite side of the large river to the west of Eden. There is a flatland area perfect for the site."

"And what happens when the humanoids reach the other side of the river?" asked Dr. Hestia. "With the genetic manipulation, they will be prone to unprovoked violence. Won't they destroy it?"

"Well," Uranus begins with a smile forming across his face. "We will be constructing a housing, in the form of a statue, for the relay station."

"What kind of statue?" Ensign Iris interjected. Uranus took a breath.

"The statue will be of a Pentarrian lion in a guarding pose."

"It will have to be big to frighten anyone," Iris said again.

"Rough calculations will put it at twenty meters tall and seventy-three meters in length."

"Yeah, that would just about do it," she replied. Everyone giggled. "The stones for the statue will come from a quarry several hundred kilometers to the south," Uranus continued. "We'll use a portable transporter unit to move the stones from the quarry to the statue.

The stones will be cut with laser rifles and set into place with antigravity units."

As he walked up onto the transporter pad platform, he turned to the group and said, "For all of you who haven't heard yet…About an hour ago, the team setting up the Eden station managed to capture one of the protohumans. It is on Olympus undergoing intense study as we speak." Everyone muttered among themselves in excitement. "When we're finished with the relay station, we will be going directly there."

As Uranus stepped onto the platform, Lieutenant Commander Benjamin came in with six laser cutters. He handed them to the first six he saw then replaced Poseidon at the transporter controls. Five others joined Uranus on the platform. Before the system was activated, Uranus looked at Benjamin. "Beam the others to the quarry.

Poseidon will join them as well. When they are all down, beam down the portable transporter unit from cargo bay one to the coordinates we're going to, then send down two sets of antigravity units, the communications relay system, power supply unit, and twelve sheets of deutronium with a gamma welder."

"Will do," Benjamin replied as he passed his hand over the controls and made the six people on the platform disappear. As the next six stepped onto the platform, he entered the new coordinates and beamed them down. Poseidon went down last. Benjamin then began to beam down the equipment Uranus asked for. In less than ten minutes, he was finished and on his way back to engineering.

"Uranus to Zeus. Come in, please," he said into his communicator as the rest of his team scanned the area with their tricorders.

"Zeus here. Go ahead" came from the speaker. "How is Eden station coming along?"

"All we need to do is power up the energy matrix and calibrate the computers, and we'll be open for business."

"Excellent. Send Hera's team to Olympus. Keep your team there to continue work. Contact the *Heaven* and have them power you up."

"Affirmative. Out."

Uranus looked over the lay of the land for the best position for the statue they were about to construct. The crewmen were starting to report in with their findings.

"Nothing unusual to report, professor…just rock, dirt, water, and primitive vegetation," reported Ensign Notus. The other four reported the same. Several reported primitive animal life but no humanoids.

Beep, beep, beep.

Uranus's communicator sounded to let him know there was an incoming message. He took the device out from behind his back and flipped the antenna grid open.

"Uranus here," he said into the device.

"This is Ensign Hypnos. We are ready to start cutting the stone. We just need to know how big you'd like them to be."

"Yeah. I guess that would help. Make them a meter tall by a meter wide by two meters long."

"Very good. Hypnos out."

During Uranus's conversation with Hypnos, all the equipment Uranus asked for materialized ten meters away. From what Uranus could see, everything he needed was accounted for. He walked over to the portable transporter unit and activated the system. The lights came on and the deutronic circuits hummed to life. The rest of the crewmen came around the transporter unit. Dr. Apollo and Ensign Notus picked up the gamma welders while Professor Uranus operated the transporter and beamed the sheets of deutronium into position. When the welding was near complete, there were two huge hollow squares with one wall missing on each. Ensigns Eurus and Iris grabbed two antigravity cargo haulers. They locked them into place on the communications relay and carried it into one of the boxes. After it was set down and the antigravs taken off, Ensign Hygeia went in and activated the relay. The two with the antigravs locked them onto the energy matrix and set it into the other box.

"Uranus to *Heaven*," he said into his communicator. "We are ready for you to energize our energy matrix."

"Roger that…Stand by."

Within seconds, a glowing white beam shot from the sky and hit the energy matrix. When the beam was shut off, Ensign Bakbakkar went into the box and set the power relay dish on a forty-five-degree angle aiming upward. He stepped out of the box.

"Energy matrix is powered up and the relay dish is set," Bakbakkar informed Uranus.

"Okay," Uranus replied. "Seal up that box."

Notus and Apollo went to the box with the gamma welders in hand. Uranus beamed the final wall into place, and the two men sealed it in place.

"We're finished," Apollo said when the wall was sealed. "Acknowledged," Uranus said as he activated the transporter unit. The sealed box faded into nothingness.

"Where did you beam the power matrix to?" Apollo asked. "It's ten meters underground," Uranus answered. "We'll start building the right foot over the matrix." Apollo simply answered, "Okay."

Uranus's communicator beeped again. "Uranus here."

"Poseidon here. We have fifteen blocks ready to be beamed to your location."

"Understood. Contact me when you have fifteen more."

"Will do. Out." Uranus activated the transporter, and fifteen blocks appeared spread out in front of the unit where he was standing.

Ensigns Eurus, Iris, Hygeia, and Bakbakkar walked over to the pile of rock blocks each carrying an antigravity cargo hauler. Eurus and Iris attached their antigravs to opposite ends of the first block and Hygeia and Bakbakkar did the same to another block. When they activated the antigrav units, the blocks rose half a meter off the ground. Each group of two guided their blocks to a position designated by Uranus.

Apollo and Notus went to the second box and activated the communications relay. When they were sure it was operational, they came out.

"We're ready to seal the relay," Apollo told Uranus, and he beamed the last wall into place. Apollo and Notus gamma-welded the box closed.

After Eurus and Iris laid down the block they had on their antigravs, they attached the devices to the box and set it in the location Uranus showed them. The location would put the box in the center of the statue. They then went back to moving and placing blocks.

Nine hours later, the statue was about one-third complete. The legs were in place as was the tail. The body stood three meters tall and totally covered the box housing the relay. The men and women at both locations continued to work through the dead of night and into the next day. They spent the night sleeping under the stars. They woke and continued work on the statue.

"Uranus to Poseidon," the professor said into his communicator. "Go ahead, professor" was the reply from the voice from the speaker.

"All we need is one more block. But it's got to be five meters by five meters by five meters."

"What's it for? The head?"

"As a matter of fact, yes."

"Okay then. Give us a few minutes, and I'll call you back."

Elapsed time was thirty hours over two days. All that remained was to carve the face, attach the head, and test the relay, and the teams were ready to begin what they came here for.

"Poseidon to Uranus. We have the block you requested."

"Excellent. I'll beam it over now." Before he could take a full breath, a massive stone block materialized five meters in front of him. "Grab a laser cutter and stand by," he told Poseidon.

"I'm ready" came within three seconds.

He activated the controls, and Poseidon was now standing in front of him, cutter in hand.

Without saying a word, he activated the controls again. In four seconds, he set the power to standby mode and walked out from behind the unit.

"What did you just do?" Poseidon asked him.

"I beamed the rest of your team from the quarry to Olympus."

"Great. Now let's finish up here and get to Olympus ourselves."

"I hear that. Another hour, and we'll be there."

Uranus took the laser cutter from Poseidon and started carving the huge block of stone. In thirty minutes, the head was complete.

"Very impressive," Poseidon told him. "You should have been an artist."

"Sculpting is actually a way for me to relax. I just don't do it on this large a scale." He stepped behind the controls and powered up the transporter unit again. He activated the controls, and the huge

Pentarrian lion head vanished from the ground next to him and reappeared on the shoulders of the massive statue. The rest of the workers came to the side of the transporter unit and glared at the huge beast.

"Damn we did a good job," Ensign Aether said to no one in particular.

"That should scare the shit out of any protohuman," Dr. Hestia volunteered out loud.

"Damn fine job, Uranus," Poseidon told the professor. "Thanks to everyone, this should stand forever," Uranus responded. And he continued, "Everyone get ready. We're going to Olympus."

Everyone spread a few feet apart and Uranus began the transport sequence. Everyone was transported to Olympus except Uranus and Poseidon. When the cycle was complete, he set the controls again and stood beside Poseidon. The two were transported to the station as well.

"Lock on to the portable transporter unit and beam it into the storeroom," Uranus told the transporter operator.

"Aye, sir" was his reply, and he activated the controls to carry out the professor's request. It was done before Uranus and Poseidon left the transporter room.

Olympus Station was a bustle of activity getting the final details ready. Uranus was in the control room overseeing the activation of the communications relay. Aphrodite was assisting at the controls.

"Let's get this sucker kicked up," he said.

Aphrodite tapped out a series of commands on the section of the console to the right of the screen in front of her. Information started scrolling across the screen as a thick red line slowly rose up along the far left side of the screen.

"Power cells are climbing, sir," she said to Uranus. "Twenty percent…twenty-five…thirty percent, and rising."

"Good," he replied. "At seventy-five percent, we can activate the relay."

"Another fifteen seconds." Time crept by as the red bar rose steadily higher on the screen. Then finally. "Seventy-five percent, sir."

Uranus tapped out commands on the console section in front of him under his screen. Data started scrolling through, indicating that the different parts of the relay were coming to life.

"Power cells at one hundred percent," Aphrodite said as she tapped out more commands. "I'm disengaging the power transfer. Power cells are maintaining at one hundred percent."

"Good, good." Sixty seconds later. "The relay's systems are at full power. Shall we test this thing?"

"Absolutely. Shall I contact the *Heaven*?"

"No. This relay needs to keep us in full contact with Mars station, so contact them."

"All right." She tapped out even more commands, and within seconds, Lieutenant Molpe's face was on Aphrodite's screen.

"Hello, Lieutenant." Aphrodite smiled politely to the image on the screen. "We just activated our communications relay and need to link with your computers for data transfer."

"All right," Molpe replied. "How long are you going to need?"

"About fifteen minutes."

"Start when you're ready."

"Great," Aphrodite replied as she keyed in the final commands. "Starting now." Data started streaming across the screen in front of Professor Uranus.

About fifteen minutes later, data transfer complete flashed across the professor's screen. Lieutenant Molpe was back on Aphrodite's screen.

"The data transf—" The image of Lieutenant Molpe started to distort, and his voice faded out. After a few seconds of this silent distorted imagery, the screen went blank. Aphrodite started keying control sequence after control sequence, but to no avail. The screen remained blank. Thirty seconds went by. Still the screen is blank.

"WHAT THE FUCK HAPPENED!" Uranus screamed in total confusion. "GET HIM BACK! NOW!"

"I'm working on it, sir!" Aphrodite yelled back loudly as she continued tapping commands into the computer. Another three minutes went by.

"What's going on, Aphrodite? How come you can't reach them?"

"I don't know, sir. I've never encountered this problem before."

Not only is Aphrodite an accomplished geneticist, but she is also a communications expert. "Give me a min—"

Beep, beep, beep.

Aphrodite tapped some controls. "We're being hailed by the *Heaven.*"

"On screen," he said more calmly this time.

Captain Jehovah's face appeared on the screen that moments ago showed the commander of the Mars monitoring station.

"What is it, Captain? We're in the middle of a slight emergency here."

"We were monitoring your communications with Mars when you lost the signal. We've been able to determine it is due to the planet's orbit around the sun in conjunction with the satellite orbit around the planet will give you two hours of blackout time every rotation."

"That is not acceptable, Captain. We need constant communications. Is there anything that can be done?"

"I'll put my chief engineer on it. We'll be in touch soon. We'll also contact Mars and let them know of our findings."

"Thank you, Captain." Uranus's tone was now more calm. "We'll be waiting…Out."

The Star Command insignia replaced the image of Jehovah. It took less than fifteen minutes to get a respond from the ship. The view screen at the communications console flickered, and the insignia was replaced by the face of Captain Jehovah.

"Lieutenant Commander Benjamin suggests we construct a

second relay station. This one should go on the satellite in orbit around the planet. Commander Lucifer is working on the coordinates now. We should have it up and running within the hour."

"That's great, Captain. Thank you very much for your diligence in this matter. Please contact us as soon as the relay is ready."

"Will do, professor. *Heaven* out." The insignia flickered back on the screen. Forty-five minutes later, the screen flickered again.

"Professor Uranus," the captain said.

"Go ahead, Captain," he said as he approached the screen. "The relay station is complete. All that's needed is a test run."

"Excellent, Captain. If you stand by, we'll test it and get right back to you. Give us a few minutes."

"We'll be waiting."

"Get me the Mars station," he said to Aphrodite.

"Right away." She activated some controls, and Jehovah's image was replaced by that of Lieutenant Molpe.

"Ah, professor." Molpe sounded surprised. "What happened? Our last transmission was cut off."

"It seems due to the orbit of the planet and the orbit of the satellite, there is a two-hour blackout period during every orbital rotation."

"How did you overcome the problem?" Molpe asked. "If it's a two-hour blackout, we shouldn't be able to communicate for another seventeen minutes."

"Captain Jehovah and his crew solved this little dilemma. They constructed a relay station on the satellite to counteract the problem."

"That's great news. Now the mission can proceed as planned."

"It's proceeding far ahead of schedule."

"In what respect, professor?"

"We've captured one of the protohumans and have already begun preliminary studies. We are very near the end of phase one."

"That's even better news, professor. I'll spread the word to my men."

"All right. We'll talk to you later. Out." The screen went to black, and the insignia of the Space Command appeared. On Mars station, Lieutenant Molpe informed the rest of his crew about the progress of the mission. Everyone was excited.

On the *Heaven*, Lieutenant Kohath had a report. "Captain, I'm intercepting an encrypted message being beamed to the planet. I cannot get a lock on the origin or the destination. Whoever sent this is a communications expert."

"Keep trying and keep me informed." A few minutes passed by. "I still can't get a lock on the signal, sir."

"Lucifer, what about you?"

"The signal is in a scatter pattern. Sensors can't obtain a lock either."

"Is there anything else we can try?"

"Logic dictates that if we can't find the source, then maybe deciphering the signal will give us a clue as to where it comes from or where it is being sent to."

"Excellent idea," Jehovah said after a few seconds of thought. "Let's get it done. The sooner the better."

"Right away, sir." He went silently to work trying to crack the mysterious signal from where no technologically advanced civilization is supposed to be.

CHAPTER

Captain's log: Stardate 9665.10. The great mission begins. The last three weeks have afforded us every opportunity to advance this project. We have completed construction of all three bases. Lieutenant Molpe has his crew on the Mars Monitoring Station, and it is fully operational. Professors Uranus and Cronus are assigning teams to their various tasks as I record this log. I pray to the gods that this phase of the mission goes as smoothly as the first phase.

Of the thirty-three crew assigned to the project, all but five were present in the central hub of Olympus Station. Missing from the group were Ensign Baal, communications officer, who was checking his station. Lieutenant Hercules and Ensign Aeolus, the station security team, were checking out their work area, and Lieutenant Morpheus and Ensign Fama were getting the mess hall ready.

Professors Uranus and Cronus, each holding a padd, were the center of attention.

Professor Cronus spoke first, "We need to learn everything that we can about this *one* creature before we can start the next phase. So the study of her is paramount. With this in mind, Dr. Zeus, your team will concentrate on unlocking the gnome of this creature. You will be in gamma section. Dr. Poseidon, your team will be working on the biology of the creature in alpha wing. Dr. Hera, your team will be responsible for the study of the gnome of some of the larger land animals as a fallback in case the *one* creature doesn't work out. You will be in beta labs. Dr. Hermes, your team will be working on a sedative for these creatures that will not have any lingering effects. You will be working at Eden station. As teams finish their assigned tasks, they will be sent to help those not finished. This is pure research for now. Let's do our best to finish quickly and thoroughly. I'd like to collect what we need and get home."

He heard mumbles of agreement throughout the gathering. The people separated and headed to their respective labs. Dr. Zeus and his team headed for gamma wing. Dr. Poseidon and his team went to alpha wing. Dr. Hermes and his team stepped into the transporter chamber and were beamed to Eden. Dr. Hera and Dr. Apollo went to the control room as the rest of Hera's team went to prepare the labs. In the control room, Hera and Apollo are tied into the *Heaven*'s sensors to search for several large animals to start testing. Fortunately for the pair, Utorian technology in optics was the best in the known worlds. The *Heaven*'s visual sensors could read the writing on a matchbook cover from high orbit.

"Use the thermal imaging scanner, and cover the area of woods where we found *One*, it's as good a place to start."

"Switching to thermal imaging now," replied Apollo as he tapped the controls on the console. When he tapped in the last command the screen in front of them, which is displaying an aerial view of the target area from about ten thousand feet, due to the magnification, suddenly turned a deep blue as the trees grew larger. Within the target area, tiny red dots, indicating body heat, grew larger as the image magnified more. Tiny dots started to take crude shapes. Crude shapes started to take on defined forms.

The red images are scattered over the entire screen, some in twos and threes, others in larger groups.

"Lock in and enhance this area," Hera said as she pointed to a spot on the screen off-center to the left. In that area were three groups of three and four images. Suddenly, the screen filled with the section that Hera pointed to. "And switch back to normal viewing." The colors on the screen changed to a normal view, and the two could clearly see, close to the upper left corner, a group of five animals.

"Magnify them another fifteen percent." The screen zoomed in on the five animals. The two stared wide-eyed. These animals are big four-legged creatures. They have a thick hide with a long protruding snout. They have flared nostrils. They have long straight hair from the back of the head, running down the long neck and ending at the shoulders of the front legs, just at the base of the neck. The tail appears to be the same type of hair as is on the neck. The group consists of two large animals and three smaller ones.

"Those big ones must stand two meters from the ground to the top of their heads," Hera said in amazement.

"I just scanned those animals. The smaller of the two big ones is the female…a family perhaps," Apollo said.

"Can you get a transporter lock on one of those from here?" Hera asked.

"Sure," Apollo said as he started keying in commands. "I just have to link into the transporter control circuits and…got it. Which one do you want?"

"The female, of course."

"Of course…Got her."

"Don't beam it up now. Just maintain a lock until we're ready."

"Reduce magnification to show the whole area again…And go back to thermal imaging."

"Okay."

Apollo keyed in some commands, and the screen showed the blue overview with scatted red shapes.

"Now this group. Nice tight close-up in normal view," Hera demanded nicely as she pointed to a thick area of trees just to the right of center. When the image on the screen finished zooming and switched its view, the two saw a group of tree-dwelling simianlike creatures swinging around. These creatures are very nearly simian, yet their movements are more refined. They measure just over a meter tall and have very short fur.

"I have got to have one of them. Get a lock on any female.

Those things are fascinating."

"Transporter locked and ready."

"Good."

They spent the next ten minutes looking at the other animals in the area. None impressed the two scientists like the two they found. The rest of Hera's team completed programming the force fields in the two beta labs a few minutes before Hera and Apollo finished looking at the indigenous life-forms.

Apollo moved to the transporter control panel and tapped in a long series of commands. When he was finished, he moved his hand over the activation control sensors. The unit hummed to life. When it had completed its task, the unit powered down. Apollo repeated the process one more time and shut the machine off when it finished powering down the second time.

"The two animals are in the labs, and containment fields are up and holding." The disembodied voice of Dr. Aphrodite, speaking from beta wing's office, was heard saying after Apollo shut down the transporter unit.

"Excellent," Hera said into the intercom system. "We'll be back there in a few minutes. Hera out."

As she walked out of the room, she turned to Apollo and said, "I'm hungry. How 'bout you?"

"Absolutely," He replied as he got up and followed her out. "Hecate, can you get me a gram of calcerite and half a gram of sodium phosphate, please?"

"Sure…yeah, give me a sec," she replied as she spun around and headed to the cabinet across the room. In less than two minutes, she returned. "Here ya go." She handed two small containers to the attractive young Dr. Athena.

"Let's get started," Athena said to Hecate. And to herself, she said, "This could take a while."

Dr. Zeus and Dr. Hephaestus, along with Ensign Dionysus, were at Eden station preparing to transport *One* to gamma lab while Dr. Artemis and Ensigns Eros and Hades stayed in gamma lab making preparations for her arrival. Everything was going along smoothly, and it was expected to be about an hour before the protohuman was in the lab and ready for testing.

In beta lab, the team had completed extracting the genetic material from the simian-type creature, figuring they would do the easy one first. Now it's time for the big one.

"So…how do you figure we sedate this one?" Ensign Boreas asked Hera with a dry wit.

"Ten cc's of hydroxylin should do it," she replied. Ares prepared the hypospray.

As they lowered the force field and stepped closer to the beast, her eyes showed the fear and anger the animal was feeling. When the two got a few steps in, Aphrodite reengaged the force field. As Hera and Boreas approached the animal from the front, moving slowly and making soothing sounds, Apollo was approaching from the rear, very quietly. Hera started softly stroking the animal's snout as Apollo got closer. Aphrodite, watching from the opposite side of the force field, took a step to the side and inadvertently knocked a padd from the console.

Startled by the noise, the huge beast turned its head toward the sound and saw Apollo with the hypospray. In fear, the creature kicked its hoofed front legs high in the air. The boney hoof of the left leg nicked the side of Hera's skull, sending her to the floor, after bouncing off of a cabinet, an exam table, and two trays of medical equipment. She was nearly unconscious. The creature's right hoof hit Boreas in the head as well, with a sound similar to a bowling ball hitting concrete. Boreas's body flew about four meters and crashed into a glass cabinet.

The animal reared its hind legs in an attempt to hit Apollo. He side-stepped the huge beast and applied the hypospray to its neck. He pressed the button on top of the unit, and the device emitted a slight hissing noise. In less than three seconds, the animal fell to the floor unconscious, which was bad for Hera. She was on the floor with her left leg right in the spot where the animal fell. Before the echo the creature's fall could fade away, Aphrodite got the force field down and is nearly to where Hera is on the floor. Unfortunately for Hera, she cleared her head just as the beast hit the floor, and her leg. A loud *snap* could be heard when the beast hit the floor.

"AAAAAAAHHHHHHHH!"

The only sound that could be heard for at least a kilometer, at least that's what Aphrodite was thinking.

"Get this fucking thing off of me!"

Apollo and Aphrodite tried to get the huge beast off of Hera, but to no avail. Dr. Artemis, in the lab next door, heard the commotion and rushed over with Ensigns Hades and Eros. The four were able to lift the creature enough for Eros to pull Hera out from under the massive beast, with a very loud scream. When Hera saw the torn, tangled lump of flesh and bone her leg had become, the shock and pain overwhelm her, and she slipped into unconsciousness. When she was freed, the four let the beast go and rushed Hera to the next lab for treatment. Eros followed along behind, helping Ensign Boreas, who was just starting to come to.

"Lucifer. Please come into my ready room." The captain's voice echoed throughout the bridge.

"I'm on my way," he responded as he rose and headed to the door leading to the ready room.

With a swooshing sound, the door behind the commander closed, and he and the captain were alone in his ready room. Lucifer walked to the front of his commanding officer's desk.

"You wanted to see me, Captain?"

"I've been reviewing the medical procedure."

"You found a problem?"

"I don't see any projections on what the results of the cellular extraction would be to the organism having the procedure."

"What would you like to do about it?"

"Nothing directly. Not yet." Lucifer looked confused.

"I want one of our sensor arrays locked onto the research teams at all times. I'd like you to assign several people to monitor those sensors. I want to know about anything out of the ordinary, no matter how trivial or insignificant."

"Right away, sir." Lucifer turned and left the room. He knew what the captain was up to, and the people to do the job.

Zeus came running into lab gamma three, nearly knocking over Ensign Boreas who just woke up from the realm of unconsciousness and had one hell of a headache. Zeus slid by him using his two hands on the injured man's shoulders for support.

"Hey!" Boreas screamed, as loudly as he could with the headache he had, angrily. "What the fuck!"

"I'm sorry…Excuse me." Zeus never lost pace.

"Nearly trampled twice in one afternoon," Boreas said to himself. "Hell of a way to start a mission." He headed to his quarters for a bit of a rest.

Zeus made it to the opposite end of the room when what he saw brought him to a grinding halt. His eyes were bigger now than when he first heard about what happened. She lay on the exam table. She was pretty banged up. Her right leg was a lump of torn flesh and protruding bone.

Dr. Hephaestus was scanning her torso with a tricorder. She stopped.

"Three broken ribs, a punctured lung, internal bleeding," she said coldly and professionally. A lump grew in Zeus's throat. "There is a subdermal hematoma on the right side of the brain…Must have been from hitting her head on the hoof," she said as she ran the tricorder over her head.

"There are also multiple contusions, various abrasions, and broken bones," Dr. Artemis said as he attempted to reset the pieces of bone in Hera's leg. As he held the two pieces together with his hands Doctor Ares, having recovered from the horse's attack, was using a bone fuser to repair the damage.

Once the two doctors had the bone fused together, Artemis held the gaping wound closed while Ares closed it with a dermal regenerator. A dermal regenerator healed the wound by accelerating cell growth to the wounded area. It leaves no scar.

"Will she be all right?" Zeus asked, the lump in his throat making it hard to speak. "We can repair the injuries, but the hematoma in her head is another story." Hephaestus answered as she used the bone fuser that Ares just finished with to repair the broken ribs. When he finished with the bone fuser, he switched it for a sonic subcutaneous regenerator. He started waving the device in small circles over the region of her chest where the puncture is in the lung. It took a few seconds before anything happened.

"The hole is closing." Ares told everyone after he scanned her with a tricorder.

Hephaestus continued the circular motions until "The punctured lung is repaired" came from Ares. Hephaestus moved the device to Hera's abdominal area and started the process over again. The pitch of the humming noise produced by the medical device in Hephaestus's hand suddenly changed.

"The internal bleeding is under control," she replied as she rested the regenerator on the table beside the bed holding the unconscious form of Professor Hera. Ares slowly waved the scanning section of the medical tricorder over the other side of her abdomen as Hephaestus looked at the results on the tiny view screen on the main tricorder.

She picked up the regenerator and waved it in a small circle over the lower section of her right side. When the tone changed, she stopped, and once again Ares waved the small scanning device over her entire torso. After interpreting the images on the view screen, Hephaestus said, "All the internal damage is healed, and the bleeding is stopped. Now it is time for the head wound."

She moved a few steps closer to Hera's head and took the scanning unit from Ares. She tapped a series of controls on the tricorder and within a second, the large view screen above her head flickered to life. She put the scanner to Hera's head just above the large lump, which formed over the spot where her head struck the floor.

The outline of Hera's head appeared on the screen. Replacing what should have been a picture full of hair was the image of her inner workings, which we call the brain. The veins and arteries were clearly visible, and the capillaries were thinner than a hair.

Over the spot that struck the floor was a red hazy area. The color was dark and deep. "This could take a few minutes." Hephaestus said in a nonchalant but serious tone as she brought the epidermal regenerator up to the wound. She used her finger to key in a sequence on the buttons on the top of the regenerator as she brought it up.

As she slowly moved the device around the outer perimeter of the wound, the pitch of the sound emanating from the unit started low and deep. At the fifth (or is it the sixth) revolution, the pitch started to rise. The image on the screen, of the deep dark red contusion appeared to be lightening up around the edges.

The color at the edge of the bruise started to match the surrounding tissue as the tone went up. Hephaestus started closing the circle slowly.

"That's getting it," she stated the obvious and continued to close the circle as the colors started blending together. The process was long but progressing steadily.

An hour later, the dark red bruise is the size of a grape. The regenerator hummed at a steady pitch, but now a pulsing tone started in the otherwise steady tone.

"That's as much as I can do," Hephaestus said as she turned the regenerator off. "The rest is up to her. The next few hours are the crucial ones."

She keyed a command into the tricorder, and all of Hera's vital signs were displayed on the large view screen, brain wave patterns included.

Hephaestus stood straight and began walking around the table. She looked up at what was around her for the first time since she started.

"Will she be all right?" Zeus asked, his voice hinting of fear.

Fear for what could happen. Fear for what will happen.

"Well, if she wakes up within the next few hours, we'll be able to better diagnose her condition. Until she wakes up, I can't even guess as to how she'll be." That was the answer he received. He walked up to the bed and stood beside her. He took her hand in his. For the next ninety minutes, he stood by her bed.

Like waking from a long night's sleep, Hera's eyes slowly blinked to life. After a few seconds, she turned her head toward the figure near her. "Did anyone get the license plate of the truck that ran me over?" She asked softly and slowly, a slight smile rolling over her face. "Welcome back," he responded with a slight tear welling in his eyes. "How are you feeling?"

"Like shit," she replied with the smile on her face growing a little bigger.

"I'm hungry too," she said as she exhaled the breath from her lungs.

"I'll get Hephaestus. You just lie back and relax."

"It's not like I can do anything else," she replied.

Zeus left the room, his head turning to look at her one last time before he was out of sight.

In two minutes, he was back, and Hephaestus was with him. Hera sat up a little straighter when the two came in. The doctor in the white lab coat picked up the medical tricorder on the table beside the bed. She took the scanning device out from the front of the unit, and as she started to open the tricorder unit to activate the machine, she began to scan Hera.

The scan Hephaestus made took about fifteen seconds. When she was finished, it took her another ten seconds to interpret the data on the small screen. To Hera and Zeus, this time seemed to be an eternity.

"Well," Hephaestus said with a slight lightness in her voice, "there doesn't seem to be anything else wrong with your lungs. The rib is healed fine. All the internal injuries are healed."

"So far so good," Hera said. The look on her face showing a very slight concern about what was coming next.

"The hematoma is not quite healed yet. You're going to have to rest in bed until tomorrow at least. You may feel a little dizziness for a couple of days, but that's expected. The external bruise will fade soon enough. Just take it easy and don't make any quick movements for a few days and you should be fine."

Hera started giggling at those words, and Zeus smiled as the tension flowed away from the both of them. Zeus took Hera's hand, and the two stared into each other's eyes for a long minute.

"I'm going back to work," Zeus told her. "You follow your doctor's orders and get your rest. I'll see you after my shift."

"Okay" was her only response as she closed her eyes and slowly faded off to sleep. Zeus headed back to his lab to continue the mission at hand.

"It seems today was the day for surprises," Professor Uranus addressed the group of people seated at the conference table. The two division heads were seated beside the two project coordinators.

The four researchers who lead the teams sat on the opposite side. The exception at this meeting was Professor Hera, who has yet to be discharged from sick bay. "How far have you gotten, Dr. Hermes?" Uranus asked the man at the end of the table.

"We've tried twenty-two hundred various degrees of formulas. Not one reaction was any different from another. We'll try again tomorrow." The disappointment in his voice was reflected in the faces of those around him, and he saw this. "But what the hell? There's always tomorrow." His optimism is genuine. "We've only got two million seven thousand five hundred more combinations to try." He started laughing a stupid little laugh. So he thought in the back of his mind until he realized that everyone else in the room was doing the same thing.

"Are you serious, or are you screwing around?" Dr. Coeus asked, his smile still fresh.

"About?"

"Two million seven thousand five hundred more combinations? I didn't know there were that many drugs in all of creation."

"There aren't that many drugs," Hermes explained. "Actually there are considerably less…But when you take into account all the different percentages, the combinations become staggering."

"Do such small percentages make such an impact?" Zeus asked as he tried to keep his mind focused on what he was there for. That was tough seeing as the only woman on the expedition, in his eyes, worth fucking was lying in a bed in sick bay recovering from a near deadly mistake. He felt his slacks getting tighter around the crotch. He tried focusing on the answer he was expecting.

"Yes…a micron over or under on some tranquilizers, and they go from being sleep aids to toxic biochemical nerve agents."

Everyone in the room was a bit taken aback by this new awareness. "I had no idea there is such a delicate balance. At least not in the pharmaceutical aspect of life."

"I didn't think so either until I accidentally dosed the entire auditorium at the academy with what was supposed to be laughing gas but turned out to be a gas agent, literally. This stuff made everyone fart uncontrollably for an hour and a half." He laughed again, and everyone followed in his path once more.

When the laughter died down, which took a little more than a few minutes, the meeting came back to order. "How did the rest of the teams fare?" Uranus's voice boomed in command as he still laughed.

Poseidon decided to answer the question at hand first. "We've got our sample stored and cut. We've got five thousand usable portions to test with."

"We've also got the same stats as Poseidon," Zeus spoke second. And he continued, "When Poseidon and I finished with our sections, we all got together and completed Hera's sample. We're all ready to move on to the next stage."

"Most excellent," Uranus began. "Tomorrow we begin the controlled advancement of the indigenous life-forms. Have your daily logs downloaded to the mainframe. That's all. Good night and good work."

"Professor," Hermes said with a raised voice to get the attention of the man who just adjourned the meeting.

"Yes, Hermes. What is it?"

"I'd like to send two of my assistants out on a scouting mission tomorrow, and I need your authorization for the use of a shuttlepod."

"What are they to be scouting for?"

"As I said earlier, with all the combinations we need to test, we need raw materials. Our scans showed everything we need is on the surface. It'll take a day to collect all the materials we need. We'll have to do this once a month."

"That's not a problem, Doctor. I'll clear your men for shuttlepod two for first thing in the morning. You'll have access to it for as long as you need. All I ask is your men keep an open com-link so we can keep a trace on them in case something should happen."

"We've already discussed it, and my men would like it if you could maintain a transporter lock on them at all times. They don't know what's out there. They don't want to take any chances."

"Hell, I couldn't ask for anything else. Happy hunting. Just keep them within transporter range."

"Thanks," Hermes said as he walked away and headed to his quarters. The rest of the men were already well on their way to rest. Tomorrow is another day.

Personal log: Day six. This has been the first complete day of research. Even with Hera's injuries, we still have all the samples we need from the chosen animals. Tomorrow begins the genetic manipulation of these animals. Only the gods know if we are doing the right thing. I only pray we are. Cronus, biological coordinator.

Things on the *Heaven* were only slightly out of the ordinary. Two ensigns, a Bar'klaan and a Chandraken, were studying computer monitors. Chanani, the Chandraken, and second-shift biologist, was on the west wall, two monitors on his console showing female simians. The one on the right was the simian behind the force field on Olympus, and the one on the left was a female in the wild.

Ensign Bukkiah, the second-shift physicist was seated to the left of Chanani. His monitors showed two horses, one on Olympus and one in the wild.

"Does the animal on the station have anything peculiar going on with her eyes?" Chanani asked Bukkiah.

"The blinking," Bukkiah said without looking away from the monitors. "The horse on Olympus is blinking her eyes way more than the one in the wild…And there's a blankness about her look."

"It has to be from the operation," Chanani started. "Now we have to determine the condition that has these symptoms."

"We'll have to use the medical scans made when the animals were beamed aboard and compare them to ones you should be doing right now." Bukkiah smiled. "I'll search the transporter logs."

They each started their own projects at their stations. It took a few minutes to get the data. The monitors at the workstations were showing two images on their screens. The lower sections of each screen represent the brain wave patterns of the corresponding animal after the removal of the brain tissue. The upper sections represent the brain wave patterns when they were brought on board, before the removal of the tissue. The lines represent the alpha, beta, and gamma wave patterns of the brain, in that order, top to bottom.

"Damn," Bukkiah said in a voice of shocked disbelief. "This scanner must be malfunctioning."

Chanani responded, "No. We recalibrated the system during the last shift."

"Take a look at those readings," Bukkiah said, pointing to a series of numbers in the bottom. "If I'm reading this right…synaptic function is deteriorating."

Chanani leans over Bukkiah to get a closer look at the number patterns. "You're reading them right. Synaptic function is deteriorating."

"Computer…" The lights on the primary interface began to blink and the whirring sound of processors coming to life indicated the computer was ready. Chanani continued, "At the current rate of deterioration, how long will it be before all synaptic function ceases?" The computer's cold, emotionless voice answered after a few minutes, "Nineteen hours, forty-two minutes." Ahijah sat for a long second staring at the screen of squiggly lines.

"What is causing the synaptic functions to fail?"

A few seconds later, the computer answered, "Sufficient neuropathways of the frontal lobe have been interrupted to cause insufficient cognitive function, and the buildup of fluid in the frontal cavity is causing irreparable damage to the surrounding tissue."

"What frontal cavity?" Bukkiah spoke next.

The computer spoke again, "The cavity was created when a section of the frontal lobe was removed in order to obtain the proper DNA."

Ahijah continued, "Extrapolate and deduce…If the same procedure was done to the protohuman that was on Olympus Station a while ago, what would the outcome be?"

The computer whirred to life once again. "Computing."

"Insufficient data to extrapolate hypothesis," the computer responded after a few seconds of analyzing.

"What constitutes *sufficient data?*" Bukkiah spoke to the machine again.

And again the clicking and whirring of the internal circuitry could be heard as the machine went to work, and again it spoke after a few seconds, "A seven-hour continuous level-five medical scan would constitute sufficient data for extrapolation and formulation of hypothesis."

"Then begin."

"Affirmative."

Zero six hundred hours came quickly. Even though it was the tenth hour of the medical scan, for Ensigns Eris and Hecate, it could have held off a couple of hours longer. The two met in the mess hall for coffee, and to plan the day's events.

"Starting in the east seems to be the most logical course," Eris said without her eyes leaving the padd she was looking at. "With the abundance of resources along the huge river, we should be fully loaded in a few hours. We may even be able to make several trips."

"I'm glad you said that," Hecate said with a smile starting to form across her face. She gave Eris another padd. "This is a revised cargo manifest. We'll be going out three times today. The final time out brings us along the southeast beaches of the large body of water to the north."

"Most excellent," Eris responded. "Get some time in the sunshine and away from here…Most excellent." A smile came across her face as well. Their eyes locked for a brief moment. The two gathered their belongings and headed toward the shuttlepod, which was several hundred yards away from the main complex that they are in.

It took the two about five minutes to get from the mess hall to the shuttlepod. Eris pressed a button on the side of the shuttlepod, and the door beside the button opened with a whoosh. The two women got inside and prepared for departure. As Eris started prepping for takeoff, Hecate made sure everything they needed were on board.

"One laser drill…Check," she said out loud to herself as she looked over the list on the padd in her hand and compared it to the supplies in the corner of the pod. "Twenty supply containers… Check. One portable transporter unit…Check. That's everything we need." She deactivated the padd and headed for the copilot seat.

"Are we ready to go yet?" Hecate asked her partner as she strapped herself into the seat. "I'm doing the final engine check. Would you check the navigational system?"

Eris answered without looking at her, "Sure."

Hecate said as she started keying commands into the console in front of her. After a few minutes, she said, "Navigational system checks out okay."

"Then we are ready to go," Eris said as she engaged the lift thrusters and propulsion units. Looking out the window, Hecate saw the door of the landing bay open as the shuttlepod headed for it, steadily picking up speed as it approached the slowly expanding orifice leading to the outside world.

The small spaceship tilted to the left as Eris guided it to an open area amidst a huge forest surrounded on three sides by huge mountain ranges and a kilometer-wide crevice that seems to drop forever. Hecate checked the chronometer and found that they had been in flight for nearly an hour.

How far away are we?" she asked.

"About two hundred and fifty kilometers from the base," Eris answered.

Hecate remained quiet, silently acknowledging her response.

Eris broke the silence. "This area holds thirty-two elements we need in a two-kilometer radius. If we set up the transporter unit half a kilometer to the southwest, we will be able to collect twenty samples from the same spot."

The ship softly landed. The door opened as the two women unstrapped themselves from the seats they were in and moved to the back of the pod. Eris picked up a square case measuring a meter cubed. Hecate picked up a case slightly larger. The two exited the shuttlepod with Eris in the lead, case in one hand and tricorder in the other. She followed the signal emanating from the small device.

The two walked for about twenty minutes, chatting about everything and nothing at all. They did agree on one thing, it seemed. Both were against using the protohumans for this project. The tricorder started to beep wildly.

We're here," Eris said as she set the case on the ground by her feet. She put the tricorder in its holder, attached to the belt she wore around her waist. Hecate set hers down as well, and the two knelt down and opened the hasps that secured the cases. They took the covers off in near synchronicity.

Hecate's case housed the transporter control unit and its stand. She adjusted the stand, which came out of the case then simply sat the case on top of the stand. The controls, you see, are built into the case.

In near the same manner, Eris opened her case. The cover of the case she carried was the transporter pad and the rest of the case was the power matrix needed to operate the unit. She connected the two side to side. They connected with a snapping sound, like two magnets slamming together.

Hecate slid the stand of the control unit to the opposite side of the power matrix. The same snapping sound was heard. The women stood and smiled at each other. "Okay, here goes." Hecate said as she engaged the unit. The panel on the control unit lit up and a slight glow emanated from the transporter pad. "We are in business," Hecate said happily.

"All right," Eris said as she patted Hecate on the shoulder, giving it a slight rub after a few pats.

Hecate entered a command into the control unit and activated the system. Within a heartbeat, five sample containers appeared on the transporter pad in the machine's usual way. Eris removed the containers from the pad and set them by the unit. This went on until there were all twenty empty supply containers in the grass.

"Let's get these suckers filled," Eris said. She took out her tricorder and, after tapping a few of the controls, started panning the unit to the right. Hecate handed her the laser drill, and she started walking slowly to the left. Hecate put one of the supply containers back on the transporter pad, then went back behind the control console.

"I'm sending coordinates for the first mineral now." She pressed a button on the tricorder. "It's close enough to the surface for direct transport." The control console beeped with the acceptance of the tricorder's data.

"Transporting," Hecate said aloud as she activated the unit.

The glass supply container on the transporter pad is now full of a luminescent orelike mineral. She activated the unit again after keying in another command, and the full container dematerialized. "Supply one is aboard the shuttle," she said to Eris, who tapped two buttons on the tricorder and started waving the tiny device around slowly.

"Good, 'cause I've got two more," she responded. One tap on the tricorder. The transporter control once again beeped with approval. Hecate set a container on the pad and repeated the transport cycle.

"The next one will need a little help to get out," Eris said in a somewhat comical voice that made Hecate laugh slightly but noticeably.

As Hecate put another container on the pad, Eris took aim with the laser drill. A fluorescent blue beam fired from the tip of the rifle-like drill. The beam lasted for about five seconds, during which time the only sound that could be heard was the explosion of rock occurring at the beam's impact site. "Now we're ready," Eris said as she pressed one button on her tricorder. Again, the beep of approval.

Again, the transport cycle was repeated. Another container appeared on the shuttlepod.

This went on until the two had filled and stored all twenty supply containers, about ninety minutes time. "We're making excellent time," Eris said happily as the two stood around the portable transporter.

"I know…" Hecate responded with a smile. "At this rate, we'll be done in no time." She put her hands together over her head and stretched back, showing off the curves of her full solid body under the uniform she wore.

"Let's leave the transporter set up," Eris suggested. "We're coming back here for the other twelve minerals." She couldn't help but notice the figure under the uniform when the material tightened around her large round breasts as she bent slightly backward when she stretched. She shook off her stare and stepped onto the transporter pad. Hecate set the controls and stepped onto the platform with Eris. The two stood close together as the transporter cycle beamed them from the mining site to the outside of the shuttlepod.

Eris and Hecate climbed into the shuttlepod and strapped themselves into their seats. Eris engaged the lift thrusters and propulsion units. The shuttlepod lifted off the ground and headed for the station. Forty minutes later, Eris activated the communications console.

"Shuttlepod to Olympus Station…Come in, please."

"Olympus Station here…Go ahead, shuttlepod."

"We've got twenty supply containers of mineral ore that needs to be stored on Olympus until it is needed on Eden."

"Copy that. We've been expecting your cargo." The twenty containers dematerialized and immediately afterward, twenty empty ones appeared where the others were. "We're sending you twenty empty containers so you can continue your field trip."

"We copy that. Containers are here. See ya." The shuttlepod turned one hundred and eighty degrees and headed back to where the portable transporter unit sat silently waiting to be used again.

Forty minutes later, the shuttlepod landed on almost the exact same spot it rested a little while earlier.

When the two women stepped out from the confines of the ship, Hecate took out a small black box with several buttons on it. She stood close to Eris and pushed the largest of the buttons on the box, the one in the middle. The women dematerialized and within a second were standing on the transporter pad at the mining site. It took about a minute and a half to transport twelve supply containers from the shuttlepod to the site.

It took about an hour for the women to mine the last twelve minerals that were in the area they were at. They deactivated the unit and packed it in its cases. Then they started out on their twenty-minute hike back to the shuttlepod. When they arrived at the ship, they secured the cases and took their seats.

The trip to the next mining site took about a quarter of an hour. The nose of the small craft lifted slightly upward as the vehicle slowly settled on the soft earth. Once the ship's systems were locked on standby, the two women grabbed the cases housing the portable transporter unit and headed outside, Eris with tricorder in hand.

"Approximately ten meters that way," Eris said as she pointed to the right. "Tricorder reads eight mineral deposits within half a kilometer. All the ore is on the surface…at least enough to fill our containers."

"Well then…" Hecate answered. "Let's get these containers full and get outta here."

Eris looked at her with a strange expression on her face. "What's your hurry?"

A smile widened across Hecate's face. "The beach, I can't wait to get to the beach. Right before we left to come here, I was on a deep space survey mission. I haven't been on a beach in two years."

A smile came across Eris's face as well. "I hear that. Let's get 'er done." The trees are getting denser. The two walk along silently for several minutes.

"Aahhh!" *Thump!*

Hecate found herself facedown on the ground, her face smeared with some dirt and leaves in her hair. The case she was carrying slid a few meters in front of her.

"What the hell happened?" Eris said with a slight panic in her voice as she spun around to see what the scream was about.

"I tripped over that tree root," Hecate told her, pointing to the thick brown root, half-exposed from its muddy food source, at her feet. Eris started laughing uncontrollably, apologizing the whole time she was doing it. After a few seconds, Hecate joined her. The two laughed for several long minutes before they could regain their composure and continue with their mission. Within ten minutes, the two were setting up the portable transporter unit. This took less than five minutes.

Keying in a command on the tricorder, Eris signaled coordinates to the transporter control console. The beep of approval came within a heartbeat. "Energizing," Hecate said as she slid her fingers over the control, and the ever-present blue sparkles of the annular confinement beam of the transporter filled the container on the pad.

When the sparkling was complete and the container filled with ore, she slid over the controls again, and the container slowly dissipated in the usual way. The container rematerialized on the floor of the shuttlepod beside the twelve others collected at the last mining site. She slid over the controls one more time and the last six empty containers appeared on the pad. She took five of them off.

Beep. The green light flashed with the sound. "Ready with the next one," Eris shouted from a dozen, or so, meters away.

Thirty minutes later, the two women were strapped in their seats and prepping the shuttle for launch. The twenty supply containers and the two cases housing the portable transporter unit were secured in the space behind their seats. Eris manipulated the controls, and the pod rose above the tree line before moving forward for the forty-five-minute flight to Olympus.

The shuttlepod landed in the small (smaller than the one on the *Heaven*) landing bay attached to the cargo section of the base. The women left the pod and headed straight to the mess hall. On the way, they came across Dr. Hestia, who was assigned to Dr. Poseidon's research team currently working on the biological aspect of the she-creature One. She was also headed for the mess hall, being currently on an hour lunch break. The three walked together.

"So…What's it like out there?" Hestia asked the two.

"Reminds me of Utoria," Hecate responded. Eris agreed and added the story of the tree-root incident. The three laughed the rest of the way to the mess hall. After a lunch of a Barcarrian sandwiches and Rigelian salads, Hecate and Eris headed back to the shuttlepod to complete their assignment and take a little break. When they entered the pod, they found ten empty supply containers in place of the twenty full ones that were there when they arrived. The transporter unit was right where it had been.

"Where to now?" Hecate asked, and without comment, Eris handed her a padd with topographical data on it.

"The last remaining ores are at the ocean." A smile formed across her face. "Six are on the southern edge. That's where we are going first. The other four are approximately one hundred and thirty-five kilometers to the north. Thankfully, they are in two main groupings. I'd have to bet that this has been the easiest mining assignment in the history of the multiverses."

"I'd have to say it would be a good bet that you're right," Hecate replied and continued. "I didn't know you are a multiversist."

"We can travel to the far side of the galaxy in twenty seconds, yet some people still can't, or don't want to, comprehend the existence of parallel dimensions and a multitude of alternate universes… hence *multiverses*."

"I can see it," Hecate told her. "Like you said, 'Across the galaxy in twenty seconds.' Everything is possible…This might even be probable." Then her eyes lit up and a grin came across her face.

"Wouldn't it be wild if you could slide from one universe to another at will?"

"I've thought about that more times than you could imagine. Those nights pulling the graveyard shift at a remote communications relay platform. I'd think up entirely new worlds using the worlds of the alliance as guides, just change things around. Sometimes a little…Sometimes radically different, just depended on my mood. Saved my sanity plenty of times. That's why it's so easy to believe in."

"I'll have to try that the next time I'm really bored." She rested her head on the headrest of her seat and closed her eyes. She allowed her whole body to rest. "I think a few hours in the sun and surf and I might feel a whole lot better."

"Oh, you'll feel a whole lot better when this mission is over. I guarantee it," Eris told her as she placed her right hand on Hecate's left thigh and lightly caressed it. Hecate's eyes never opened, but the feel of Eris's caress made her think of things she'd sooner shrug off.

When her eyes opened, the shuttlepod was on the ground, and Eris was unstrapping herself from her seat. Through the window in front of her, all Hecate could see are two shades of blue, the blue of the sky and the blue of the ocean, the latter being a deeper, richer hue.

"Welcome back," Eris said with a smile when she noticed Hecate had opened her eyes. "I thought I was going to have to do the whole job myself," she continued jokingly.

"Are you kidding?" Hecate replied. "And do the last load alone while you soak up the sunshine longer?" She squinted slightly as she answered her own question, "Not a chance." She unstrapped herself and started to get up. "Let's get this show on the road. I need some sun." She smiled at Eris. She picked up the two cases that were the portable transporter unit and head out the open hatch.

"We've got six down here and four at the northern end of this ocean, one hundred and thirty-five kilometers away," Eris told

Hecate as she rose a hand over her eyes to shield them from the brightness of the sun and spied the terrain in all directions around the tiny craft.

"I know, I know," Hecate told her as they walked away from the pod and headed toward the woods. "Most of them are about ten meters beyond the tree line ahead." The collection of trees to the north of the shuttlepod is enough to constitute a small-sized forest. Eris turned toward Hecate. "Try to watch your step this time," she said laughingly.

"Yeah, yeah, yeah, fuck you too" was her response. They continued along laughing hard.

It took the two women about five minutes to get to the tree line and a few minutes to find a good spot for the transporter unit.

Seven minutes later.

Eris took aim with the laser drill and fired. The beam that was emitted from the nozzle of the riflelike tool lasted a long fifteen seconds. She spun nearly three-quarters of the way around to the left with the laser drill tucked under her right arm and the tricorder in her outstretched left hand.

She had been still only a nanosecond when she pulled the trigger of the laser drill again. This time, it was merely a ten-second beam that was emitted. A second explosion was heard from the point on the ground where that beam made contact with the rocky earth.

While Eris was digging ore (if any sentient being would call what she was doing digging), Hecate transported the six containers she would be using from the pod. "Two ready to go!" Eris yelled from her location as she relayed the coordinates to the transporter control console computer. She continued searching for the other four ores.

One beep and one green light. Second beep and a second green light.

One hand-slide over the controls and the empty container was full. A second hand-slide over the controls and the full container is gone, tucked away on the shuttlepod where it will sit until the arrival at Olympus Station. Hecate repeated the procedure a second time.

As Hecate placed a third container on the transporter pad, she heard a third beep. "Damn…she's fast," she said aloud to herself as she walked up to the control console.

It took about fifteen minutes to transport the other four ores. Ten minutes after that, the two women were in their respective seats preparing to lift off. "I hope I didn't rush you back there," Eris said as the craft silently rose off the sandy beach and headed over the trees, to the north. "I just want to finish the work and begin the play."

After checking the navigational computer, Hecate reported her analysis, "We'll be there in twenty-five minutes."

In slightly over twenty-five minutes, the pod set down again. They are some one hundred and thirty-five meters north of their last position.

"The last four minerals are on the beach here…well, make that three are on the beach and one is…" She keyed a command into the padd and the view screen showed a topographical close-up of the area they were at. There were seven lights blinking on the screen. Two blue lights, representing the two women were right beside the red light, representing the shuttlepod. There were three green lights in close proximity, about twenty meters away to the west, and one green light within the edge of the blue.

"Where is the fourth one?" Hecate asked, knowing the answer already.

"The fourth one is about five meters beyond the surf, under approximately one and a half meters of water." Her tone was light but serious as she looked out into the ocean at the spot she thought the ore would be. At that, Hecate started laughing. She just couldn't help herself. Eris looked at her with an expression of mock anger.

"You bitch!" she said in an *I don't believe your laughing at me* tone. She, too, started to laugh.

In the better part of ten minutes, the two were outside, cases in hands. They set the transporter unit up right outside the shuttlepod. Hecate went back into the pod for the four remaining containers while Eris, laser drill in one hand and tricorder in the other, started scanning for the three ore deposits on land.

Hecate placed three of the containers on the sand and as she placed the fourth on the pad, *beep,* a green light on the console.

"All right," Hecate said out loud to no one but herself. She firmly placed the container down and moved behind the control console. A wave of her hand over the controls, and the empty container filled with shiny blue sparkles. The sparkles faded and were replaced by gray metallic-looking ore. With another wave of her hand, she made the container vanish. She walked around the console and reached down for another container. As she placed this one on the pad, *beep,* another green light.

As she walked around to the console, she started saying something to Eris and looked around to find she was nowhere to be found. She started to repeat the transport procedure and, *beep,* a third green light. "This bitch is too fucking fast," Hecate thought to herself with a feeling of admiration behind it. The sooner they finish, the sooner they can relax. By the time she finished the thought, she had completed the second transport.

As she completed the third transport, Eris was back at the transporter unit.

"Last one, huh?" Hecate asked, trying to hold the smile back.

She doubted any success.

"Yep." Eris replied as she made some adjustments to her tricorder. Now there was only one dot on the view screen—the ore in the ocean.

Hecate, standing less than a meter away, could see that the dot was not that far off shore.

"Well, here I go." Eris put the tricorder on the control console then rested the laser drill on the transporter pad. She braced herself on the console with her right hand as she leaned slightly and kicked off her left boot with the toe of the right boot.

After the boots were removed, she leaned over more and removed the black cotton socks covering her bare flesh.

Hecate was kneeling down finishing the reenergizing of the power matrix. When she finished, she instinctively looked forward before getting up. Her eyes locked on to the figure in front of her.

With both feet in the sand, Eris wiggled her toes, allowing the warm tan sand to sift between them. She placed her thumbs into the waistband of her uniform slacks and slowly slid them down, gyrating her hips and ass cheeks to get them off easier.

As the uppermost part of her slacks cleared her hips and slid past her ass smoothly, her cream-colored underwear was revealed. Hecate notices that the G-string–style underwear just barely covered the deepest regions of her ass crack. For a moment, it appeared that Eris might be naked under her uniform.

Eris bent over further as she lowered the black slacks, revealing her, what most including Hecate would consider, a perfect ass, along with her long firm milky white thighs and slender calves.

The more she bent over, the more exposed the puffy skin that was her intimate area became. Hecate could see the darker pink flesh of her love tunnel and the dark brown pubic hair that surrounds it protruding from the sides of the tiny patch of fabric that was her G-string.

She pulled the slacks off of one foot then the other. She set them down on the shuttlepod floor by her boots and socks. She crossed her arms and grabbed her tunic by the bottom, on the sides. She peeled the uniform top up over her tight stomach then over her large round breasts. It took an extra effort to get the tunic over the firm mounds of muscle and flesh.

The tunic got caught up on the underside of Eris's double-D breasts, pulling the sports bra supporting them over the top and releasing the breasts from their cotton prison. This caused another problem for Eris.

Hecate started laughing when Eris realized that all the bunched-up material tucked under her chin, and her arms still three-quarters of the way in the sleeves left the center section of the tunic covering her face. She started struggling with her situation, and after a few minutes, her arms came free. Even with her head caught up in the tunic, she could feel the warmth of the sun on her barely covered nipples. The two red orbs hardened in the sunlight as Eris enjoyed the warm feeling.

The tunic came off with one more good yank. She threw it down with mock disgust. As she started to pull her bra back over her breasts, she froze in thought of half a second. She decided quickly that she enjoyed the sun's warmth on her naked breasts. She pulled the bra off it, and put it with the rest of her cloths.

Armed with a tricorder in one hand and a laser drill in the other, dressed only in a pair of G-string panties, Eris was ready to locate the last ore supply needed for the project.

This was Hecate's first realization of just how beautiful the female body is. She, too, felt a warm glow, but not from the sun.

It took Eris about two minutes to reach the site of the deposit. By the time she reached the coordinates, she had both arms raised to protect the equipment. Her breasts looked like a pair of thirty-eight double-D buoys floating in front of her. She one-handedly keyed in the command into the tricorder, and the green light on the command console flashed on.

Hecate did for the last time what she'd been doing all morning and early afternoon. She packed up the portable transporter unit and brought it onto the shuttlepod. Just as she finished securing it, she noticed what could have been a laser drill fly by the open door. Seconds later, a tricorder went flying by. Both hit the ground with a dull, dry thud.

She stepped outside to see Eris flat on her back in the sand, sunlight bathed her now nude body. Hecate felt a little flush now that her partner of the day was completely naked. Eris tipped her head back and opened one eye when she heard Hecate come out of the pod.

"Hey, this is great," Eris said. "Come on and join me."

"I don't know," Hecate replied. "The sun looks pre—"

"Oh, don't be an old fart," Eris interrupted. "Get naked and get over here." She patted the sand beside her. After a few seconds of thought, she looked around with a cautious eye.

"Don't worry. There's no one around for over a hundred kilometers of us in every direction."

After a few seconds, Hecate said as she started to undress, "Ah, fuck it." As her clothes came off, the body that's revealed was equal in beauty to Eris's. Hecate maintained a pair of thirty-six D breasts, not much smaller than Eris's, along with a twenty-six waist and thirty hips. Her legs are long and supple, yet firm and toned, a golden tan covering her body, all together, a perfect package.

"Well, well, well," Eris said, choking back a nearly uncontrollable laugh but letting a smile peek through.

"What's wrong?" Hecate said with a slight panic in her voice. "You just looked mighty apprehensive about taking your clothes off, but I don't need to be a detective to notice that you've got a very nice tan, but you have no tan lines. Obviously you sunbathe nude."

"I've got a pool back home. I also have a high stockade fence around my house. No one can see into my yard. I'm not used to being naked out in the open," Hecate explained as she rested herself about half a meter from Eris. She wiggled her body for a few moments so the soft sand under her can conform to her figure. She let her body relax as the sun's warmth engulfed her nakedness.

Eris turned her head and, looking at Hecate, noticed the perfectness of Hecate's left breast. "Damn," Eris commented, "you've got the most perfect breasts I've ever seen." There is a slight admiration in her voice.

"Oh...come on," Hecate replied with a slight giggly tone. "No, I mean it. They are perfect."

"Yours are much more perfect."

"Are yours as firm as they look?" as she rolled onto her right side.

Hecate made a sort of sound as she locked her fingers together and placed her hands behind her head. She arched her back up slightly toward Eris, implying that she feel for herself.

Eris lifted her left hand and brought it to Hecate's right breast. She placed her palm lightly on the bottom of the mound of flesh and slowly wrapped her fingers around it and began to gently caress the firm tissue.

Hecate let out a moan of approval as the fingers climbed up to the areola. At the nipple, the forefinger and thumb rolled the rockhard tissue between them. A moan of painful pleasure rang from Hecate's mouth. Her eyes remained closed, and she arched her back even more. Eris's right hand pivoted on its elbow and rested on Eris's left breast, caressing the nipple before pinching it forcefully.

A cry of near ecstasy rang from Hecate as her elbows rolled up, wrapping her head between her forearms. By this time, she was grinding her ass checks hard into the soft sand uncontrollably. She also began rubbing her legs together hoping to stimulate her clitoris with the motion. Eris noticed this.

Eris replaced the fingers pinching the left breast with a slight pressure of her teeth. She poked the nipple head with the tip of her tongue as she rolled her teeth left to right, in juxtaposing directions, grinding the nipple between them. Her left hand softly slid off the breast meat and glided over the stomach slowly.

"Your ab muscles are so tight," Eris said between her teeth and started clawing her nails across the firm area of flesh just above the pubic area. Hecate's hips went into convulsions for several moments, as her love juices boiled intensely deep within her, nearing eruption. "Do you taste as perfect as you look?" Eris said after she released the swollen nipple. Hecate's hips convulsed several more times before she unlocked her fingers and brought her arms forward. She grabbed two handfuls of Eris's hair and firmly guided her head down to the wet, hot area between her legs. Hecate's legs spread quickly, invitingly.

Eris let the tip of her tongue run down Hecate's body while her head was guided by the woman on the verge of orgasm. When Hecate felt Eris's tongue in the right location, she stopped applying downward pressure.

Eris's tongue went to work gently messaging the outside of Hecate's clit while she ran two fingers lightly over the two tender puffs of flesh that protected her love tunnel. The fingers gently probed the crease between the two puffs and, within a few strokes, opened them enough to release a small amount of love juice. Hecate's entire body convulsed in pleasure as the warm breeze of ocean air blowing over her stimulated clit and entering the outer edges of her canal as the fingers opened the passage slowly and deliberately. More juices flowed.

Hecate screamed out a cry of pleasure in a voice that quivered in unison with her body. The tone of her voice implied extreme pleasure; her body proved it. She lifted her ass cheeks and began gyrating in time with the messaging fingers. Then, with little warning, the fingers entered her pussy and started sliding in and out, slowly at first, but increasing in speed and intensity with each thrust.

In a matter of minutes, Hecate had what she would later describe as the best orgasm of her life. It grew slowly and steadily until she thought she was going to lose her mind. Her juices exploded from her body with enough force to cover most of Eris's face. Eris kept licking up the juices until there was no more. Eris's continued tongue-lashings were more than Hecate could stand, and before all her juices were licked up, she exploded again, and again Eris's face got soaked.

Hecate reached out and grabbed Eris's thigh, pulling her body into her own. She guided Eris's thigh over her body, wanting to give Eris what she was giving her.

Now Eris was on her hands and knees on top of Hecate. Her tongue never missed a stroke the whole time she was moving into her new position and now her pussy hovered over Hecate's face. She reached up and caressed Eris's ass cheeks and applied a gentle downward pressure. Eris allowed her body to be manipulated because she knew what's about to come—her.

"Lieutenant Korah." The voice came from behind him, from the science station.

"What is it, Lieutenant?" Korah, the night-duty commanding officer and tactical officer, replied from the tactical duty station.

"Scanners show a shuttlepod is leaving Olympus Station.

Heading is two, seven, eight, relative."

"Six forty-five," Korah noted. "Kinda early for resupply, but it was on the schedule." He thought for a moment. "Make a note of it in the ship's log and keep an eye on it for a while. Program the computer to alert us if the pod has any problems or the occupants run into trouble."

"Done," responded Lieutenant Aaron, the science officer, after a few seconds and finished the task in under a minute.

At zero seven fifteen hours, the familiar female voice of the computer came to life bringing the two crewmen back from their light sleep.

"Level-five medical scan complete." The two are startled awake. "Good…good," Chanani said. "Now can you answer my question?" he asked sarcastically.

"Affirmative," the computer replied coldly, then silence.

"Well?" Chanani asked, this time annoyed.

"The test subjects are exhibiting physiological and emotional changes. The end result will consist of increased hostility, mental retardation over prolonged duration, as well as increased tendencies toward violence."

"Can you include all data obtained of the protohuman and, using this medical scan, extrapolate and hypothesize the outcome of the mission we are currently undertaking?"

"Affirmative. Analysis will be complete in twenty minutes."

"Okay. Begin."

Twenty minutes later. "Analysis complete."

"Let's have it."

"If mission continues, the hybrid species will be prone to excessive violence, increased hostility to the point of brutality, retardation of most higher level cognitive functions as well as a genetic flaw that will bring the species to extinction in approximately six thousand to six thousand two hundred Terran years."

The two crewmen sat silent, then Bukkiah asked, totally astonished, "Did you say 'extinction'?"

"Affirmative." The coldness of the computer's voice along with what it said made the hairs on the back of their necks stand up and sent shivers up their spines.

"We've got to get this information to Dr. Anak right away," Chanani said.

"Don't you mean Commander Lucifer?" Bukkiah responded.

"Not yet."

"Why the fuck not? This is important."

"I know…that's why we need the doctor to confirm this data before we bring it to the commander."

"I don't know, Chanani."

"Look, if we bring this to the commander and he brings it to the doctor for confirmation and there's a mistake, we'll be scrubbing toilets for a month. Remember, it's only a computer."

"Yeah, since you put it that way, I'll download the data." Bukkiah picked up a padd and keyed in a few commands. In a few seconds, the transfer was complete.

The day-duty shift took control of the ship at zero eight hundred hours. The day progressed at its usual pace. The crew was still performing detailed scans of the solar system they were in. This place that was so alien. This place that was so far from home.

As of now, only the two inner planets have been fully scanned and documented. Scans of the outer planets began today, but there wouldn't be any usable data available for several hours. Those hours couldn't pass fast enough for any crewman. At eleven hundred hours, the first data streams became available.

The total diameter of this star system is nine thousand million kilometers, and the outer twin planets take two hundred and forty-eight years to orbit the star at the center. There are five planets beyond Terra, and they all have satellites, some two while others have up to a dozen. There was enough work for several months.

At twelve thirty hours, everything changed. The captain took the call in his ready room. After only several minutes, he came out again.

"Put me on shipwide intercom, please," he asked.

"You're on, Captain" came from Kohath, the young lieutenant at the communications console.

"All hands, this is the captain. May I have your undivided attention, please." Looks around the bridge became more serious and alert. "I have just received a communication from the Mars station. They will repeat the information that they have relayed to me. Go ahead, Lieutenant Molpe."

The voice of the commander of the Mars station begins to echo throughout the ship. "You're not going to believe this one, *Heaven*, but I repeat…long-range sensors have detected a planet heading toward the solar system."

Everyone on the ship froze to listen. Only Commander Lucifer could manage speech. "What do you mean…planet?"

The lieutenant continued, "It's as big as the sixth planet and has two satellites…Hold on a second. There's more data coming in now…Planet has a sustained gravity…and atmosphere…"

Groups mumbled in astonishment throughout the ship.

"I repeat…a breathable atmosphere…There are also faint signs of power distribution planet-wide…Still too far away for life-sign scans."

"Is there any telemetry data coming through?" Captain Jehovah asked the officer.

"Telemetry coming in now, Captain. Data shows the planet will pass within three point five million kilometers of Terra…There is a possibility that one of the satellites could impact on Terra. Tidal forces will be affected drastically at the very least."

"How long, Lieutenant?" Lucifer asked coldly.

"Five and a half months…maybe six…our months."

The captain cut in, "We must now engage the spacefold drive and investigate this planet in order to determine our next course of action. All hands, prepare for spacefold." He waved his hand across his throat.

Kohath disengaged the intercom. "You're clear, sir."

"Get me Professor Uranus."

"Ready."

"Professor?"

"Yes, Captain. What is it?"

"Apparently there is a rogue planet headed into the star system. ETA is five to six months. The *Heaven* needs to leave here for a few days to investigate while it is far enough away for whatever we do has time to take effect. We shouldn't be gone for more than half a week."

"Okay, Captain. Thanks for letting me know. We'll be fine here. See you in about half a week."

"Very good, professor. Out." He walked over and sat in his seat, the center seat. He pressed one of the buttons near the end of the armrest of the chair. "Lieutenant Commander Asher. Come in, please."

"Asher here, Captain" came from the little speaker/microphone just above the buttons on the armrest.

"Engage spacefold drive when we are five hundred thousand kilometers from the planet."

"Aye, sir. Engagement at five hundred thousand."

The captain pressed the button again, turning off the intercom. "Lieutenant Levi."

"Yes, sir," he said without turning around.

"Lay in an intercept course for the planet and engage at full impulse. Notify Asher when we reach five hundred thousand kilometers."

"Yes, sir," he replied as he started manipulating controls. The ship started moving forward then banked to the left and in the direction of the alien world.

"Bridge to spacefold control," Levi said into his intercom. "We're at five hundred thousand kilometers. Engage spacefold drive."

"Copy, bridge" came a reply over the tiny speaker. "Engaging spacefold drive." In less than a minute, the star patterns began to streak and fold onto themselves in the nauseating feeling that everyone in front of a view screen watching the event remembered from the first time. The smart ones looked away from the screens avoiding the shitty feeling.

As quickly as it started, the process was over. It took a few minutes for the wave of nausea to pass.

Back on the bridge. "Long-range sensors reading the planet, Captain," Lucifer reported, still looking into his scanner view screen. The planet is ninety thousand kilometers in diameter. It has a gravity, point nine six percent that of Terra and a nearly identical atmosphere. Hundreds of power signatures covering the entire planet. We will not be able to scan for anything else for at least an hour."

"How is that possible that planets of such different sizes could have gravity and atmospheres so nearly identical?" The captain asked.

"Unknown. In our section of the galaxy, this cannot exist."

"But out here?"

"Everything is possible."

"Is this planet in the same temporal realm as the star system?"

"Unknown."

"What about life signs?"

"Unknown."

"Is there anything that is known?" Annoyance was heavy in his voice.

"Yes…the planet exists. It is heading for the Terran system. And no further scans will be possible for two hours."

"Your point is well taken. Sorry." Lucifer nodded in acceptance.

The next forty-five minutes went by uneventful. Data of all sorts came in on every scanner and sensor that was available. The most important data, other than the indication of life, was only now been completed and was ready for viewing.

"Captain." When Jehovah turned, Lucifer motioned him to his station. When the captain approached, he motioned him to the view screen right above his instrumentation.

"Captain, we've finally calculated the orbital path of this planet." He looked at the screen. The display showed the star system that they were currently working in. It was located in the lower right corner, taking up about one-third of the screen. All the planets with their satellites were represented as was the mysterious asteroid field lying between the fourth and fifth planets. All are slowly moving in their appropriate orbits, like watching a movie in slow motion. The two things that dominate the remainder of the screen are the planet they are approaching and its elliptical path around the star.

"As you can see, this orbit brings it out to a distance of twelve thousand million kilometers. Two and a half times the distance of the tenth planets."

"So…if the planet's orbiting so far from its sun, how can it maintain an atmosphere? How come it looks like it supports life?" The captain's face showed the puzzlement that everyone was feeling at this discovery.

"We'll find out in just over five minutes," Lucifer stated coldly. The five minutes went by slowly, very slowly. The next few minutes after that, even slower. Now, it begins.

"We're getting readings from the sensors," Lucifer said while he was looking into the screen, interpreting the data coming in. "There was an abundance of planet life." After a few more seconds, he said, "There are also hundreds of animal species and thousands of species of insects…There also seems to be—"

"Captain, we're receiving a signal," Lieutenant Kohath said. "From where, Lieutenant?" The captain responded.

"The planet, sir. We're being hailed." Jehovah looked at Lucifer.

"—intelligent humanoid life," Lucifer finished the sentence he had started when Kohath interrupted. Jehovah turned and headed toward his chair.

"All right, Lieutenant," the captain said as he sat down. "Open a channel."

Kohath made a quick movement of his hands and said, "Channel open, sir."

The commanding officer stood, tucking at the front of his tunic from the bottom as he took several steps forward, toward the view screen. "I am Captain Jehovah of the USS *Heaven*. We are on a mission of peaceful exploration."

There is no response. A full thirty seconds passed.

"What is your purpose in our star system?" came over the intercom system in a deep male voice that the universal translator had converted to Bar'klaan.

"We are on a research mission. Our species is suffering from a noncontagious medical emergency. There is a possible cure on the third planet. We hope to be finished before your planet enters the primary system."

"Is there anything we can do to assist?" The voice seemed less formal this time.

"You can start by answering some questions we have, help to expand our understanding of this part of the galaxy."

"You…and several of your crew, are more than welcome to join us here for a discussion. We'll radio the coordinates right now."

"Confirmed," Lucifer said. "Coordinates received."

"We will be in transporter range in"—he looked at Lucifer again—"two minutes, forty-seven seconds."

"We'll beam down in ten minutes."

"Excellent, Captain. We'll see you then…Out."

The captain pressed on of the buttons near the end of the right armrest of his chair. A voice acknowledged his call.

"Doctor, meet me in transporter room one in five minutes.

Bring a padd with all the data on our current genetic affliction."

"Will do," the doctor replied. "Where are we going?"

"To a planet that shouldn't exist."

"Great," the doctor responded. "I had to ask."

Jehovah grinned as he turned off the intercom with the push of a button.

"Lucifer, you're with me. Simeon, you've got the bridge." The captain and first officer left the bridge.

Five minutes later, the captain and first officer were in transporter room one. Dr. Anak came in and two security officers, Lieutenant Abaddon and Ensign Gabriel, right behind him. Anak turned quickly, not realizing until now that the two men were behind him, his mind still with the padd on his desk.

"Okay, the gang's all here. Let's go." Jehovah stepped up onto the transporter platform. The four other men follow. Lieutenant Commander Benjamin was, once again, manning the transporter controls, as he does every time the captain or first officer needs to transport anywhere, at any time.

He manipulated the controls, and the five men vanished in the blue haze of sparkles. In less than a second, the green light, indicating that a transport has been successfully completed, flashed on. Benjamin put the unit on standby and patiently waited for the orders to transport the group back to the ship. He spent his time reviewing technical schematics of the spacefold drive.

When the transport cycle finished, the five men found themselves in a rather expansive foyer of some larger, much grander building.

By the looks of it, this building must be some sort of government center.

"Captain, captain!" came from the lead man in the group of three heading toward the *Heaven*'s crew. They're about fifty meters away and closing fast. The man who spoke, obviously the leader of the group, had a look and outward appearance not unlike proconsul Jacorrian. The leader held out his hand as he approached.

Ten meters. Five meters. One meter.

The group stopped. The captain reached up to meet the outstretched hand with his own.

"Hello, Captain. My name is Takel Ra. Welcome to Marduk, gentlemen."

The man standing in front of Captain Jehovah stood an average height of just over two meters. Humanoid in appearance with long slender arms and legs. In fact, his entire muscular development is almost nonexistent. It is as if the limbs are just a long cylinder that's hinged in the middle. A four-fingered hand adorned the end of the cylinders called arms, the fingers are also long hinged cylinders.

His eyes are slightly larger than the Bar'klaan, and all black. The rest of the facial features remained like those of the landing party. The back of the skull protruded slightly, giving his head a more oval shape. Hair is minimal, light on the eyebrows and none on the head. The rest of his body is covered in a silvery garment with the exception of the hands.

The suit looked like it could be a uniform of some kind, but nothing else about it is clear. There is no rank insignia or department IDs. There are no markings of any kind. The material, though silvery in color, seemed to shimmer in the light. It seemed to be alive. It could be well possible that the uniform is part of the being himself.

The two beings that are with him are a different story. They stand nearly three meters tall. Their physic is similar to the shorter man doing the talking as in that there musculature is underdeveloped to the point of looking like hinged cylinders. The same four-fingered hand ended their arms' length. Their torsos are wide yet bony, the ribs pressed up against the skin, each one perfectly outlined by the tight flesh. The abdomen areas are smaller than the ribbed upper halves and flat, leading down to a large, nearly protruding pelvic bone.

Externally, the two large aliens had no visually defined sex organs, at least none that the Bar'klaans could identify. Nor do they wear clothes of any kind.

Their heads are larger with more pronunciation than Takel Ra's, and bald. They have no ears other than a tiny slit on each side of their head. Their eyes are much larger, to a point that the socket bone of the skull expanded during evolution to allow for their unusual size. They have no noses to speak of and slightly larger slits for mouths. Larger, that is, than the slits they used for ears. Their skin tone is an eerie shade of gray.

"These are my associates," Takel Ra continued as he waved his hand to acknowledge the two behind him. "This is Unaka, and this is Larkoh." His hand returned, and he locked his fingers together in front of him. He continued, "Unaka is our head of internal affairs, and Larkoh is our head of external affairs."

"I am Captain Jehovah of the starship *Heaven*. This is my first officer, Commander Lucifer." He turned his head slightly to the right. "This is Dr. Anak, chief medical officer. The two men behind him are security officers Abaddon"—who nodded his head—"and Gabriel"—who nodded his as well.

"Now what is this problem your race is having?" Takel Ra asked as the group started walking in the direction that the three had came from. Jehovah took the padd from the doctor, glanced at it quickly, and handed it to Takel Ra. "Hmmm. This could be a problem," Takel Ra said dryly after quickly looking over the data on the padd for a minute. He handed the padd to one of his associates; none of the Bar'klaans knew which one. The alien with the padd turned and headed in another direction.

"Unaka is going to check your data with our medical database. We'll know something in a little while. Until then, let's go to my office. We can continue our conversation there."

"Would it be possible for the security officers and myself to look around for a while? Check out this magnificent city of yours?" Anak asked Takel Ra.

"Absolutely. Feel free to go anywhere you like."

"When Unaka returns, we'll call you," Jehovah added. "Collect as much data as possible," Lucifer requested.

The men agreed and headed off on their own, Larkoh following behind them. Jehovah and Lucifer followed Takel Ra. They walked for about ten minutes.

Takel Ra's office is rather large, fifteen meters by fifteen meters at best guess. The view of the city is spectacular from the window to the right of Takel Ra's desk. Being eighty-five stories up, every view is spectacular.

The three men sat down, Takel Ra behind his desk in the over-sized leather chair and the Bar'klaans in the two chairs on the other side. Takel Ra's secretary came in to offer the two strangers a beverage. His secretary looked exactly like the two men they had met upon their arrival. Neither of the men could determine if the secretary is male or female. Both men refused for the time being.

"Now, Captain. What is it you would like to know?" He asked with a large toothy smile that reminded the two men of proconsul Jacorrian.

"Well," Jehovah began. "About this planet, for one thing. How does it maintain a comfortable atmosphere while its orbit is so far from the sun?"

"We don't have it worked out totally yet, but what we do know holds our curiosity for now," Takel Ra explained. "As we travel through the temporal barrier around this star system, our atmosphere and gravity processing systems increase. When we exit the barrier to complete our orbit, our environmental systems start to deteriorate, but the rate of decay is slow enough so it doesn't affect our daily lives. There are some components in combination in our atmosphere that protects biological life from being affected by the barrier. It is still a mystery to our scientists, but we hope to be able to explain and exploit it someday."

"Exploit in what way?" Lucifer asked, not trying to hide the deep concern in his voice.

"If we can artificially recreate the elements of the temporal barrier, we could accelerate the processing of life on worlds with very, very minimal life and open new planets for colonization."

"Artificially recreate?" he repeated with the same deep concern. "Of course," Takel Ra said. "With the development of intelligent life on the third and fourth planets in our system, we cannot jeopardize the delicate balance and risk killing everything on two worlds."

"So you know about the life-forms?" Jehovah asked. Lucifer looked much more relieved.

"Oh yes. We've been monitoring their development since life formed on both planets."

"Just how old is your race?"

Takel Ra answered, "Our civilization has been around since before the birth of the primary solar system. Well over a billion years by any standard. Even after we attained the ability to travel faster than light, we could not find a civilization as technologically advanced as ourselves. We gave up looking thousands of our years ago." A slight smile spread across his face. "I'm glad you didn't give up on us."

"Actually we weren't coming to see you," Lucifer stated. "What do you mean? What else could be of interest?"

"The third planet," Jehovah started to explain. "One of our probes landed there some years back. We discovered then that the protohumans there have the same reno-aminoclades combination that we do. That makes them the only known life-forms that can help us."

"In what way can *they* help *you?*"

"In a more advanced state, the DNA from the protohumans

can be used to filter out the disease," Jehovah continued. Just then, Unaka walked into the room. He moved up to Takel Ra's desk. Both closed their eyes and seemed in simultaneous trances. This lasted for about two minutes. They opened their eyes. Unaka turned and left the room. Takel Ra's expression looked glum.

"What is it? What's wrong?"

"Unaka has reviewed our medical database. He found nothing there that can help you. I'm sorry."

"Don't be sorry. It was a chance. We'll continue with our current course of action."

Takel Ra continued, "Oh yes. You were starting to tell me."

"The process is called electrodinucleic transposition. I don't know it fully, but I understand it is a combination of DNA that is altered, and at that point, the disease is removed, and the DNA returned to normal then injected into the patient. The new DNA resequences the body's DNA until the patient is cured."

"I apologize for my ignorance, Captain, but what do you mean by 'more advance state of DNA'?" His face was twisted in confusion. "If the tests we are currently conducting fail, we will genetically advance the humanoid species there until they are several millennia ahead." The look on Takel Ra's face suddenly became a blend of shock and anger.

"Captain, you must not interfere with the intelligent life-forms, the ones you call protohumans! We will not allow you to do that!"

"We plan to only use two, and there won't be any change to the beings they are. We have enough people with us to make enough vaccine to treat all of our infected people. Takel Ra, I'm talking one hundred and forty trillion people. Our original plan involved manipulation of the beings themselves, but new techniques allow us to have the females give birth to a newer form, and we will use them. We will create a newer, more advanced species."

"And what will that do to the indigenous life. Won't your newer species eventually phase out what's there now?"

"It's quite possible…but there can be no assurances."

Dr. Anak came into the room with Abaddon and Gabriel. The atmosphere in the room suddenly changed, like a cold snap of wind across the face.

"Captain…listen…I see your side of this. I don't agree with it, but I see the need for what you do. Give me some time, and let me take up your dilemma with the scientific community. You must understand. We've been studying the evolution of life on both planets since the earliest of time…since life actually developed on both worlds. That you want to genetically alter some of the life there may not take well with those scientists who prefer to keep evolution natural."

"I understand, and I respect your position, but understand this… we are a desperate people," Jehovah said quite calmly.

"Give me thirty days, Bar'klaan time, and we will have a decision for you," Takel Ra answered.

"Realize that we could be finished this entire project and be gone before you get close enough to do anything about it. I may not be able to stop those directly involved with the procedures, but I will stall them for thirty days. Beyond that, I cannot guarantee any results."

"That may be all the time you need to lose," Takel Ra said in a more pleasant tone.

"No," Jehovah answered. "Not just now…we should get back to our people and inform them of our discussion."

Jehovah and Lucifer stood and met the doctor and security men in the open space between the desk and door. "We'll see you in thirty days." He opened his communicator. "Jehovah to *Heaven*. Ready to beam back." The group sparkled away into nothingness.

Takel Ra pushed the button on his desk connected to the interoffice communications system. "This is Takel Ra. Set up an emergency meeting of the Scientific Community Council. I want it for no later than tomorrow afternoon. Stress to them it is an emergency."

A voice from the little speaker answered, "Right away, sir. I'll notify you as soon as I get it organized."

The grave expression Takel Ra wore seemed to smooth out very slightly after he hit the communications system button again, deactivating the unit. He sat in his seat, his eyes staring into the unknown realm of thought. He would get no sleep tonight.

"Jehovah to the bridge," the captain said from his ready room. "Get us back to Terra right away. Notify me when we arrive."

The five men from the landing party sat in various seats around the ready room. Abaddon and Gabriel were seated on the sofa to the left of the door leading to the bridge. Dr. Anak was seated in the overstuffed chair to the right of the door leading to the corridor of deck one. Lucifer was sitting in the chair in front of the captain's desk. Jehovah occupied his usual seat.

"What were you able to find out, doc?" Jehovah asked.

"Their medical records date back well over a million years. I managed to download the treatments for six diseases back home still labeled 'incurable' and data on alternate treatments to dozens of other conditions. Nothing to help us, though."

"What about you, Abaddon?"

"These people have had faster-than-light travel for five hundred thousand years. Advancement in technology is pretty much at a snail's pace. They're only slightly more advanced than we are." The captain looked at his first officer.

"I guess what Takel Ra said about holding their curiosity involves all aspects of their lives." Lucifer nodded in agreement. "Gabriel?"

"Their databanks house information from eons past. During one of the earlier recorded orbits, one of the moons collided with a planet in the system. The moon was totally destroyed and became, along with some of the smaller pieces of debris, the asteroid belt just beyond the fourth planet. The rest of the planet broke into two pieces, one was about twenty times bigger than the other. The larger one became the third planet. The smaller one became the satellite."

He took several breathes then continued, "Marduk orbits the star every six and a half years. With the time it spends outside of the temporal realm, four thousand years passed on the planet Terra. They've got an actual, physical sample of the primordial ooze that spawned life on Terra, along with samples of all life from the planet…and I mean every form of life, right up to the friends we mean to exploit." *Beep, beep, beep.* The intercom alerted the captain of an incoming message. He pressed the button to engage the system. "Bridge here, sir. We are entering the Terran system."

"Understood. Contact Professor Uranus. Tell him I'll be down to see him in about ten minutes."

He replied into the air, "Yes, sir." A beep was faintly heard as the intercom system shut off automatically.

The captain scanned the room, looking at his men. "Dismissed. Lucifer, you're with me." He keyed the intercom again. "Jehovah to transporter room two. We're beaming down." The two left the ready room through the door leading to the hall.

The office door opened with a whoosh as Jehovah and Lucifer walk in during Uranus's meeting with Dr. Cronus. Jehovah ignored the meeting and sat in the chair beside Cronus. Lucifer sat on the cushioned bench against the wall a few meters away.

"I'm sorry for the intrusion, gentlemen," Jehovah began, "but our business is rather urgent."

"What can we do for you, Captain?" Uranus said, hiding his anger and annoyance well. "How was your trip to the new planet?"

"That's what we're here about, professor." His tone became more serious. "All tests on the protohumans must be suspended for thirty days, our days, that is, or there could possibly be hell to pay."

"And to what do we owe the honor of your gloomy forecast?"

"The planet we went to maintains a species of humanoid hundreds of thousands of years in advance of our own," he continued slow and firm.

"They have been studying the life-forms on Terra since life

began there. They are so old that their recorded history tells of the creation of Terra and other parts of the star system."

"So?" Uranus asked.

"So, professor"—sarcasm heavy as he spoke—"the planetary leader is convening a meeting of their scientific community to get us authorization to use some protohumans for our project. I told them we wouldn't do anything until we met again in thirty days."

"With all due respect, Captain," Cronus jumped in now. "We will be bringing *One* back on the station to begin preliminary testing in two days. Just who do you think you are telling them we'd stop working? Thirty days will put us behind schedule."

"Behind schedule?" Jehovah looked at the two scientists with an expression of curious disbelief. "Unless something happened in the last day, we are still, at best estimate, five months ahead of schedule. Thirty days is bullshit. I gave my word that no testing on the protohumans would happen for thirty days. Since the threat is from external sources, it falls under military jurisdiction. What I say, goes."

"What external threat, Captain?" Uranus now. "They're six months away. What possible harm can they be."

"When I said hundreds of thousands of years older than us. Well, it's closer to the order of a million years. Now let me ask you two this…" He paused more for dramatic effect than anything else but passed it off as collecting his thoughts. "If we made contact with a primitive race that comprehended space travel, would you show them all our technological advancements on their first visit?"

"No, of course not," Uranus answered.

"We didn't see very much of their technology. What we did see was impressive. Do you really believe we could adequately defend ourselves against a race nearly a million years more advanced than we are?"

"Well, since you put it that way, I guess thirty days wouldn't be asking too much." Professor Uranus finally agreed, as did Cronus.

"Then it is agreed? No testing on protohumans for thirty days.

Scan her and study her but don't remove even a drop of blood or do anything else invasive."

"Thirty days, Captain," Uranus said as the two men headed for the door. "No more."

Without turning around, Jehovah said, "Agreed."

He and Lucifer exited the room and walked down the corridor. The door closed behind them.

"Cronus," Uranus said to the man across from him after the door closed and he was sure Jehovah and Lucifer were well down the hall. "Get everything ready for *One*, then get it up here."

"What about what Jehovah asked?" Cronus looked at him oddly. "What about it? These Nephillium are six months away. What the hell can they do? Just get everything ready."

"All right," Cronus responded, with worry hanging tightly on his word.

CHAPTER

Captain's log: Stardate 9814.70. Our first meeting with the life-forms called the Nephillium. Other than looks, they seem unremarkable. For being nearly a million years older than we are, this concerns me. My gut feeling says they are much more than they lead on. It is understandable that they not reveal their full capability on our initial visit, but there is a feeling of darkness one need not be an empath to sense.

"Captain on the bridge," Lieutenant Simeon said from the tactical station when the door of the turbolift opened and Jehovah and Lucifer stepped out. The captain sat in his command chair as Lucifer stood on the captain's right side.

"Do you think Uranus will keep his word and wait the thirty days you asked for?"

"I certainly hope so, number one. There's no telling what the Nephillium would do…what kinds of technology they didn't show us."

"It is quite possible that they have weapons far beyond our comprehension. The big question is, will they use what they haven't showed us?"

"Exactly, number one. Exactly."

The sparkles of the transporter faded away revealing the hairy apelike protohuman known as *One*. As soon as the containment field dropped and movement was restored, *One*, still a brainfull of emotion and instinct, started flailing and charging toward the transporter operator.

Before the operator could react, she heard a high-pitched sound coming from somewhere behind the charging creature. Suddenly, *One* let out a roar of pain rather than the roar of fright and anger that was just coming out. The creature's face became distorted. Then, in half a heartbeat, her eyes closed as her face became more relaxed. *One* slumped to the floor and lay there unconscious. Behind her, standing in the doorway, is Professor Oceanus, his phaser still pointing at where the beast lay.

"Thanks for the assist," Ensign Dionysus, one of Dr. Zeus's assistants who was pulling extra duty as the transporter operator, said to the man who just saved her life. "You just saved my ass."

"You're welcome," he said. "It's a good thing I came in when I did."

"You don't have to tell me twice."

Oceanus tapped at the control of the station's intercom access system panel located on the wall just over his left shoulder. "Oceanus to Zeus…Come in, please."

"What is it?" The voice on the PA asked. "Would you come to transporter room one?"

"I'm on my way."

"Bring a couple of assistants with you."

"Okay. Anything else while we're at it?"

"As a matter of fact, Doctor, there is."

"You're kidding, right?" the voice said, sounding a little annoyed. "No." A slight pause. "Would you stop by sick bay on your way and grab a gurney?"

"Is someone injured."

"Not injured, Doctor, unconscious. Just get your asses down here. Gods damn it!" His voice was loud and stern.

"We're on our way. Out." The voice on the other end that once sounded annoyed was humbled.

It took a few minutes, but Zeus finally came into the transporter room followed by Ensign Hades, who was pulling a gurney. It took all four people to lift *One* onto the gurney and two to push her. It took nearly ten minutes of straining to roll the gurney straight down the halls to get her into a special lab set up just for her. The group strapped her to the table in the middle of the room and exited, turning on the force field in the doorway. Just as the hum of the force field became evident, the group could hear the grunts of *One*, who was just starting to regain consciousness. "Just in time," Hermes stated.

"I don't want to cut it that close again," Hebe said. All agreed.

Professor Cronus came to the force field–protected door about ten minutes after the three men left. He just stood there staring at the female man-beast. He was not aware of the passing of time. Professor Uranus showed up an indeterminate amount of time later. He woke Cronus up from his waking dream.

"Is everything all right?"

"Yes…fine. I didn't hear you walk up, that's all." He shook his head in hopes of clearing out the cobwebs that have taken up residence in his mind.

Uranus opened the medium-sized gray bag that he was holding. Cronus recognized it at once as an ancient medical bag used by doctors centuries ago to carry their supplies in when they had to visit patients in their homes.

Uranus removed a small type-one phaser from the bag and held it with a firm grip. He saw the wide-eyed look of confusion and distrust grew on Cronus's face. "It's set on stun. In the event *One* should break free of her restraints. Nothing more." Cronus relaxed with visible relief.

Uranus nodded his head, and Cronus pressed several buttons on the control panel on the side of the door. The blue lights and hum that denote force field activation fell dark and silent. The two men stepped into the room, and at once, Cronus hit buttons on his tricorder and the force field hummed back to life. They approached the table in the middle of the room. The one that the protohuman, in all her ugliness, was strapped down on.

"Captain to the bridge" echoed throughout the *Heaven*. It took a few minutes, but the turbolift door opened, and the captain stepped onto the command deck. He looked around and saw Lieutenant Aaron looking at him. He was motioned over to the science station usually occupied by Commander Lucifer. He walked over.

"What is it, Lieutenant?" he asked as he approached and stood beside the young officer. "I was doing routine scans of the surface, and when I scanned Olympus Station, I picked up an anomalous reading. When I concentrated the scan, I picked up a protohuman on the station.

"*One*," the captain whispered to no one in particular. "Where on the station is she?" Aaron looked down at the screen and replied, "That data will be coming through in a minute." Jehovah stood silent, waiting for information. It came quickly. "The protohuman is in gamma wing…lab number two…force field is in place."

"We'll see about that!" Jehovah said in a voice thick with restrained anger. If only Aaron could conceivably realize just how restrained the captain was actually being. Jehovah turned and walked back toward the turbolift in strong, deliberate steps. He entered the lift without saying another word.

"Where is One, professor?" Jehovah asked sternly but calmly, suppressing his anger well. Uranus could see in the captain's eyes what the rest of his features are able to hide, the intense burning anger still boiling, not unlike the lava in the shaft of an active volcano, ready to explode without warning.

"I don't know wh—"

"DON'T FUCK WITH ME, PROFESSOR!" the captain screamed in Uranus's face. He paused now and regained his composure. "We wouldn't be here if we didn't know."

"Captain…I, by no means, want to fuck with you. But this is not your decision. It is ours."

"To hell it is, professor," Jehovah came back. "You haven't met with the Nephillium. You have no concept of what they're capable of. Hell, I have no concept of what they're capable of."

"What does that have to do with our research projects?" Uranus asked, oblivious to the possible consequences of his actions this day. "Are you fucking kidding?" Disbelief booming from his voice.

"You are kidding, right?"

"No, I'm not," he responded with serious conviction.

The captain let out a laugh. Not that he found it humorous, but it was either laugh or explode at this man's lack of compassion or common sense.

"Unbelievable," Lucifer stated coldly.

"Let me fill you in again, Professors Moron and Dimwit," the captain interjected. Then he continued, "The Nephillium are at least a millennium more advanced than we are. Do you remember me telling you this yesterday?" Uranus and Cronus nodded silently in acknowledgement. "Now, doesn't that set off the warning bells in those pea brains of yours?" Neither said a word. Both men looked dumbfounded. The captain continued, "These Nephillium didn't want us to experiment on the bipeds here."

"All right, all right," Uranus said in a sigh of defeat. "We figure the Nephillium are, what, about six months away? We can be done and gone by the time they get here. What the hell is wrong with that?"

"Did it ever occur to either of you, incredible morons, that it will take that long for the fucking planet to get here. Their ships could be here in an hour. We have twenty-three teraquads of data from these people, and we still don't know dick about them. What part of all that didn't you and Dr. Dopey over there"—he motioned to

Cronus with a lift of his right arm—"understand at our last briefing?" The captain's face reddened up quickly then he screamed, "IT TOOK US TWENTY FUCKING SECONDS TO GET HERE!"

Neither of the two men seemed at all concerned about the captain's ranting. They sat with their expressions changing very little during the whole thing. Uranus ended a brief moment of silence.

"We've looked over your data, Captain. We've found no evidence that they will ever be of any consequence to this mission." His voice was flat and dull. He continued in a matter-of-fact manner, "There is no way I could stop it even if I wanted to…even if you tried force as persuasion." The captain's expression showed he's on the verge of understanding.

"Yes, Captain," Uranus helped him along. "We've already impregnated *One* with the first-generation DNA. In less than a day, we will have the first byproduct from *One*. So you see? You're too late…as will the Nephillium be late."

"You may have condemned all of us to death, professor," the captain said as he turned and walked toward the door, Lucifer following. "I think not, Captain. You'll see," Uranus said, trying to sound reassuring.

Captain's log: Supplemental. Not two hours after getting Professor Uranus and Dr. Cronus to agree to the Nephillium demands, we have discovered that not only did they bring the biped known as One to the Olympus Station, but they have already begun the experiment. All we can do now is sit back and wait for some response from the Nephillium.

Lucifer walked over to Jehovah who was sitting in his command chair on the bridge. The day rotation was only an hour in. Everyone on the bridge was tensed—in waiting. It's amazing, in hindsight, Jehovah would later say, that the Nephillium had so much control for being so far away.

"Ten hours and still no response from the Nephillium. We may be able to take that as a good sign," Lucifer said.

"With an estimated hour and a half until the first birth, we've still got a while to go," the captain replied. He then turned to the communications officer. "Lieutenant Kohath, contact the Mars station and get a status update."

"Aye, sir," Kohath replied as he worked the controls to do what the captain instructed. Everyone on the bridge was quite. The only noise heard were the machines humming life as they keep the ship's systems alive. It took about three minutes.

"Mars station reports all quiet. Nothing to report." The tension let up slightly but not to anyone's relief. Time slipped by slowly. Seconds seemed like minutes, minutes like hours. Nearly ninety minutes later...

"Olympus Station is hailing captain...It's professor Uranus... He reports that it's time." Kohath breaks the silence. "Okay...reply that we're on our way then contact Dr. Anak. Have him meet us in transporter room one. Lucifer, you're with me. Lieutenant Simeon, you have the com."

The captain and first officer disappeared into the turbolift.

A few minutes later, the two men entered lab two in the gamma wing of Olympus Station. One was strapped to the exam table in the middle of the room. Her howls of pain could be heard throughout the entire complex, this there was no escaping from.

Professor Coeus, the lead researcher of the genetics division, was sitting on a stool in between One's legs waiting for the imminent arrival. The swollen belly of the beast partially hid the doctor from the two men. The sweat was building on his brow as he awaited the baby at the end of its internal journey. The captain and first officer took a position near the outer ring of spectators, just within view.

Another howl-like scream came from the primitive being on the table.

"It's coming out," Dr. Coeus said in a voice of anxiety. An echo of the events of less than a day before. Everyone in the room wished silently that the end result was better than before. Another howl/scream filled the complex, and the roar followed. "It's just about there…It *looks* Bar'klaan." He chose his words carefully.

"The head's coming out," he said in less than a minute after his last statement. "Holy shit." His voice was a dull monotone of disbelief in an elevated whisper. His eyes were wide, his mouth gaping open behind his surgical mask. "Here comes the shoulders," he muttered in the same voice. "My gods! This is horrible!"

As the infant came out, everyone in the room wanted to stare at the deformed baby with curious disgust. All who saw it reeled back. The deformities ranged from large oozing sores to huge cysts to twisted limbs and missing digits. Tears flowed from a few in the room. Without another word, Coeus took the infant into another lab.

Jehovah and Lucifer followed Uranus and Cronus to Uranus's officer. A mirror reaction to the last time the two men visited the lab complex. A different tone hung in the air this time.

In the office, the four men were seated. "Where did he take the baby?" Jehovah started the meeting. "Lab three. For an autopsy. We have to wait until we get the test results from Coeus."

It took about fifteen minutes.

"Well, here are the results." Coeus handed Uranus the padd he was carrying.

"Give us the overview, will ya, doc?" Lucifer asked.

"Sure." He started, "The tests show that we are on the right track, but we had some unexpected cellular reproduction that caused the deformities."

"So what now?" Jehovah asked.

"I've got Hera's team working on isolating the root cells and correcting the problem. We're hoping it won't take too long."

"Is there anything we, on the *Heaven*, can do to help?"

"No, Captain. Thank you anyway. We have more than enough people to do the job."

"Okay, then. We'll be on our way. Contact us when you've isolated the problem and are ready to try again." He took his communicator from behind his back and flipped the top open.

"Will do, Captain," Uranus said.

"Jehovah to *Heaven*. Two to beam up." The two dematerialized.

The next full day brought no news from the surface. Now as the end of the day shift drew to an end, Lieutenant Kohath answered a beep that indicated an incoming transmission. "Captain," he started, "incoming message from Professor Uranus."

"On screen," Jehovah replied. The image of Professor Uranus appeared on the main view screen.

"Captain, we think we've isolated the flaw, but we need to bring three more females to speed the process along."

"That may not be a prudent course of action, professor."

"Maybe not, Captain, but the process has begun. I'm simply informing you so the next time your crewman scans the station, you won't be surprised."

"Understood. Is there anything else, professor?"

"No…" After a brief pause, he said, "Captain, using three more will get us out of here much faster."

"I understood that the first time, professor."

"But you don't approve?"

"No, sir, I do not."

"Look, Captain, we've already violated your agreement. We might as well get it over with as quick as possible."

"Is there anything else, professor?" the captain said coldly. "Apparently not, Captain. Uranus out."

"Good-bye, professor," Jehovah replied and sat in his seat quietly.

In Olympus Station, the lab that held One was a bustle of activity. The bed that held the protohuman was no longer the only one in the room. Now there were three more beds with female protohumans strapped down on them. Two of Professor Hera's assistants, Ensigns Boreas and Zephyr, entered the room. Boreas was carrying a hypospray.

"Are you ready to get this shit going?" Boreas asked Zephyr. "Sure. Why not?" was Zephyr's reply.

Boreas walked over to the protohuman on the bed farthest from One. He injected the beast with the hypospray, and the protohuman fell silent and limp, unconscious from the drug in the hypospray. He moved down the line, injecting the other three.

"Let's get their eggs and get out of here," Boreas said after injecting the last one.

"Already started," Zephyr responded from between the legs of the second female.

"Cool" came from Boreas.

It only took a few minutes to get the four eggs. The two left the room with the protohumans still unconscious.

Entering lab three, the two brought the four containers holding the precious cargo to Professor Hera. "Place those containers on the table over there." She pointed to workstation two, away from her own. "I'll be there momentarily."

After a few minutes, Hera made her way over to where the eggs were. She placed the dish holding the eggs under a microscope and, using a tool similar to an eyedropper, began to examine the eggs. After a couple of minutes, she was done. All four eggs were in perfect condition.

"Now the serious shit begins," she said to the two men still standing there. She placed a dish under the microscope and, using other instruments from the same collection as the eyedropper was from, began the careful, delicate procedure of genetically manipulating the egg with cells from a Bar'klaan male's sperm.

It took Hera nearly an hour to work her scientific magic on each egg. Aeolus and Zephyr stood silently watching her perform the delicate tasks. The workday ended with the completion of the fourth egg.

"Will you two put these dishes in stasis for the night?" she asked the two men, still amazed by what they just witnessed on the view screen that's linked to the microscope.

"Sure," they responded. "Okay."

When the four dishes were away, the three left the room, Hera turning off the lights as the door closed behind her. The three headed to the mess hall. In the mess hall, the trio broke up. Hera went and sat with Professor Coeus and began to inform him of the day's events. Boreas and Zephyr go sit in a corner booth where Ensigns Hades and Dionysus, who work under Dr. Zeus, were finishing their dinners.

Captain's log: Stardate 9887.10. Four new attempts at the experiment were born several hours ago, three females and one male. All four were failures. One came close, and Professor Uranus seems optimistic. The other three are horrible mutations ranging from physical to psychological. The four have been placed in an isolated area away from the station. On a personal note, I cannot help but feel pity for these mutations, forced to life…forced to suffer.

In the office of Professor Uranus. "Captain, I just received the results from the DNA tests on the children." Uranus's voice was thick with excitement.

"What do you make of them, professor?" The captain's voice sounded cautious.

"Well, the disfigurements in two of the beings are obvious. There is no disputing them." He pressed a button on the terminal in front of his computer, and four images filled the view screen. They were pictures of the four beings born just over two hours ago. The top two beings were deformed over their faces.

"There was an unbalanced decay in a series of protons that overlap each other when the two strands of DNA were combined," Uranus said looking at the padd in his hands. "The flaws vary but are very similar." The two faces on the top of the screen showed inflated cheekbones and enlarged foreheads reminiscent of caricatures drawn by artists at county fairs back on H'Too Bar'kla.

"The deformities include hardening of the bones, tighter

muscular development, which will allow for only a reduced mobility, spinal curvature, as well as a hostility quotient much higher than we expected." The jawbones were grossly enlarged with teeth crooked and pointed. The eyes of the creatures were glossy and dull, denoting a serious lack of intelligence.

The same abnormalities were clearly visible along the neck and down along the shoulders. These same deformities covered the entire bodies of the unfortunate beings. The four men looked at the screen, and an aura of somberness filled the room. The captain's eyes watered slightly.

After a few minutes, Uranus continued, "Subject three, the girl in the lower left corner, shows very minor deformities, but only on the body and limbs. The rigid facial features of the mother are less noticeable. This brings her one step closer to what we are aiming for."

"But?" Lucifer asked.

"Pardon?" Uranus responded to his one-word question. Jehovah continued for his first officer, "What's her drawback?"

"It seems our number three here has the ability to move objects with her mind…at will…and has been able to do so since about the age of five minutes. Her brain activity is quadruple that of any of the other subjects, even the first ones."

Cronus interjected and explained, "That is why she is not in isolation with the others." Jehovah and Lucifer looked at each other, puzzled.

"Why keep her here?" asked Lucifer.

And Cronus continued, "We must eliminate her mental ability right away. We have no way of determining what could happen in, let's say, ten thousand years from now if we let these beings evolve with these abilities."

"Is there a chance the power will fade as the child grows?"

Now Uranus answered, "It might, but if it doesn't, we've given these beings the chance to develop the power without the understanding of how to use it. It is possible that someday, with a single thought, they could wipe out the universe."

"I see your point, professor," Lucifer responded. Jehovah agreed then added, "What about the last one?"

Uranus's facial expression became more upbeat. "Now this one looks most promising. As you can see, the physical changes are more subtle than the girl, but he is completely without deformities."

Jehovah's eyes widened, as did Lucifer's. "None at all." There was a short pause, then.

"There is one problem. His ESP quotient is much higher than the girl's. He can make you think what he wants you to think. Do what he wants you to do. And at a little more than two hours old, just over six weeks in his years, he has the mental capacity of a young adult."

"Now that's a dangerous little boy," Jehovah said with disbelief spewing through every word.

"That's why he is not only isolated but sedated as well," Cronus told them. "And he'll stay that way until we can counteract the ESP effect."

"So. What's next on your agenda, professor?" Jehovah asked, looking into Uranus's eyes.

"Well," he started. "I've got Zeus's team working on the boy and Hera's team working on the girl. Dr. Coeus is overseeing their progress." Looking a little confused, his eyes quickly scanned the desktop. After a second, he saw what he was looking for. A padd off-center and to the right. He picked it up and glanced over it. "Ah yes," he continued, "Poseidon and Hermes's teams are correcting the genetic flaws in the DNA. They figure they'll be able to impregnate the protohumans tomorrow morning sometime."

"Professor?" Lucifer asked, looking out of the window in the center of the office door. "I'm just noticing. Why is it so quiet around here? No one has walked past this door for, like, five minutes."

"We've got half of Hera's and half of Zeus's teams observing the progress of the mutations, who have been relocated to the west side of the western river, beyond the lion's statue. Until the ESP problem is corrected, we thought it best to keep the number of people on the station at a minimum. We nearly lost three men just discovering that they had these powers."

"The next births are expected day after tomorrow, late in the afternoon," Cronus volunteered. "We'll save the two of you seats," he stated with a light laugh.

"Oh, we'll be there. Don't you worry," Jehovah responded with a little more seriousness in his voice.

Lucifer looked at Cronus with a stare that, with his goatee and thick bushy eyebrow, made him look evil. *In fact, very nearly demonic,* Cronus thought to himself. After a few moments, a devilish grin swept across his face. Cronus breathed easier.

After a brief moment, Jehovah stood up. As he rose, he extended his right hand toward Professor Uranus, who accepted it into his right hand. Lucifer followed suit.

"Well, professor, until tomorrow," Jehovah said. "Until tomorrow, Captain" was his reply.

"Professor," Lucifer said as he turned toward the door. "Doctor," he said to Cronus, giving his head a slight downward tilt.

"Professor," Jehovah followed. The two exited the office and turned right, toward the transporter room.

"Well," Uranus said to Cronus, "I'm ready to call it a night." Cronus replied, "So am I."

The two men exited the office and went their separate ways. Back on the *Heaven.*

"What are your plans for the rest of the night, sir?"

"Dinner. Then bed." They walked silently for a few seconds.

"Ya know, Lucifer? Every time I see one of those mutations, I feel ten years older, and that much more worn out."

"So do I, sir. So do I." He hung his head down, displaying what could be construed as shame. Not for him but for his people. Another silent second went by. "Good night, Captain," Lucifer said as he turned down the corridor on the left, which leads to his cabin.

"Good night, number one." The captain headed into the mess hall for the day's last meal.

The next morning came much too quickly for the captain. He mechanically went through his morning routine all along wondering what kind of biological monstrosities he would be faced with today. It was almost too much to bear, and he sat on the corner of his bed, staring emptily into space beyond the transparent aluminum panel that makes up the windows on his ship.

He rose from his bed slowly and took a few steps toward the door. Exhaling in a loud sigh, he left his cabin and headed for the bridge. The doors of his cabin closed and locked behind him.

Jehovah's empty demeanor lasted for the entire shift. To the rest of the bridge crew, it was like serving under an android. The shift's end was just under an hour away and still no news from the surface. Then with about forty minutes left, Lieutenant Kohath announced, "Incoming message from Professor Uranus." The captain's spell broke.

"On screen." Uranus's image fills a full half of the main view screen. "Greetings, Captain. How are you doing on this fine day?" the image on the screen said.

"Good. Good. And yourself?" Jehovah responded.

"Not bad" was the reply. "But I am not good either." He continued, "I am told that the corrections in the genetic material will not be ready until sometime tomorrow evening." He looked a little saddened by the comment he just made. Jehovah, however, seemed a bit elated. "We won't be able to fertilize for several hours after that."

"I'd still like to be present if possible."

"Not a problem, Captain. I'll contact you again when we are ready."

"Very good, professor. Out." The view screen returned to the image of the top slope of the planet with the darkness of space beyond it.

Once again, the night passed too quickly for the captain. He walked onto the bridge at zero eight hundred hours.

"Uranus hailed about five minutes ago," Lieutenant Reuben, the night-shift communications officer, said before the turbolift doors closed. He then continued, "He said they're ready to begin when you get there. Commander Lucifer is waiting in transporter room two."

Without stopping and before he got to his chair, he made a U-turn and got back on the turbolift, not saying a word the whole time. A look of confusion spread across his face after he received Uranus's message, as the scientists are twelve hours ahead of the projected schedule.

When the doors of transporter room two opened, Jehovah saw Lucifer standing in front of the control console. He was talking to Lieutenant Commander Benjamin, who was getting the system ready. "Good morning, sir," Benjamin said, alerting Lucifer of the captain's arrival.

He turned and said, "Captain, I trust you slept well?" Only half-asking.

"No. Not at all," Jehovah answered abruptly. "I don't think I'll get another good night's sleep until we get home." His tone was almost apologetic now.

"Nor I," Lucifer replied as he stepped onto the transporter platform, following his captain.

The two materialized in the transporter room then make their way to lab beta two on Eden. Everyone involved in this aspect of the mission was present to see the four protohumans impregnated with the modified DNA. Uranus and Cronus approached Jehovah and Lucifer. "Welcome, Captain, Commander" came from behind the two men. They turned to find Uranus and Cronus standing not a meter and a half away.

"How are you two this morning?" Cronus asked.

The captain and first officer spun around, startled at first, then relaxed when they realized where they are. "Very good, professor. How about you two?"

"I'll let you know when we're finished here." Lucifer retorted with, "I hear that."

"Professor, I was under the impression you wouldn't be ready for another six hours or so."

Uranus grinned slightly as he responded, "It's Dr. Athena's fault. She is one of our newest and youngest members. She recognized a degradation pattern familiar to a disease on gamma prime that she helped eliminate. If it wasn't for her, we could have been looking for the solution for weeks…maybe even months. That twelve-hour estimate I gave you yesterday was way premature."

"Why are we on Eden instead of Olympus?" Lucifer asked as the men entered the lab.

"We decided to move here after we started working with our young patients with telekinetic powers," Cronus answered. And he continued, "The two kids are at the other end of the complex under the guidance of Dr. Hestia and Dr. Ares. Once this procedure is finished, all nonessential personnel will be beamed to Olympus." The men took their seats in the front row.

In the center of the lab were four beds. Each bed had a protohuman strapped to it. The beasts were sedated but not completely under. All four of the protohumans had their legs strapped to harnesses that force the knees to bend and legs to spread, exposing all the bodily parts needed for this procedure.

Dr. Athena rolled a small table to each of the four beds. On each table was a small dish containing an impregnated egg and a long thin needle at the end of a syringe. Athena started with One and moved across the row of tables. She used the syringe to remove the egg from the dish. She then slid the syringe into the vagina of the protohuman. Carefully guiding the long needle inside of One, she reached the womb. She slowly injected the egg into the body of the beast.

She removed the needle and moved on to the next one. All four were finished in about seven minutes. Now the hardest part of this procedure began. The nine-hour wait until the birth of the next phase. Jehovah and Lucifer returned to the *Heaven*. The routine on board the ship was somehow different for the two men.

"Captain Jehovah to the bridge." The voice over the PA system blared throughout the ship.

"What is it?" Jehovah said into the intercom panel on the desk in his quarters.

"I've got Professor Uranus on the line, sir," the voice said. "Pipe it through to my quarters."

"Captain Jehovah? Are you there?" The disembodied voice of Uranus asked.

"I'm here, professor. What is it?"

"We're ready to induce labor. Would you like to attend?"

"Lucifer and I will be down momentarily."

"Very good, Captain. Out."

The captain and first officer materialized on Eden station once again, and once again Uranus and Cronus were in the transporter room to meet them. The four exchanged greetings and headed to the lab without delay. They entered the lab to find Dr. Athena with Dr. Hermes and the four protohumans.

"Professor?" Lucifer asked. "Yes?" Uranus responded.

"It just dawns on me. Where is everyone?"

Uranus explained, "Because of the psychic power exhibited by the other children, we thought it would be safer to move everyone to Olympus for a while.

"Good idea, professor," Lucifer commented. "Who is left here?" His curiosity getting the better of him.

"The six of us in this wing and Professor Hera with the two children from the last birth cycle are in Alpha wing."

"How are they doing?" Jehovah asked.

"Very well. For children of nearly three years." A look of surprise swept across the faces of Jehovah and Lucifer.

"Damn," Lucifer said in a low tone. "Three already. I thought I would adjust to this temporal difference more easily. Strange."

"Yes, it is," Uranus answered Lucifer's statement. "Only a few people, a very few people here have made the transition smoothly. I'm not one of them."

"Neither am I," Cronus interjected.

"Excuse me, professor," Athena half-yelled from across the room. "We are ready to begin if you are."

Uranus turned to face the woman by the beds. "Yes, I'm sorry, Athena. We'll begin right away." He turned back to face the captain. "Will you excuse me, gentlemen. We must get this show on the road, so to speak." Uranus and Cronus walked to the beds in the center of the room.

Dr. Hermes took a hypospray off the tray beside the first bed. He programmed a code into the small control panel on the top of the device. Starting with One, he injected all four protohumans in the neck. All was quiet.

Five minutes into the silence, One started screaming in intense pain as her large swollen body began to convulse under the restraints. Within seconds, the second, then the third, and finally the fourth started screaming. All four were now in labor. The four scientists took positions between the spread legs of the beasts. The babies came at different rates, but all were delivered within minutes. Jehovah and Lucifer watched intently.

The whole event took ten minutes, two and a half days for the mothers who will never see their children. They, the children, were whisked away by Athena and Hermes. "The test results will be ready in about an hour," Uranus informed the two men. "Shall we wait in my office?" The four left the lab. The four protohumans were sedated on the beds.

The four reached the central hub of the complex. The hub consisted of the communications center in the middle of the open area. To one side was the corridor leading to alpha lab. Opposite that was the corridor to beta lab. On the northern side of the communications center was the storage bays and shuttle bay. The southern side consisted of the transporter room and a cargo bay. To the right of the transporter room was a double door leading to the outside.

"If it's all the same to you, professor, I'd like to take a walk outside. Our duties confine us to tritanium bulkheads for a great deal of time. The fresh air is a welcomed change," Jehovah said after spying the doors.

"Certainly, Captain," Uranus replied. "Excellent idea." The four men exited the station and headed toward the tree line just south of the complex, to where the Eden proving grounds are located.

Ninety minutes later, the double doors opened as the four men returned. As luck would have it, Dr. Athena was passing through the central hub as the men came in. The doctor stopped quickly when she saw them. Breathing heavily, she started, "Professor. I've been looking for you."

"And apparently you found me" was his reply.

A smile swept across his face when he saw the expression on her face. She relaxed a bit and handed Uranus the padd she was carrying. "Here is the report on the babies." Jehovah noticed Athena was elated, near ecstasy, but trying to hide it.

"Dr. Athena." Jehovah looked dead into her eyes. "How about the short version for the rest of us while Uranus reads the details?"

"Oh sure." She began, "One infant died about ten minutes after we got her to the lab. We're waiting on the autopsy report. One infant has minor deformities. All internal and correctable." Her smile broadened. "The other two, a boy and a girl, are free of all deformities. They are also ESP free. There is also sufficient synaptic retardation to limit the intelligence to within the approved parameters." Now everyone looked as elated as Athena.

"They even look more like us than the protohumans they came from. The cranium above the eyebrows is greatly reduced, the jawbone is smaller and less pronounced and the back of the skull is much rounder. The skin pigmentation is a lot lighter, nearly halfway to our tone. There are a few more subtle differences, nothing of consequence, but you can see them for yourselves." She turned, motioning the men to follow.

The five walked into the lab at the end of the hall and approached the two beings standing at the far end. Three beeps sliced through the light silence. There was a slight pause and then three more beeps. Jehovah reached behind his back, and when he brought it around again, he was holding his communicator. He flipped the metal antenna lid, and the unit chirped to life.

"Jehovah here. What is it?" the captain said into the little black box.

"Dr. Anak here, Captain. I need to speak to you and Commander Lucifer as soon as possible," the little black box said back to the captain. "Well, we're in the middle of something right now. Is it important?"

"Not life threatening, so to speak, but it is important, and it is relevant," the doctor replied.

"Okay then. We'll come to see you as soon as we get back to the ship. Shouldn't be more than about thirty minutes."

"Excellent, Captain. I'll see you then. Out." Jehovah returned his communicator to where he took it from.

"Sorry, gentlemen." the captain told the others. "And lady, shall we continue?" The five continued walking toward the two beings. They entered the room where the children are, and the door closed behind them.

"The boy's name is Adam, and the girl is Eve," Athena told them. The four men could only stand in amazement at the children in front of them. Each child had a temporal discriminator on.

"We allowed the children to reach six years old, then we put the discriminators on until we decide what to do next." It was still a few more minutes before the four have the ability to speak. Jehovah was the first.

"What's your next step, professor?"

"Well." Uranus seemed flustered. "To be perfectly honest, I haven't detailed the next phase yet. I was going to get with Cronus, here, after dinner tonight and take care of that. I hadn't expected these two to come along so quickly."

"That's okay, professor. We've got things to do onboard ship. Contact me when you've got an outline."

"Very good, Captain. We'll be ready in several hours." Jehovah and Lucifer turned and walked toward the transporter pad.

"What shall I do with them, professor?" Athena asked in reference to the children.

"Well, get them some dinner, and get them settled in. I'm sure we'll be working by morning."

Three hours later, in the captain's ready room.

"Good evening, gentlemen," Jehovah said as the two men entered the room. "I trust you have some good news?"

"Yes, Captain," Cronus said as they sat in the chairs in front of the desk. "Well, we have an outline at least. I think we covered everything."

"Good, good. Let's have it."

"Since the children and the protohumans have been issued temporal discriminators, we can hold off any work until we've all had a good night sleep."

"Amen to that," Lucifer jumped in half-jokingly.

After a short light pause, Dr. Anak continued, "In the morning, we're going to teach the children basic communication skills along with certain survival skills. When they are ready, we will put them in the garden and monitor their progress. While this is going on, another team will be impregnating the protohumans enough to get seven more males and seven more females. They'll be taught the same skills and released with Adam and Eve. We feel having eight couples will allow enough *interaction*, shall we say, to expand the DNA base much quicker. After that, we get the DNA we need and we are outta here."

"What kind of timeline are we looking at?" asked Jehovah. "We figure about four months, maybe a little less. Remember, the longer we wait, the more DNA we'll get, and a better quality, closer to our own."

"Let's not forget about the Nephillium," Lucifer jumped in, more serious this time.

"We haven't, Commander," Cronus said. "But because of the effort of all the men and woman on this mission, we are incredibly ahead of schedule. We will be long gone before the planet gets close enough to be a real threat."

"Doc," Lucifer stepped in, "the *Heaven* got to their planet in just a few minutes."

"Well, with that vision in my head, I can tell you that by dinner tomorrow, we will have seven new boys and girls, and by tomorrow evening, they will be ready to live on their own and start reproducing."

"Holy shit, doc!" Lucifer said with surprise. "That is great!"

"I concur, Doctor," Jehovah threw in. "Send the specifics to my terminal so I can add them to my logs and—"

"I have a padd here, Captain," Uranus interjected as he passed it to Jehovah, who took it.

"We'll then, gentlemen, we will see you tomorrow for dinner," Jehovah said as he stood.

Captain's log: Stardate 9897.5. The second phase of the project is complete! We have not two, but eight advanced protohumans to begin breeding. Uranus and Cronus give us a four-month timeline to completion. We still have serious concerns about the Nephillium making good on their threat. Only time will tell. We hope to be out of here before they arrive.

The following day went by without drawbacks, unfolding the way it should. For the officers and crew of the *Heaven* and the crew on Mars station, the day went along at a snail's pace. On Olympus, things were incredible busy. Dinner that night was on Olympus.

"Congratulations, gentlemen," Jehovah said as he raised his glass, "to a job well done!"

"Here, here!" said the others in the room. Dr. Anak arrived to the celebration just as the toast was over. With a look of dire seriousness, he handed a padd to Commander Lucifer, who was sitting by the captain and a padd to Professor Cronus, who was beside Uranus. She stood there while the men read. The two groups finished within a few seconds of each other.

"We should go to my office," Professor Uranus said as he stood. The three follow suit, and Anak fell in with them. The rest of the room fell quiet. As soon as the five were out of earshot, the volume in the room increases as whispered questions overtake the guests.

"This MUST be a mistake," Cronus said just as the office door closed behind the group.

"No mistake," Anak responded. "I ran the tests over twice more to confirm. That's why it took so long to report it. I had to make sure it was irrefutable?."

"We have to stop this. NOW!" Lucifer nearly screamed, anger heavy in his voice.

"We can't stop it!" Uranus answered back in the same loud tone. Lucifer started to shout back when he was interrupted.

"Wait, wait. What do you mean you can't stop it?" It took a second or two for it to sink into Lucifer's and Anak's heads. Chilly silence swept over the room. "What do you mean you can't stop it?"

"It's already been started, Captain. Just before dinner. We sent the children out into the wild. There are crews monitoring them now."

"You only have eighteen beings out there. Don't let it spread," Anak said. "When we started this mission, I was all for it, but not anymore, not if it means dooming this race to extinction!"

"I agree with the doctor, Captain," Lucifer started. "We have to end this now and find another way!"

"We can't stop the mission, now," the captain replied. "Why the fuck not!" Lucifer responded in utter disbelief.

"It's already under way, number one…and with the threat of the Nephillium, we can't risk losing the time to go back to square one."

"So you're just going to sit back and let an entire race go extinct?" Anak half-shouted at the captain.

"It's them or us, Doctor. I'd rather it be us."

"They're the innocent, Captain!" Anak, now shouting, answered back.

"We brought about our own destruction," she continued in a bit more calmed voice, after taking a second to breathe.

"These people did nothing wrong. Nothing to warrant a death sentence." She took the two padds and left the room. She's heading to the transporter room, via the galley.

Anak entered the galley where the celebration was continuing. She turned to the right and chose the table with the most people congregated around it. She walked over and, without a word, dropped a padd onto the table. One of the occupants picked it up. The rest of the group gathered around. She went to another crowded table at the other end of the room and did the same thing. She headed off quietly yet angrily toward the transporter platform.

Back in Uranus's office.

The door closed behind Anak. As she left, the room was quiet for a long second.

"Captain," Lucifer said, breaking the cold silence. "We cannot let this mission continue."

"I agree, number one. But there are bigger considerations here. I have to follow my orders."

Cronus interjected, "Commander, it's only a computer extrapolation formed from a lot of data that's still speculative at best. You can't possibly believe thi—"

"I've believed it from the beginning!" Lucifer cut him off. That statement brought another hush to the room. This time, it's Uranus who broke the silence.

"Commander, after our little party in the galley is over, we'll be monitoring all sixteen beings continuously, around the clock. I give you my word, if any of the symptoms in Anak's report become evident, I'll terminate the project myself, and we'll search for another way."

"That's it?"

"What do you want me to say, Commander? I'm going to stop the project? I can't do that! Not now!"

Lucifer left the room without another word.

"What do you think, Captain?" Uranus asked. "Is he going to be a problem?"

"I don't know yet."

"Captain, we can't let anything stand in our way."

"Don't you think I know that!" Jehovah said as he slammed his hand on the desk. "I don't like it. But I know it!"

Deciding to forego the party, Lucifer instead went directly to the transporter controls. He set his coordinates and adjusted the delay time. He activated the controls and stepped onto the platform. In a few seconds, he dissolved away in blue sparkles accompanied by the familiar, high-pitched hum of the containment beam.

"How's the research coming, Ensign?" Lucifer asked Eris, junior member of Dr. Hermes's team, therefore expendable from the party and able to work.

"We had some delays getting things going, so they've only progressed a few months."

"Learn anything of cultural values?"

"It seems that several couples have joined together, a little community, just like that."

"Is that all?"

"Some have already established fundamental religions"—she paused to take a light breath—"based on us."

"What are you saying?" Lucifer looked totally dumbfounded. "I know it sounds fucked up, sir. It's like an inbred need for spirituality, for guidance from higher beings. They pray to specific people, people I know."

"Like who?"

"The largest community worship Uranus, Cronus, Hera, Zeus, and a handful of other doctors…as a group of gods."

"Adam and Eve, who are staying isolated from the rest, to themselves, worship Captain Jehovah as a single god. There's even a four-person group worshipping Ensign Boreas, one of Dr. Hera's assistants, for god's sake, but they mispronounce his name. They call him 'Buddha'."

"You're right, Eris. That does sound fucked up."

"You can review the logs if you don't believe me."

"No, no, that won't be necessary, I believe you. Just busting your ass."

He stared at the monitor showing Adam and Eve sleeping under a large shade tree. He fell deep into thought.

These people need a chance was the only thought that filled his head.

In the minutes that passed as years, on the surface, Lucifer made a decision that will forever change the future course of events.

It was early morning in the garden, east of Eden station. Adam was still asleep while Eve was happily observing a snake slithering along the roots of a large tree bearing oval red fruit. As Eve rolled the snake over with a long stick, the area above the snake filled with blue sparkles. The high-pitched whinnying noise was so loud she had to cover her ears as she dropped the stick and backed away, falling to the ground. Eve looked up to see the sparkles had quickly taken the shape of a person. She looked in awe.

Lucifer looked down to see Eve quivering on the ground in front of him.

"Stand up, Eve," he said to her. "Do not be afraid," he continued with a comforting voice.

It took a few minutes, but Eve slowly stood up. She had a look of total bewilderment on her face.

"Do you understand me?" he asked as he looked into her eyes, searching for a spark of enlightenment. Her eyes widened as she gave an unsure nod.

You understand, but you're afraid, he thought for a second, studying her face while she studied his.

"You don't understand how I got here. I bet that's it." He got her attention, eye to eye.

"Someday you will understand," he said softly and slowly. He looked up and spied a piece of red fruit hanging within arm's reach. He reached up, grabbed it, pulled, and handed the fruit to Eve.

"Eat this," he told her as he handed it to her. He made an eating motion with his hand to his mouth."

"Eat this. Eat this, and you will understand faster than you could ever imagine."

She took the first bite. She looked to Lucifer for approval as she chewed the piece. Lucifer nodded in agreement and smiled with approval. She took another bite. He stepped back as he activated his communicator.

"Computer. Beam me back."

As Lucifer walked into the mess hall, Jehovah came up from behind him. The commander grabbed his first officer by the shoulder. "WHAT THE FUCK DID YOU JUST DO!" he started screaming. "WHAT THE FUCK GIVES YOU THE RIGHT!" he screamed again.

"Did you read the doctor's report, Captain?" Lucifer responded in a raised voice. Not that it mattered, since the door to the mess hall was open when the captain started screaming, the twelve or so people in the room were spellbound, waiting for the scene to play out.

Lucifer handed the captain the padd he had been holding since he received it some hours back.

"Six thousand to six thousand five hundred years!" he said, his voice still raised so everyone can hear.

"That's how many years these people will have to live if we complete this project. In six thousand five hundred years these people will be in the same situation we are in now. I've given them the chance to live out those years without being held back!"

The captain's communicator beeped. He stepped back and answered it.

"It's Aaron on the bridge. Are you somewhere private, sir?"

"One minute," he said as he looked up to Lucifer. "I'll catch up with you soon." He motioned for the first officer to go into the mess hall. He did.

When the door closed, the captain said, "All right, what is it?"

"Captain, it has begun. Sensors show Eve has given the fruit to Adam. What should we do?"

"Aaron, go to the transporter room and beam that tree out of there. Send it to the far side of the planet. Are Adam and Eve around any of the others?"

"No. They are alone."

"Meet me in my ready room when you get rid of that tree."

"Aye, sir."

The captain headed to his ready room. Lucifer sat in the mess hall, enjoying a cup of coffee.

"Come," the captain said just after his doorbell rang. The door opened and Lieutenant Aaron, science officer in the absence of Commander Lucifer, entered the room in rigid military demeanor. The captain noticed.

"At ease, Lieutenant, relax. Did everything go okay with the tree?"

"Yes, sir. Everything went fine."

"But?" the captain added.

"But that's not the problem, Captain. It's Adam and Eve. They've eaten the fruit and have already started going through biophysical changes."

"To what extent?"

"We don't know. Changes are minute but rapid and continual."

After a moment of thought, the captain asked, "Can we project a holographic image on the surface?" A slight pause. "An image about four meters tall?"

"I don't see why not. I need some time to align the emitters—"

"How much time?"

"What do you want to project?"

"Me. I want to project an interactive message to Adam and Eve."

"Give me about ten minutes. Meet me in the holosuite."

"Let's get started."

Aaron left the room hurriedly. In the holosuite.

Jehovah's entry into the holosuite startled Aaron, who had his back to the door as he keyed commands into the wall-mounted access panel.

"Didn't mean to startle you, Lieutenant."

"That's okay, sir." He keyed in some final commands. "All set, sir. Stand in the middle of the room to begin transmission." The captain complied. When he got to the center of the room, Aaron keyed more commands.

"Can you put the coordinates of the broadcast point on the monitor? I want to see what is going on when I'm transmitting."

"I can do that just before we start."

There was a pause of about five seconds—the time it took to read these two lines.

"All set, sir. Ready to go," Aaron started. "View screen on, now."

On the view screen, Adam and Eve were studying the intricacies of a flower.

"Begin transmission," ordered the captain. Twelve points of light appeared on each wall. These light are the projectors that are capturing the image of the commander to be beamed to the planet in a three-dimensional image that will move as he moves.

On the view screen, Adam and Eve were visited by a likeness of Jehovah just over twice the height of the two beings.

"Adam, Eve," Jehovah said in a stern voice. The two trembled and fell to their knees in stark terror.

"Look at me!" The two looked up reluctantly, slowly.

"Look at me!" Jehovah ordered more sternly. The two looked up quicker. More terrified. From the point of view of Adam and Eve, they saw a semi-transparent image of Jehovah. He stood approximately ten feet tall. When he spoke, his voice sounded like thunder. "You have eaten from the tree I told you never to eat from.

There can be no excuse for this! Because of this, the two of you will leave this place, never to return!"

The two beg for forgiveness, but Jehovah was not deterred. The two left the fertile garden and headed off into the hot desert. The giant image of Jehovah slowly faded away as the holoprojectors powered down. The holosuite darkened slightly.

"Damn! You scared the shit out of them!" Aaron said, somewhat awed at the captain's plan.

"That'll guarantee they never come back."

"That was the idea." The captain headed for the deck one looking somewhat saddened.

After sitting in his ready room for an undetermined amount of time, Jehovah hit the communications button on his console.

"Lucifer, come to my ready room."

It took a few minutes, but a chime echoed through the ready room. "Enter." The door slid open, and Lucifer came in.

"Have a seat," Jehovah said without looking away from his monitor. He continued reading silently. Lucifer was looking slightly uncomfortable, but he knew not to speak until spoken to. Minutes ticked by slowly, seeming more like hours. With each beat of his heart, Lucifer grew more uncomfortable as he sat in silence.

"What you did with Adam and Eve was totally reprehensible," Jehovah said without warning and with the sound of contempt, only now looking up from his monitor to his first officer.

"I'm sorry you feel that way, sir," Lucifer defended himself. "I felt they needed to fully develop given the allowable duration of their existence."

"Don't go there with me, Commander. I don't like this any more than you do, but it must be done, for the greater good."

"And what makes our existence over theirs the greater good?"

"Look, Lucifer, we can discuss this till we're blue in the face, but the fact remains. Orders are orders. You had the chance to back out before we left, you didn't. Then you pull this shit."

"Captain, I can't change what I did. But now, what becomes of Adam and Eve?"

"Oh yeah, that." Sarcasm was starting to set in. "Since we couldn't change what you did, I had to expel them from the test area. They are on their own in the desert."

"Why did you do that?" A crippling sadness overtook Lucifer. "We couldn't have them contaminating the others. I had no other choice."

Lucifer closed his eyes as he dropped his head. A tear rolled down his cheek.

"As for you, Commander," Jehovah continued, "here I also have no choice. You are hereby relieved of duty."

"But, Captain…"

"I don't want to hear it, Lucifer. Be thankful I'm not throwing you in the brig or confining you to quarters. I'll deal with certain formalities once we have a more definitive timeframe, but right now, you are relieved. Dismissed." The captain looked back down at his monitor as Lucifer stiffened up for a second, turned around hard, and walked out the door. Jehovah was only slightly aware of the *whoosh* of the door that announced the departure of the former first officer. A single tear rolled down his cheek.

CHAPTER

Captain's log: Stardate 12418.50. It has been two months and seven days since beginning phase three…one thousand six hundred and twelve years on the planet. The population has reached one million nine hundred and fifty thousand. Adam and Eve have somehow managed to survive and flourished a line of their own. Unfortunately, not all is as we hoped…The aggression we expected is inherent, though it is curious that the degree of hostility varies from individual to individual. There is one group, apparently a family unit, that shows no aggressive tendencies at all…and they are from the line of Adam and Eve. Those of their line have shown little hostility in comparison to the others. The data we've collected will keep our scientists busy for decades. Our mission is nearly complete, yet tempers over the morality issue continue to escalate.

"Captain, I'm receiving a transmission from Mars colony."

"Put it through, Lieutenant."

"This is Lieutenant Aglaophonos, I need to speak to Captain Jehovah."

"This is Jehovah. What seems to be the problem?"

"I've just started receiving a signal at the outer edge of my sensors. Scans show it is a powered vessel, and it is on an intercept course."

"Thank you, Lieutenant. We'll take it from here." The captain turned to his communications officer. "Contact all ground personnel, and tell them we'll be back as soon as possible." Then he turned to his navigator. "Plot an intercept course, and get us to that vessel."

"Aye, sir" came from both crewmen.

As the ship sped out of orbit, tensions on the bridge grew.

Nothing could be done until the ship reached its intercept point. "Captain, the alien vessel will be in range of the Mars station five minutes before we arrive."

"How can that be?" the captain said with astonishment. "Either there is a glitch in our computers or they are really flying four times faster than we are."

"Amazing" was his only reply.

"Captain, this is Lieutenant Aglaophonos again. I'm receiving a transmission, audio only, from the vessel. They would like to speak to you. I'm patching it through the relays." The static from the speakers was replaced by a familiar voice, a voice that was sending dread through the captain's body.

"Captain Jehovah. This is Takel Ra of the Nephillium." His voice was stern and angry, yet restrained.

"What can I do fo—" Jehovah started.

"Don't insult me, Captain!" His anger was now slipping through. "Do you think you could get away with this! Did you think we wouldn't find out!"

"Takel Ra, let me explain," Jehovah started quickly. "When we returned after your initial warning, we discovered the only possible course of action was to minimize the contamination to the rest of the life-forms."

"Even that is untrue, Captain! Despite this, once the first was violated, the species was condemned! All the years of work my race has done is now wasted! There can be no forgiveness! Retaliation is inevitable and swift! This is on your hands!" The speakers abruptly returned to static.

It was only a couple of heartbeats later that the main view screen sparkled to life. It was Mars station.

"Captain, Lieutenant Aglaophonos here. The Nephillium ship stopped in the field of asteroids by the next planet."

"What are they doing, Lieutenant?"

"Nothing, just sitting th…hold on."

"What is it, Lieutenant?" Silence. "Report, Lieutenant."

"Sensors picked up a strange energy reading several kilometers from the Nephillium. Computer analysis indicates it was a temporal singularity, but on a quantum level. But it was only there for a few seconds."

"A quantum temporal singularity?" the captain mumbled to himself. "But for what?" He will soon regret asking that question.

"Captain!" Lieutenant Aglaophonos continued, now with panic in his voice, "I've picked up the same readings one hundred thousand kilometers away from Mars. New signal, Captain. Oh my gods!"

"What is it, Lieutenant?"

"Holy shit! Two asteroids, repeat, two asteroids, approaching planet at twenty-three thousand miles per hour. One is four miles wide! Other just over five! Iron cores! impact in one and a half minutes!"

"Sound red alert, Lieutenant!" the captain shouted. "Evacuate the base, now!" Jehovah turned to Lieutenant Reuben, the beta-shift communications officer, mildly shouting, "Get Lucifer up here." Then looking at Lieutenant Aaron, beta shift's science officer, he asked, "Any shuttles leaving?"

"None yet, sir."

"Time till impact?"

"One minute, fifteen." The next fifteen seconds seemed like an eternity. The *whoosh* of the turbolift broke the silence as Lucifer hesitantly stepped onto the bridge. Jehovah spun to face him.

"Despite recent events, an emergency has arisen, and I need you at your station."

"What's up?" Lucifer asked as he headed to his station, a station Lieutenant Reuben was more than happy to surrender.

"The Nephillium have transported two asteroids one hundred thousand kilometers from Mars on an impact course. I need to know what to expect."

"The data is coming from our link to the stations computers," Reuben volunteered.

"Interesting" was all Lucifer could manage as he buried his face into the scanner's viewer.

"Oh. Did I mention we have less than a minute."

"Great" was his muffled reply.

It took all of twenty seconds for Lucifer to formulate his theories. "This isn't good, Captain."

"Let's have it."

"When they impact, it will be at opposite sides of the planet. The shock waves will encircle the planet from opposite sides, and when they meet, the atmosphere will be completely ripped away from the planet and send out a level-eight shock wave, right toward Terra."

"What happens then?"

In a few seconds. "The axis will shift by approximately three degrees. There will be flooding over half the planet."

"Where?"

"About two thousand kilometers centering around Eden. All the Terrans and protohumans will be killed."

"Can we evacuate?"

"Between shuttles and transporters, we could move about ten percent."

"How can we buy more time?" The bridge fell silent except for the sounds of the ship's systems humming with life.

"Captain," Lucifer said, "I have an idea. Let me see if it's feasible." As he fed data into the computer.

"Lucifer," Jehovah said anxiously. "One moment, Captain."

"Lucifer." The captain was now even more anxious. "We don't have a moment."

Still silence.

After a few seconds. "Got it!"

"What?"

Ignoring the captain, Lucifer hits the intercom button. "Bridge to engineering."

"Engineering here," Chief Engineer Benjamin said over the intercom.

"In fifteen seconds, two asteroids are going to destroy Mars. The impending shock wave will destroy Terra as well. I need you to get us to full impulse now. Helm, get us between Terra and Mars." Jehovah nodded when the helmsman looked at him for approval.

The ship tilted slightly to the left as she responded to the helmsman's commands.

"Now as we are getting there, I need you to transfer power from the spacefold drive, channel it through the temporal discriminator, then run it out of the navigational deflector, and set it to disperse in a wide angle in front of the shock wave. I will readjust the discriminator so it will slow down the shock wave.

"That'll take some time."

"We have about three minutes."

"Oh, then I guess we don't have time. I'll get going then."

"How much time will this buy us?" Jehovah asked with a bit more calmness.

"I don't know, Captain. That all depends on how far I can adjust the discriminator. I will need some time."

"Do it."

Lucifer returned his attention to the scanner view screen. "*Heaven…* Impact in five…four…"—the voice started crackling—"three… two…" The sound started fading as static overtook the sound waves. "One." a loud low-pitched roar could be heard. "Impact at coordin—" Static was all that was left coming over the speakers.

"Put Mars on the view screen." In half a heartbeat, the small blue and green orb appeared on the screen. Everything looks normal. Then from the far side of the planet, a plume of dirt and debris started to rise over the northern horizon. Then from close to the surface but in front of the plume, four shuttlecraft could be seen.

"They're getting away, sir." The helmsman observed.

"As long as they can achieve orbit before the shock wave hits, they'll be…"

Before Jehovah could finish his sentence, a dark band, nearly as high as the plume, appeared on the horizon. In less than a second, the dark band was seen around the entire planet. Before anyone could react, the shuttlecraft disappeared into the dark wall of debris one at a time. As they disappeared, a small flash of light was seen as they exploded. In two seconds, the blue and green orb became a desolate, lifeless body.

When the shock wave met, it exploded outward into space, toward the *Heaven* and toward Terra.

"Lucifer, are you ready yet."

"Yes, Captain. These are the final equations," he responded as he keyed in the last commands. "Helm, swing us around so we are facing the wave. Engineering, are you ready?"

"Ready, Commander."

"Okay, then. Here we go," he said as he looked at the view screen while pressing the button.

Again, eternity seemed to overtake the crew.

Lucifer's head shot up quickly as his right hand keyed the intercom controls.

"Commander Benjamin, this is Lucifer."

"Benjamin here. Go ahead."

Jehovah gestured to interrupt, and Lucifer lifted his hand with finger raised in a gesture for him to wait, which he did. Lucifer continued.

"Listen and work quickly. Put the ship five million kilometers in front of the shock wave. Then adjust the output angle of the deflector dish to seventy-two degrees all around. After that, set the power output of the spacefold drive power converter to ninety-eight percent. You have two minutes."

"No problem." Benjamin's voice echoed through the bridge. "Almost there."

Thirty seconds.

"Ship moving into position." Sixty seconds.

"Deflector output angle set." Ninety seconds.

"Spacefold converter power level set. Go!"

"Tell me when we are in position, Levi," Lucifer asked the *Heaven*'s helmsman.

"Be there in three…two…one…there."

"Benjamin, engage."

"Engaging!" Benjamin said as Lucifer's eyes focused on his monitor. Jehovah looked at the main view screen as the oncoming shock wave was immersed in a brilliant blue light.

Jehovah turned to Lucifer as he lifted his head from the console and turned to his captain. "This is only a temporary solution, Captain."

"How long?"

"Roughly three hours," Lucifer answered. "About six Terran months."

"Now, we need to figure out how to save the Terran population without letting them know what we are," Jehovah thought out loud. "Not only the Terrans, sir," Lucifer said, still looking into the science station view screen, "but all of the life-forms on the planet."

"Explain," Jehovah ordered.

"The scans of the shock wave show it to be more powerful than originally computed. I just finished the calculations of the damage to Terra, and new data shows that ninety percent of the planet's surface will be flooded, killing off ninety-five percent of the animal population as well as all of the humanoid life."

"Why don't we just beam the Terrans up to the ship until the planet is clear?" asked Lieutenant Simeon, the tactical officer.

Jehovah answered, "Because they are advanced enough to know what technology is, and we don't know what the influx of such technology will do to such a primitive culture's evolution."

"But wouldn't that be better than extinction?" Lucifer asked with a touch of anger in his voice. "Then we would never get what we came for."

"Well, then. Find a way to save them without exposing ourselves."

"Yeah, I'm working on it," Lucifer responded with a bit more anger. "And fuck you" came out under his breath enough not to be heard by the object of his anger.

Business as usual went on as Lucifer worked on the problem at hand. Jehovah worked on it also, from the computer mounted to his command chair. The engineering department was also working on it while they monitored the systems, keeping the shock wave in a sort of temporal flux. All the personnel not on duty were using their off time to give suggestions and assistance.

An unusual suggestion came from an unlikely place. About forty-five minutes into this research project, Ensign Bakbakkar, the night-duty chef, offered a solution. "Instruct the Terrans to build a ship." A simple enough solution.

"But how can they build a ship big enough for all the Terrans plus all the animals? It would have to be miles long, and they don't have the technology to do it," asked Lieutenant Merah, the second-shift helm officer.

Everyone was stymied. It took some time, but Merah, the question asker, becomes the answerer. "Collect DNA from every living organism on the planet and store it on a ship. Allow a small group of Terrans to watch over the samples. When the planet's ecosystem stabilizes, we can reconstitute the DNA."

"Excellent idea, Merah," Lucifer responded. "The ship wouldn't have to be all that big. We can find people who show little signs of the rage issue and have them build the ship and watch over the DNA."

"Excellent," Jehovah stated. "Unless anyone has a better plan right now, this is the one we'll work with. Lucifer, coordinate with Dr. Anak. Find out how big this ship would have to be, then start the DNA extraction procedure. Take any crew members you'll need to expedite the process. I'll work on finding the candidates to man the vessel."

For the next several hours, everyone on board the *Heaven* worked at a feverish pitch. Crew members were beamed down all over the planet in an attempt to secure DNA from every living organism, from the smallest blade of grass to the largest tree in the forest, from the smallest insect to the largest animal on land as well as in the seas. Jehovah found those he was looking for as well. He found a carpenter named Noah. He, along with his wife, three sons and their wives were the only people who didn't show signs of the rage. Noah was alone in a wooded area near his home when Jehovah picked him up on the scanner. According to the readings, there was no one else around. Jehovah found this to be the most opportune time. He moved quickly to the transporter room.

While Noah was looking for just the right tree to use for his next project, his attention was drawn to a high-pitched sound and sparkling blue lights. He looked into the light and saw a strangely dressed man appear out of thin air. Noah, in awe, dropped to his knees and bowed his head.

"Please," Jehovah started. "Stand up. I must speak to you." Noah stood up and hesitantly asked, "Are you the creator?" Jehovah thought about it for a second and answered, "In a manner of speaking, well, yes, I guess you might say that. What is your name?"

"I am called Noah."

"Well, Noah, I have a very special job for you. The survival of this planet depends on you successfully completing this job."

"What is your will, creator?" he asked, flirting his eyes. "Please," Jehovah said calmly, "call me Jehovah."

"What is your will, Jehovah?"

"I need for you and your three sons to build a large ship."

"A ship!" Noah asked in awe. "For what purpose? There are no bodies of water nearby."

"In three of your weeks, a flood will envelop the whole of the planet. On the ship, you will care for the seeds of all life on the planet."

"All life! On all of the world! Why me, creator?"

"I have chosen you, your wife, your sons, and their wives to tend to all the life on the planet. Only the eight of you can be on the ship."

"Why must we do this, creator?"

"The reasons are far beyond what you are capable of understanding at this time. However, in the future, your people will be in awe of this accomplishment."

Noah smiled at the stranger and said, "How big must we build this ship?"

Jehovah grinned and said, "Here's what must be done."

Over the next two hours, Jehovah gave Noah every detail about the ship that was needed to be built.

Captain's log: Supplemental. I've just beamed up from the surface after giving Noah directions on how to build the ship. I've only been back on the ship for three minutes, yet the ship is nearly complete. I'll have to watch it later. Only time will tell what the future holds…What all of our futures hold. A personal observation: I don't think I'll ever get used to the feeling of disassociation…of disconnection I get every time I shut off that damned temporal discriminator. As useful as it is, that thing really sucks.

Beep. Beep. Beep.

"Computer, off," Jehovah said. "Yes. What is it?" he said again, this time to the door, and the door to his quarters opened, revealing Lucifer.

"Captain, Noah and his family are on the ship. All the DNA samples have been loaded and secured. They took a lot of ridicule for what they did for us down there."

"Well, they can take solace in the fact that they'll be the last eight life-forms on the planet very soon…with some luck."

"About that, current calculations have the discriminator going off-line in"—he looked at his watch—"about twenty seconds."

"Thanks for letting me know," Jehovah said sarcastically. He hit the intercom button on his desk.

"Bridge, this is the captain. Disengage the temporal discriminator, and steer the ship away from the shock wave. I'll be on the bridge momentarily."

"Yes sir, right away" echoed in the captain's quarters.

The captain and first officer arrived on the bridge in about thirty seconds, and the shock wave was just reaching the outer edge of the atmosphere. Lucifer double-timed it to his science station as the captain took his seat.

"Report," the captain barked.

And Lucifer answered, "Data coming in now, sir. The shock wave has slowed down by a factor of five. Projections indicate eighty percent of the planet's surface will be flooded. At this magnitude, the ship will have no problems surviving the storm."

Everyone on the bridge heard what the science officer said; they are all just mesmerized by what is on the screen before them. The narrow band of energy swept from one side of the planet to the other and forever changed the surface of the planet in its wake. On the ship, the whole incident was over in a few seconds, but on the surface, the fierce weather raged on for forty-three Terran days. By the time the rains subsided, 87 percent of the planet's surface was under water. The magnified images of the research facility area showed thousands of corpses, humanoid and animal alike. Among the carnage floated a large rectangular ship, still in its upright position.

"Scanners show eight humanoids, still alive and apparently

healthy," Lucifer informed everyone. He then adjusted his scanners and focused on a series of readings at another location. He slightly grinned and returned the scanners to their previous position.

"How long before the flood waters recede enough for the ship to make landfall?" Jehovah inquired and was promptly answered with "Approximately twelve minutes, sir."

The next eleven minutes went by routine, power-level checks, station statuses, the usual. It was the next minute when things started to get tenser and tenser, in a slow, steady pace rather than a quick spike. More like the anticipation of things to come.

The last fifteen seconds of the countdown brought the whole ship in a surreal scene from a second-rate science fiction movie. Throughout the entire ship, all that could be heard was the sound of computers, and onboard sensors show absolutely no movement. Every crew member was fixed on a view screen, a view screen that shows a large rectangular ship gently settling down on solid ground.

In the ship, however, that wasn't at all what it felt like. The ship slid onto a large rock face, making the ship look like a toy in a child's bathtub. Loose items fell off of tables and shelves. Those who weren't holding on to something suddenly found themselves flat on their asses.

On the ship, it had been several days since that fateful moment. Noah and his sons slowly lowered the side door. It landed on a mound of mud. The eight humanoids walked slowly down the ramp and gently stepped into the solid ground. As soon as all the humanoids were on solid ground, Noah fell to his knees as he lifted his arms and head to the sky, praying for their survival. All his family members followed. Jehovah felt a bit embarrassed and flushed.

As Noah and his family started building shelters, activity on the *Heaven* began to get fast-paced. Systems needed to be checked and damage needed to be assessed. It took about fifteen minutes to determine that there are no major issues with the ship.

"What next, Captain?" was asked by someone behind him. "Now I need to go down there."

"Why?" Lucifer asked with a little hint of nervousness in his voice.

"They believe I'm some sort of divinity, so they won't think twice when I ask them for the DNA samples. I'll bring them to Olympus Station so Dr. Zeus and Dr. Hera can begin to repopulate the planet."

"So we are going to continue with this damned project?" Now sounding angry, Lucifer's attitude made Jehovah stop in his tracks. "The project is why we're here. Or have you forgotten?"

"No, I haven't forgotten, but our interference has condemned this species to imminent destruction in six thousand years and nearly caused their extinction now. How much more bullshit do you plan on putting these people through?"

"As much as it takes to complete the mission. Do you have a problem with that?"

"Yes, sir. I do."

"Well then, thank you for saving these creatures, now get off my bridge until you can put your personal feelings aside and carry out your duties."

Lucifer just stiffened up and silently left the bridge. The rest of the crew just sat in silent disbelief.

After an eternal minute, Jehovah took a deep breath and, with commanding authority, began, "Lieutenant Kohath, notify transporter room that I will be beaming down to the settlement, then notify Zeus and Hera of my impending arrival. Lieutenant Aaron, begin scanning the rest of the planet for survivors. When sensors show they are asleep, have them beamed to Noah's location."

"Aye, sir" came from both crewmen. "Lucky for us, Lieutenant Aaron has joined forces with Zeus and Hera."

Jehovah headed for the turbolift. As he stepped inside, he turned to face the bridge. "Lieutenant Aaron, you have the bridge."

"Aye, sir." The captain heard as the door swished closed.

On the surface of the planet, the captain stopped materializing as Noah and his family fell to the ground and bowed their heads.

"Please," Jehovah said to the group as he lifted his hand in a halting manner. "Stand, I must speak with you." He motioned to Noah. Noah stood up and walked with Jehovah. They were gone for a few minutes, and upon their return, Noah went to his family and Jehovah went straight to the ark. When he was aboard, he closed the door.

"What is god doing on the ark, my husband?"

"He is using his mighty powers to bring the animals and plants back to life from the vials on the ship."

"Oh, I want to see that!" Shem, the eldest son of Noah, said with a voice riddled with excitement as he and his younger brother Japheth ran toward the ark with their wives.

"No!" Noah said loudly and angrily. "Jehovah said we must stay away from the ship, and the word of god is law!"

In the ark, Jehovah was looking around, completely amazed at the construction technique of such a primitive people.

"Jehovah to *Heaven*," he said after tapping his communicator. "Beam the DNA samples to Olympus Station in batches. I will be transported with the last batch."

"Yes, sir," replied a disembodied voice, and within seconds, a large amount of containers turned into blue sparkles and faded away. It took twelve transports to get to the last load, and with that the ship is empty, Jehovah being gone as well.

After roughly twenty minutes, Noah inched his way to the massive vessel.

Jehovah, my god, are you there?" When he heard no reply, he lowered the door and went onboard, his family following slowly behind him. When they saw that the ship was empty, they stood in silent awe.

"Jehovah is truly the all powerful god," Noah's wife said.

"We have truly witnessed a miracle," Shem, the eldest son, said. Olympus Station was buzzing with activity. Dr. Hera was directing a group of a dozen scientists who were reconstituting the DNA samples from the ship into living creatures. Dr. Zeus was directing another dozen reconstituting every plant on the planet.

"Dr. Zeus, I need to talk to you," Jehovah said while still walking. He stopped a few steps into the room, keeping an intended distance. When Zeus realized this, he stepped back from the people working.

"Continue working," he said to no one in particular. "I'll be back," he added in his best foreign muscleman accent. No one noticed. He approached Jehovah.

"What can I do for you, Captain?" he asked.

"I want your people to start increasing the humanoid population right away."

"Sure. No problem." He turned and leered at the two groups of scientists for a long minute. "Dr. Apollo, Dr. Athena, come here, please." After a few seconds' pause, he said, "Ensign Hades, Ensign Eros, come here as well."

"What is it, Doctor?" Apollo asked when the four had reached the two.

"We need to get back on track. This team is to start increasing the humanoid population immediately. Use every means necessary."

"Yes, sir," the four said in near unison. They headed off together to another lab.

After just under four days, ninety years on the planet, the humanoid population was up to nearly two thousand three hundred, mostly women. All the plants and animals that were alive before the flood were back thriving in the wild. The region appeared as it did before the Nephillium attack, just a bit more spacious.

"Dr. Zeus. Status report, please," Jehovah asked as he walked into the lab where Zeus and his team were just finishing up the in vitro process to a humanoid female.

"Sure." He started walking toward the captain. "We've been monitoring the first two groups of offspring. Even though they still hold the violence gene, they are able to suppress it easier. There have only been a couple of incidents but nothing at the previous levels.

"I need you and your senior staff on the *Heaven* in ten minutes," Jehovah said as he keyed his communicator. "Jehovah here. Beam me up."

"We'll be there, Captain," Zeus said as Jehovah sparkled into nothingness.

The ten minutes went by quickly. Jehovah walked into his conference room to find it full. Zeus was there with ten scientists including professors Cronus and Uranus as well as seven of the *Heaven*'s crew, including Lucifer. Even though he had been relieved of duty, Jehovah still needed his expertise.

"Ladies and gentlemen," Jehovah said as he walked in and sat down, "how do we minimize the violent tendencies in these people?"

The room became as quiet as the vacuum of space.

"This isn't a rhetorical question, folks." Everyone started looking around the room. Faces got a little nervous.

"Any suggestions?"

"Why don't we spread them around the planet. Thin out the population" came from Lieutenant Nazay, head nurse.

"Not a good idea, Lieutenant," Lucifer interjected. "Only because as they grow isolated from each other, there will become an inherent distrust in those outside of the community. This will lead to constant conflict as the groups meet." Everyone started to mumble as ideas get tossed around.

"Why don't we get them involved in a common pursuit? Something that will involve all of them," Professor Oceanus said aloud. "What could be so massive a project?" echoed through the room from several people.

"Building projects. We can have them work on building projects. It'll teach them teamwork," said Dr. Ares.

"First, they need to develop a rudimentary language," Dr. Athena said. "Then they'll need to learn math and science skills." Then the ideas started to click. The construction of a school large enough for five thousand students at a time.

The crew of the *Heaven* along with the scientists of Olympus began building the school with several hundred humanoids who showed gifted intellect. It took two Terran weeks to get the buildings built. The visitors found fatigue growing the longer they wore their temporal discriminators.

It took another two weeks to get the classrooms and equipment readied.

"Dr. Anak to the bridge," a disembodied voice broke through the normal day to day sounds of the bridge.

"Jehovah here, Doctor. What is it?"

"I need to see you right away." Her voice was calm, businesslike.

"In that case, Doctor, I'm on my way."

It took less than five minutes for the doors of Dr. Anak's office to swish open, and Jehovah came walking in. He sat down in the chair in front of Anak's desk.

"What's up, Doctor?"

"I've been running routine tests on the crew members that built the school."

"For what, Doctor?"

"Nothing specific. None of our people have ever worn a temporal discriminator for the amount of time these people have."

"It's barely been half an hour."

"For us, yes, but for them, it has been four weeks."

"Ah, I didn't think of it that way. Well, you wouldn't have called me down here if you didn't find something. So what did you find?"

"The cellular-decay rate of the landing parties is well out of whack. This is causing excessive disassociation."

'Yes. I know. I've felt that disconnected feeling. It passes."

"Not when you've been wearing one for a month."

"Okay, so what did you find?"

"The cellular-decay rate is what causes that disassociative feeling. The more the decay rate changes, the stronger the feeling. I've found that after a month wearing the damned things, our crewmen are nearly neurotic, though they all think it's simple fatigue."

"So why did I have to come down here? You could have told me this over the comm."

"Yes, but I couldn't tell you this. This condition, along with the extreme stress of this mission, could cause an escalation of the tendency to resolve conflict with violence among our own people."

"Our people are highly trained to handle high-stress situations, Doctor. What's your point?"

"This isn't your normal high-stress situation. There are a lot of emotional issues involved with this mission. Three quarters of the crew is on the verge of mutiny. That is what I couldn't tell you over the comm. If you don't tread very carefully, this mission will end in disaster."

"Your concerns are duly noted, Doctor," he said nonchalantly. "Is that all you have to say, Captain?"

"What would you like me to say, Doctor? What would make you feel better? Should I scream and jump around and carry on? I think that would make matters worse. What do you think?"

"All I meant was that you could show some concern."

"I am concerned, Doctor. I am very concerned, but I have more important things to worry about right now."

"What can be more important than your crew?"

"How about the six hundred billion people back home, Doctor. Or have you forgotten about them?" He got up and headed toward the door.

Captain's log: Stardate 13112.71. Babel university is now complete, and the humanoids are responding well to the language training program. They have built two cities along the coast of a nearby ocean, without help from any of our teams. The ingenuity of these creatures never ceases to amaze me. Our best estimate shows we'll be able to start harvesting DNA in four to six generations, barring no other catastrophes. On a personal note: The tension is increasing exponentially as we get closer to ending this project.

The past four days had gone by with relatively little incidence. Now that the second generation had been born, all the focus was on the humanoids. Jehovah was sitting in his seat of power, deep in thought, the planet on the screen rotating opposite the direction of the ship.

"Captain, there is a ship approaching. Intercept course. Bearing two, seven, three mark two, eight. Warp factor eight point six," Lieutenant Aaron, the on-duty science officer, told Jehovah.

"On screen," The captain said with slight concern in his voice. Aaron hit several controls, and the image on the main view screen changed, showing a ship seen only once before. The captain spun his chair to face the communications officer.

"Get Lucifer up here now, then open hailing frequencies."

"Aye, sir," Lieutenant Reuben answered as he carried out his orders. In two minutes, Lucifer arrived on the bridge. "No response from the vessel, sir."

"Interesting," Lucifer said as he approached his station. "The Nephillium. Maybe we'll find out why they destroyed the Mars station."

"That's obvious, Lucifer," the captain commented to his remark. "Why they are here, now, is the mystery."

The bridge remained dead quiet as the ship approached. It took up a position in front of the *Heaven*."

"Red alert," Jehovah said, slightly more tense. The alert Klaxon sounded as the bridge was bathed in a dull red glow. Throughout the ship, crew members got their stations ready for combat.

An hour went by without any word from the Nephillium ship. The bridge was silent now that the Klaxon was silenced, but the ominous red glow still filled the room.

Without warning, the Nephillium ship fired a volley of torpedoes and simultaneous phaser fire, at the planet surface. The bridge crew went into action.

"Where did those weapons hit!" Jehovah screamed to Lucifer. "Working on it, sir!" He screamed back as he planted his face into the scanner view screen on his console. "Tactical, are we hit!"

"Negative, Captain. All weapons focused on the surface!"

"But where on the surface?" the captain asked out loud but to no one.

"Oh my gods," Lucifer said as if to answer the commanding officer. "What!" the captain asked with dread in his voice.

"It's Babel."

"What about Babel?"

"It's gone."

"Gone?"

"Yes, gone. It is what the Nephillium were shooting at."

"Open hailing frequencies."

"Channel open, sir."

"This is Jehovah, captain of the *Heaven*. Why have you attacked us?" His voice was stern and unwavering. Silence was his reply. An hour passed, and nothing. The silence was suddenly broken by a beeping at the communications console.

"We are being hailed, Captain."

"On screen."

A familiar face appeared on the screen. "Takel Ra," Jehovah said as he stood slowly.

"Yes, Captain. I am flattered you remember me," He answered. "I, of course, remember you…and the warning I gave you at our first encounter."

"Nephillium ship is powering weapons," Lucifer warned. "Raise shields!" Jehovah ordered.

"Shields up," Lieutenant Korah, the on-duty tactical officer, said. The ship rocked as the dull roar of an explosion was heard. "What the hell?" Jehovah said to himself as he sat. "Tactical, return fire."

The enemy ship rocked mildly as the two florescent red bolts of phaser energy hit it.

"No appreciable damage to enemy vessel," Lucifer reported. "Okay then. Full barrage. Phasers and photon torpedoes. Now!"

The Nephillium ship rocked wildly side to side and back and forth for several minutes. When a lull in the firing occurred, the Nephillium ship started to back away while turning. It sped away, and in seconds, it was out of view.

"Where did they go?"

"Unknown," Lucifer answered.

"Unknown is not good enough," Jehovah snapped. "You are the science officer. When I need answers you give them. Unknown is not an answer."

"Do you want fact or speculation?" Lucifer snapped back.

Jehovah paused. "I see your point," he said a bit more calm. "Let me know when you find them."

CHAPTER

Captain's log: Stardate 13144.73. The Nephillium have destroyed Babel Institute. One thousand, seventy-three dead. Fourteen team members were among those killed. The ship vanished, but not before a brief firefight. Data received from that fight has allowed us to modify our weapons. Our next encounter will be considerably different.

"**A**nything yet?" Jehovah asked.

"Nothing, Captain," Lucifer replied.

"What the fuck! It's been nine days. How the fuck can they hide for nine days!" the captain half-yelled, then composed himself quickly.

"When we find them, you can ask," the science officer responded. Minutes ticked by slowly as silent tensions grew on the ship. Every crewman on the *Heaven* sat at their duty station, prepared to do whatever the captain ordered them to do. After what seemed like forever, Lucifer finally broke the silence.

"Found them, Captain," he said as he keyed several controls to manipulate the main view screen. The screen now showed a digital image of the planet and its singular satellite. Orbiting the planet but on the far side of the satellite was the *Heaven*. In a geosynchronous orbit above the satellite, on the far side of the planet, was the Nephillium ship.

"Korah." Jehovah turned to his tactical officer. "Find a way to get within weapons' range of that ship without being detected."

"Lucifer." He turned back to his science officer. "Scan the planet. I want to know if there are any Nephillium on the surface."

After about thirty seconds.

"Sensors show twelve Nephillium on the surface. There are four in one of the cities and six in the other city. And two with a group of humanoids on the far continent. No other bio signs anywhere."

"We need to know what they're doing down there."

"Agreed. But I think it would be too dangerous to go down there while they are still there."

"You're right. Keep the sensors locked on them. Let me know when they are gone." He took a deep breath and a slight pause. "Korah, any ideas about getting to that ship?"

"Well, sir. Without knowing the capabilities of their scanners, there is no way to approach without detection. Also, with the Nephillium on the surface, we should concentrate on getting them off the planet, so with all that, I recommend we do a one-eighty, come around the planet, and head to the satellite in a full frontal assault."

"And what kind of tactical advantage does that give us?"

"Their orbit is geosynchronous," Korah continued. "That tells me they are hiding. We damaged them. If we head at them head-on, I anticipate they will turn and head toward the planet to retrieve their people. At the last possible second, we cut across the front of the satellite, come in behind them, and give them another barrage when they lower their shields to be up their landing parties."

"Very logical," Lucifer added. "In a Bar'klaan sort of way." He started laughing. The rest of the bridge joined in.

"Agreed. Make it so. Full impulse."

The ship rocketed around the planet and slowly arced toward the singular satellite. The image on the view screen showed exactly what Korah speculated would happen. The Nephillium ship turned and headed away from the *Heaven*, circling the satellite and heading toward the planet at full speed, which is much faster than the *Heaven*. At the last possible moment, the *Heaven* cut hard to the right and soared in front of the satellite on an intercept course.

The Nephillium ship slowed in orbit above the twin cities. "They must still be having trouble with their sensors. They are acting like they don't know we're coming," Lucifer informed.

A few seconds later.

"They've lowered their shields."

"How long until we are in weapon's range?"

"Five seconds, sir," Korah replied. Then he continued, "Three, two, one, in range, sir."

"Full barrage. Fire!"

The weapons discharged a volley of phasers and photon torpedoes. The Nephillium ship rocked about from the onslaught. After about three minutes of continuing bombardment, there was a lull in the attack. The Nephillium ship turned and warped away. Jehovah looked toward Lucifer's station. He senses the stare from his captain. "Enemy shields down. Minor damage to their engines and hull plating. Their power output is down by fifteen percent."

"So they can be damaged."

"Apparently, but it took a lot of ordnance to do this much damage. Their engines are damaged so they must still be close by." After analyzing the data on his screen he continued, "I estimate we will have to use just about all of our torpedoes and most of our energy reserves channeled to the phasers to destroy them."

"Korah. New assignment for you," Jehovah said as he turned to face his on-duty tactical officer. "Find a way to increase the yield of our photon torpedoes. Once you've accomplished this, I need you to find a way to increase the output power of the phasers without drawing additional power from the ship. And time is of the essence."

"Right away, Captain," he replied as he stood from his position and headed toward the turbolift.

"Lieutenant Reuben, have Ensigns Michaels and Gabriel and Lieutenant Abbadon meet me in transporter room two," he commanded his communications officer.

"Aye, sir," he replied as he spun to his console and did as ordered.

Jehovah and Lucifer headed toward the turbolift together.

"We need to know what they were doing down there. I'll be back shortly. Keep things together until I get back. And find the Nephillium."

"Yes, sir" was the last thing Jehovah heard as the turbolift doors closed. In seconds, the doors were opening on deck four. A few meters down the hall was transporter room two. He entered to find the men he ordered to meet him already there. A transporter technician stood quietly at the controls.

"Good afternoon, gentlemen."

"Hello, Captain," the three respond in near unison. "What's up, sir?" Abbadon asked.

"A short time ago, Lucifer detected a number of Nephillium on the surface. Several were in both of the two cities by the coast and several on the continent on the far side of the planet. Michaels and Gabriel, the two of you will investigate the city at the northern tip of the sea. I will go to the other city. Abbadon, you will go to the far continent. We need to know exactly what the Nephillium wanted down there."

The three men gave signs of acknowledgement as the captain turned to the transporter tech.

"Chief, beam the three of us down between the two cities, then beam Abbadon down at his location. Make sure your temporal discriminators are functioning properly, and remember, one hour, no more. Then return to the beam down site."

The first three stepped onto the transporter platform. "Good luck, gentlemen," Abbadon told the three. "To you as well," Jehovah replied.

The three men sparkled into nothingness. Abbadon stepped onto the platform, and soon, he too, vanished.

On the surface, Jehovah, Michaels, and Gabriel were standing in barren wilderness. About a kilometer to the north, the walls of one city could be seen. Less than a kilometer to the south was the other. "Good luck, gentlemen," Jehovah told the two as he turned toward the city to the south and started to run.

"To you as well, Captain," they replied as they head off to the northern city.

At the entrance to the city, Michaels and Gabriel waited until there was no one at the gate. Time was passing without results. An oxen-drawn cart came up to the gate. On the cart was a man and two younger women. They saw Michaels and Gabriel.

"Good afternoon, strangers," the man on the cart said. "How are you today?"

"Well, sir," Michaels answered, "to be honest with you, we'll be doing much better once we get inside the city."

"You may enter with my daughters and I," the man offered. "Climb into the back of our cart."

The two men got in the cart.

"I am Lott. And these are my two daughters."

"I am called Michaels, and he is Gabriel."

"It is a pleasure to meet you, strangers."

"The pleasure is ours, sir."

"What is your business in our city?"

"There were strangers in your city a short time ago, and we need to find out what they were doing."

The oxen pulled the cart and people through the gate of the city. "The strangers you ask about were here to see the governor. They brought strange tools with them. And strange metals. They asked to store them here."

"Can you show us where they put those things?"

"Yes, of course. As soon as we bring my daughters home."

"Agreed."

The oxen-drawn cart rolled in front of a doorway in what appeared to be a long wall with rows of doors and windows. The two girls got out, and the men continued in the cart. It was only a few minutes when the cart stopped again, this time in front of a small building. The building stood alone. It has a door in the front and one window high on the right side. The two men got out of the cart and walked to the door. It was locked. Michaels took out a small sonic device and aimed it at the lock. A red light emanated from the device, and with a low whirring sound, the door lock tripped, and the men went inside. Lott looked on in amazement.

As Michaels and Gabriel entered, Gabriel took out a flashlight and started looking around. There was only one room in the building, and it was full of crates. The two men removed the cover on the closest crate.

"Holy shit!" Michaels said softly.

"Let's check another one," Gabriel said.

They walked toward the back of the room and picked a random crate.

"What the fuck is going on here?" Michaels asked rhetorically. "We need to tell the captain."

"Yeah. Let's go."

The two left the building and relocked the door. They turned to find Lott still waiting for them.

"Can you give us a ride to the gate?"

"Yes, of course."

The two got on the cart.

"Did you find the answers you seek?"

"Yes, yes we did. Thanks to you."

"Then I am glad."

When they reached the gate, the two men got off the cart. "Good day to you, Gabriel, and to you also, Michaels."

"Good day to you, Lott," Gabriel responded.

"And thank you for your help," Michaels added.

The two men left the city behind as Lott rode toward his home. An hour later, the two men were with their captain.

"What did you two find out?"

"The Nephillium are using the city as a weapons depot."

"Are you sure?"

"Yes, sir. We opened several crates. One was full of phaser rifles."

"The other was full of what appeared to be quantum grenades."

"Now it makes sense."

"What did you find out, Captain?" Michaels asked. "Surveillance equipment and communications gear."

"What do you think they're up to, sir?" Gabriel asked.

"Looks like they are going to try a hostile takeover of the planet."

"With the help of the citizens of these two cities," Gabriel added. Jehovah flipped open his communicator and said, "*Heaven,* three to beam up." The three men sparkled into nothingness.

They stepped off the platform, and within seconds, Abbadon appeared on the transporter platform.

Jehovah walked to the communications panel on the wall. He activated it.

"Captain to crew. Senior staff meet in the briefing room in five minutes."

The four men left the transporter room, leaving the transporter technician alone again.

In the briefing room, Lucifer was sitting by chief medical officer Anak who was beside Lieutenant Commander Benjamin, the chief engineer. Lieutenant Simeon, the tactical officer, was on the other side of the table alone.

Jehovah entered the room with Abbadon, Michaels, and Gabriel. The three sat on the side with Simeon as Jehovah moved to the head of the table.

"Gentlemen. We are faced with a serious situation," Jehovah started. "Abbadon, what did you discover on the far side of the planet?" Abbadon stood. "The far side is scattered tribes of humanoids.

Everyone I encountered was friendly enough, but no one had seen any strangers. There was no evidence of extraterrestrials or advanced technology. We know the Nephillium were there, but I could find no evidence of why."

Gabriel stood. "Michaels and I went to the northern city, called Sodom by the locals. We found that the Nephillium have made arrangements with the city's leader and has a storehouse of phaser rifles and quantum grenades."

With that all eyes got big. Now Jehovah stood. "The southern city is stocked up with surveillance and communications equipment. With what Michaels and Gabriel found, I can only draw one conclusion: The Nephillium are planning an armed revolt."

"It sounds like they are preparing for a full-out revolution," Lucifer added.

"Could be, number one."

"Do you think they would wipe out the entire species out of spite?" Benjamin asked.

"Quite possible. That is what I believe they will do."

"What are we going to do?" Anak asked.

"That's what this meeting is about. Any suggestions?"

"A definitive, preemptive strike," Simeon replied. "Interesting. Elaborate," Lucifer interjected.

"Destroy the cities. Not only the storerooms, but both cities, in their entireties."

"By what justifications?" Jehovah asked in somewhat disbelief. "Doctor," Simeon continued, "are these people still hostile, or do they still have the potential for hostility?"

"Yes," Anak began. "We've been monitoring the planet, and most in our research area still show signs of violence. The humanoids on the other side of the planet, where Anak was, are more at peace and show an advanced balance and harmony with the land. A culture which is the polar opposite of this region."

"Then we should obliterate both cities and send a message to the Nephillium."

"What a minute, Simeon!" Gabriel yelled. "Michaels and I met a man and his family. They were nothing but helpful. There is no way you can justify killing them just to make a statement!" Anger stemmed from his voice.

The debate ran amok for several minutes. Voices started to get heated to the point of screaming, mostly in defense of sparing Lott and his family.

"All right, everyone!" Jehovah yelled above everyone else's screams. The room went to a sudden deathly quiet.

"When I was in Gomorrah, I saw no signs of friendly people, so Gabriel and Michaels, beam down to Sodom. Find this Lott and tell him to get out. If you meet anyone else who has a lack of hostilities, tell them to get out. You have five minutes on the surface. Go."

The two men got up and ran out of the room.

The two beamed into the city near Lott's house. As they head for his door, they were met by other people. Several of these people tried to assault them. Lott opened his door and, when seeing this, calls to the two strangers.

"Hey, my friends. Come. Quickly!"

The two men ran into Lott's house, and he closed the door behind them.

"Hello, my friends," Lott said with excitement. "It has been so long. How are you?"

"We are fine, Lott," Michaels said.

"But we come with dire news," Gabriel added. "What is it, my friends?"

"Because the other strangers came here and conspired with your city's leader, our commander has decided to destroy your city."

"Who is this commander you speak of?"

"His name is Jehovah." Lott's eyes opened wide and his mouth opened with a gasp.

"Not the Jehovah of our forefather Noah?"

"Yes," said Michaels. "The same."

"If our one true god said the city must be destroyed, so be it." Sadness spread across his face. Gabriel and Michaels looked at each other, each showing distress.

"We have good news for you, though," Michaels said. "What would that be, my friends?"

"Jehovah has sent us here to spare you and your family," Gabriel told him.

"Gather your wife and daughters and leave here at once. Keep going until you get beyond the mountains to the north. Do not stop and do not look back."

"You must leave right away," Michaels added. "And each member of your family must cover themselves in these blankets." He handed Lott four thermal blankets. "They will protect you."

"Protect us from what?" he asked.

"It is much too complicated," Gabriel interjected. "Just say they will protect you from the wrath of god."

Lott stared back in wide-eyed awe as Gabriel gave Michaels that 'What the fuck?' look. Michaels just raised his eyebrows in reply.

"Of course. Of course. Thy will be done."

"We will see you at another time, Lott."

"Good-bye."

"Good-bye, my friends."

Lott left the room, and Michaels opened his communicator. "Michaels to *Heaven*. Beam us up now." The two men disappeared in blue sparkles. Lott came back in the room and was in awe that his two friends were gone so quickly.

Michaels and Gabriel left the transporter room and took the turbolift to the bridge. Jehovah turned when the doors opened.

"How did it go?"

"They should be out of the city by now, sir."

"Okay then. Lieutenant Simeon, prepare a phaser barrage in unison with a full volley of photon torpedoes. Full yield. Wide disbursement. I don't want two bricks left together in either city."

"Yes, Captain," he answered while he manipulated some of the controls on his console. In seconds, fluorescent blue beams blasted from the phaser array, and the torpedo tubes fired missiles continuously.

On the surface, Lott, his wife, and two daughters were nearing the peak of the northern mountain range. Each was shrouded in the strange shimmering blanket. Lott reached the plateau and waved his daughters to go ahead of him. They did. As his wife approached she paused. She took a deep breath and turned to look at the city. With nothing to protect her from the photonic radiation, she stared in awe for just a second before she let out a horrific scream, and her body solidified. In seconds, she became a pillar of dried flesh without any human features.

Lott wept as he followed his daughters down the slope on the opposite side. Several meters down, Lott spotted the entrance to a cave and instructed his daughters to enter it until the firestorm was over.

For three minutes, a full assault rained down on the cities of Sodom and Gomorrah.

"Captain, phaser banks are beginning to overheat."

Jehovah sat silent for several seconds. One by one, the bridge crew turned to look at the captain. He took a long breath.

"Okay. Cease fire," Jehovah ordered. "Lucifer, what are the damages?"

Lucifer looked into his monitor and responded, "Just as you ordered, sir. Total annihilation. Both cities utterly destroyed. No survivors."

A mere two seconds passed before, Lieutenant Kohath reported, "I'm getting an incoming message, sir. It's from Takel Ra."

"On screen," Jehovah ordered. The anger-riddled face of Takel Ra filled the main view screen.

What is the meaning of your attack?" Takel Ra screamed. Jehovah winced in mock pain and turned to Kohath. He gestured to the communications officer to lower the volume. He did. Jehovah turned to pay his full attentions to Takel Ra. "What the hell are you talking about?"

"Don't give me that bullshit, Captain! Why did you destroy the twin cities?"

"That's an interesting question coming from the one who just tried to destroy the entire planet."

"That's not the point, Captain! Why did you do it?"

"Tell me, Takel. What pisses you off more, the loss of six men or the loss of all that equipment?"

"You had no right doing that!"

"After what you did to Babel Institute last week, did you really think we could let you get away with stockpiling weapons and equipment in the midst of innocent people?"

"What you have done cannot be undone. When my government learns about what you've done, I will be ordered to destroy you and wipe out the entire population."

After a brief pause, Takel Ra leered at Jehovah with an intensity the captain had never seen before.

"And to tell you the truth, Captain, I can't wait to come back here and destroy you, and I'm going to do it with a smile. This I promise." The view screen went black.

The captain turned to the communications officer. "Call the senior staff to the briefing room."

It took about three minutes for the senior staff to assemble. "We have this final generation left to advance these beings and the Nephillium have declared war against us, and that's the good news," Jehovah said. The senior staff look at each other with inquisitive looks, slightly uncomfortable.

The captain turned to the table full of officers with a slightly sly grin. The staff officers let out collective sighs of relief.

"Now that the tension is broken, how are we going to win?" A gentle seriousness came over his face.

"I think we have something here, Captain," Lucifer started. "We transported some of the supplies from both cities to examine and reverse engineer. The communicators have an unidentifiable component that I believe is a phase discriminator. There are also other devices with that same component."

"How can that be helpful?"

"If I may," he answered while he looked at his padd. "I need to go to the lab for one more test. If I'm right, not only will I know how they plan on beating us, but also how to defeat them."

"Then go. Hurry."

"This will not take long." He got up and exited the room in a near run.

"Well, while we are waiting for Lucifer, are there any issues we need to address?"

"Yes, Captain, there is," Lieutenant Simeon, the tactical officer, interjected. "Should we be successful at our mission, we will be leaving this civilization on the brink of destruction with no guidance."

"What do you suggest?"

"Lieutenant Gabriel, you said that when you told Lott the commander's name is Jehovah, he asked if Jehovah was the god of his forefather Noah. Is that right?"

"Yes, yes it is," Gabriel responded.

"You're not going where I think you're going with this!"

"Why not, Captain? It would solve so much very quickly." Everyone at the table looked puzzled.

"Absolutely not! I will not be the cornerstone of an alien religion!"

"You already are captain. Since you visited Noah, there have been writings in several cultures about you. We can use that to our advantage and give them a code of guidance to live by, helping them control their hostile tendencies."

The captain closed his eyes and bowed his head in thought. "There's not much time, Captain," Simeon pleaded. "You have much more important thing to deal with. I have a degree in religious anthropology. I can take care of this in a couple of hours."

"Okay," Jehovah said reluctantly.

"Captain," Lucifer's voice chimed in after the chirp of the communications console activating. "I have made a discovery that will give us at least a fighting chance."

"Explain."

"I'm on my way."

In less than two minutes, Lucifer walked through the doors and to the head of a table surrounded by intense eyes. In his hand was a small rectangular box with definitive curved features with a small strap on each side.

"Captain, we have the answer," Lucifer said before he is able to stop.

"I assume it is in your hand?" was the captain's reply. "Yes," Lucifer responded, "it is."

"Then by all means, enlighten us."

"This is a phase discriminator," he answered matter-of-factly. "And what is that?" Jehovah asked.

"I'm glad you asked that, Captain. This works along the same lines as our temporal discriminator, but instead of manipulating time, it manipulates space. It allows the wearer to be invisible and to be able to occupy the same space as other objects. This is how the Nephillium were able to move the asteroid that destroyed Mars station and get supplies to Sodom and Gomorrah without detection."

"So not only are we invisible, but we can walk through walls?"

"Exactly!"

"So how exactly is that going to help us win? I see a balance, that's all," Lieutenant Simeon asked.

"Used in conjunction with the modified weapons and shielding, we will have the element of surprise on our side. The modifications made from reverse engineering the Nephillium equipment have increased phaser power by three hundred and forty-seven percent, photon yield by four hundred and twenty-five percent, and shield strength by seven hundred and twenty-seven percent."

"Aahh!" Simeon let out as her eyes brightened up with knowledge.

"Are we able to integrate anything into the temporal discriminators?" Jehovah asked.

"Not yet. I have the whole lab working on compatibility hardware. It shouldn't be long."

"Good, I want to know the second they get it. Get down there and stay on them and get it done." He looked around the room. "Now that we all know about our advantage, I would like a free flow of tactical strategies, no matter how off the wall it may sound. We need to beat this, beat them and get this mission over with."

Captain's log: Stardate 13173.92. It's been two days since our last encounter with the Nephillium. The final generation has been created, and results are as we expected. Lieutenant Simeon conducted an experiment to test religious faith in those showing pacifistic tendencies. The experiment shows that enough of the beings show common traits that we can extract enough genetic material to successfully complete our mission.

"Red Alert!" Lucifer's voice screamed over the intercom as the ship rocked.

"Captain to the bridge!"

The turbolift opened on the bridge, and the captain headed to his chair. On the view screen was Takel Ra's ship along with four smaller ships.

"Damage report."

"No damage. New modifications are working perfectly," Lieutenant Korah replied.

"Lock phasers on the ship to port."

"Phasers locked," Korah answered.

"Fire." The florescent beam came into view at the bottom of the view screen as it approached the ship at the far left. The ship was obliterated instantaneously.

"Lock phasers to the starboard ship."

"Phasers locked."

"Fire."

"Incoming message from Takel Ra," Lieutenant Reuben said as the ship on the right was obliterated. The other three ships broke formation and moved away in different directions.

"Swing around…two, two, seven mark three, two. Fire as we pass." The crew executed the captain's orders, and another ship vaporized under the *Heaven*'s assault. "Takel Ra still on the comm, sir."

"Not now, swing around and take out the last ship then I'll talk to Ra."

The crew complied, and the fourth ship blew up. "Open channel."

"Open."

"What can I do for you Takel?" the captain asked sarcastically. "Congratulations, Captain," Takel Ra said as his image appeared on the view screen. "You are smarter than I gave you credit for, but not smart enough." He motioned to an unseen person. The image changed to Takel Ra's ship, alone in space. In an instant, eight other ships appeared around the lead vessel.

"You're wrong there as well, Ra. Engage phase discriminator and take up a position behind the fleet."

"Aye, sir."

Takel Ra looked at the *Heaven* on his view screen with a huge smile on his face. He was about to fulfill the promise he made to Jehovah several days earlier. He turned to a member of his crew, the smile still glued to his face.

"Lock weapons on target."

"Captain, look!" a panicked voice from another part of the bridge said.

As Takel Ra looked at his view screen, the *Heaven* headed directly at them, and as Takel Ra winced his face bracing for impact, the *Heaven* disappeared.

Those on the bridge of the *Heaven* were also wincing in anticipation of a collision. As the ships met the vague, shadowy image of the Nephillium ship passed through the *Heaven*. Once the ship reached one hundred kilometers beyond the fleet, she turned one hundred and eighty degrees and now faced the aft section of Takel Ra's ship. The fleet flank the Nephillium cruiser on both sides.

"Can we fire weapons while we're phased?" Jehovah asked. "Unknown, Captain" came from the science officer.

"Let's find out. Korah, get simultaneous locks on the smaller ships."

"All eight, sir?"

Jehovah nodded.

"That'll take a few moments," he answered as he started to carry out his orders. After nearly a minute, he said, "Weapons locked, sir. Staggered assault pattern. All weapons to bear."

"Very good, Lieutenant. Fire," Jehovah said calmly.

Korah pushed the buttons on the console, but nothing happened.

"Apparently, we cannot fire while in a phased state," Lucifer said.

"Apparently not," Jehovah mocked. "Deactivate the phase discriminator, destroy the ships, phase, then move in front of Ra's ship, got all that?"

"Yes, sir. I think I can handle that." Jehovah grinned at his mocking. "Then make it so, Mr. Korah."

"Aye, sir." He pushed the buttons.

The *Heaven* became visible in an instant and started a weapons' barrage against the Nephillium fleet. First to go was the ship farthest port from Takel's ship, then the one farthest starboard, and so on. By the time Takel Ra received the first message of a problem, four ships were lost. By the time he was sure there is a problem, two more ships were lost. By the time he called for his science officer's report, his ship rocked with the destruction of the seventh ship. Before his science officer could respond, his ship was rocked by the destruction of the eighth. The *Heaven* cloaked and maneuvered in front of Ra's ship, yet they remain cloaked.

"Lucifer, where is the Nephillium homeworld?" Jehovah asked as he approached the science station. Lucifer keyed in some commands, and the view screen above his hands flickered to life. The image showed the star system as well as the two ships and, out in a distant corner of the screen, Marduk.

"How long at warp nine?" he asked. "Four days, sir," Lucifer replied.

Jehovah contemplated his next move. The bridge was as still as a painting. Everyone was holding their respective breaths.

"Lieutenant Reuben. Open a channel."

"Channel open, sir."

"This is your only warning. Move against the planet and be destroyed." He motioned his hand across his throat.

"Channel closed."

"Lieutenant Merah, plot a course to Marduk. Warp nine."

"Course plotted" was the response.

"Okay. Hit it." Takel Ra's ship shot off to the left on the view screen as the stars blurred during the ship's turn. The blurs became streaks as the warp engines kick in when the turn was complete.

"Ra's ship is maintaining position," Lucifer said in anticipation of the captain's request.

"He's probably too scared shitless to move out of his chair right now."

The bridge crew giggled at the captain's remark.

Captain's log: Stardate 13274.08. We have arrived at Marduk, the Nephillium homeworld. We are still phased and invisible to

Nephillium technology. What we do in the next few hours will forever change the future of the life-forms we chose to alter. We must make sure that the Nephillium can never be a threat to the Terrans.

"Tactical analysis, Simeon?" Jehovah asked with eyes fixed on the view screen.

"Planetary defenses are formidable but centralized. If they can't see us, we should be able to take out shield generators and communications satellites out on a single orbit. The second orbit will give us weapons platforms and planetary ground defenses. The third pass will annihilate industry and a large percentage of the civilian populace."

The captain sat quietly in his seat still staring at the planet on the view screen. *All those innocent people*, he thought to himself. *How do I justify this?* He looked around the bridge slowly, looking at each crewman working at their stations.

"Fuck justification!" Jehovah said loudly as he stood. The crew turned and looked at the captain with faces showing slight confusion. "This is survival, and we owe it to them since they saved us.

Simeon, line up first-orbit priority targets."

"Aye, sir," she replied as she manipulated controls. And in a few seconds, she said, "Targets acquired. Weapons locked and charged."

"Well then, Simeon. Fire!"

"Aye, sir," she answered as she pushed the glowing button. The florescent red bolts of energy shoot from the phaser emitters with enough power to blast through the shield generator housings. The photon torpedoes took care of the communications satellites. After the first orbit, the defenses were down and the planet went dark.

Now the panic begins, Jehovah thought to himself. "Line up second-orbit priority targets and fire when ready."

At the end of the second orbit, all planetary defenses were obliterated and the loss of life was in the hundreds of thousands.

"Line up the third-orbit priority targets. Fire. And may the gods have mercy on our souls."

Weapons fired at an increased rate as hundreds of buildings were destroyed. The ship traveled slowly across the surface of the planet, zigzagging north to south as it traveled east around the sphere.

Florescent bolts of energized death fired from its underbelly at targets in all directions.

While obliterating the third continent, the weapons suddenly went off-line. The red alert Klaxon started blearing.

"What the hell happened?" Jehovah asked no one.

Jehovah hit the communications panel on his command chair. "Engineering, what's happening down there?"

"Engineering here. Primary EPS conduit from the warp reactor blew!" The disembodied voice answered. "We'll have to take the main energizers off-line while we effect repairs."

"How long?"

"Thirty minutes."

"You have ten."

"Captain," the voice said sternly, "I've got to have thirty minutes."

After a brief pause. "Very well. Put us in a geosynchronous orbit above the northern pole. Engineering, get us fixed now."

"Aye, sir" came from both Lieutenant Simeon and the disembodied voice on the comm.

Twenty minutes into the repair, everything was going well. Suddenly, the ship rocked violently as the dull, thunderous roar of an explosion was heard.

"What the fuck was that?" Jehovah asked as he picked himself up off the floor.

"It's Takel Ra's ship," Lieutenant Simeon answered. "He's coming around for another pass."

"How's that EPS conduit, Benjamin?" the captain asked into the armrest of his command chair.

"Working on it, sir, two minutes."

"We don't have two minutes!" he shouted. "Acknowledged."

"Tactical, status."

"Starboard shield down. Port shield at seventy-one percent," Simeon reported.

"Swing us around, keep the port shield in front."

"Ship's moving sluggishly, sir."

"Compensate."

"Here they come."

"Brace for impact!" The captain shouted as the ship rocked, even more violently than the first time. Again, the captain hit the communications console on the arm of his chair.

"Benjamin?"

"Ten seconds, sir." In what seemed an eternity, he said, "Conduit repaired."

"Systems coming back online, Captain," Simeon said. "Shield status?"

"Port shield powering up, at thirty-six percent, starboard shield at ninety-five percent, phasers back online and at one hundred percent, torpedo launchers online."

"Lock weapons on life support systems and warp engines."

"Aye, sir."

"Fire when ready." The phaser fire blasted through the shields and hit the life support systems. At almost the same instant, the *Heaven* rocked, and half a heartbeat later, the ship rocks a second time, this explosion was different, but only to a trained combat officer. Jehovah clicked the switch on his armrest console.

"Damage control. What was that second explosion?"

"EPS manifold," a nameless voice came over the intercom. "It's gone, sir."

"How long for repairs?"

"Not under these conditions."

"Okay then. How are the torpedoes?"

"Tubes still operational."

"Six-torpedo spread, center mass of that asshole's ship, now."

The front of the *Heaven* lit up on both port and starboard sides three times as the torpedoes escaped from their launchers. The missiles closed in on the Nephillium cruiser as the crew watch on the view screen.

Through the glare of the torpedoes' engines, two objects started to take shape, and they were heading toward the *Heaven*!

"Incoming torpedoes!" Simeon shouted in surprise.

"Evasive action! Shields up!" The torpedoes' impacts came a second too soon. The starship rocked to a near perpendicular angle. The bridge lights went out as computer systems and power conduits exploded around the room.

"Get the stabilizers online! Now!" the captain ordered the helmsman.

"Working on it, sir!" Lieutenant Merah screamed over the explosions around her. The lights flickered on and off sporadically as the ship started to level out. Individual workstations started to light back up after a few seconds.

"Main viewer on now!" the captain shouted to the room as he settled into his seat. The main view screen flickered on. The static on the screen dissipated slowly. The image cleared to show debris floating around the ship, a lot of debris.

"Is that all our debris?" Jehovah asked as he spun his seat to face Lucifer.

"Negative, Captain," Lucifer answered while deciphering the incoming data. "Sensors are sketchy, but I cannot find any signs of the Nephillium ship. Internal sensors show critical damage but cannot account for all that debris. Long-range sensors are okay and show no signs of Takel Ra."

"What's our status?"

"Damage control report," communications officer Reuben called out. Muffled voices started flowing through the open channels in his earpiece.

"Main engines off-line," he repeated out loud. And he continued, "Hull breach on decks three and four, aft section. Port nacelle
is damage, impulse power is available. Hangar deck is damaged but
repairable. Life support, transporter controls, and port shield generator down but under repair. Fifty-three injured, two dead."

"Best speed to Terra. How long?"

"Fourteen days, sir," Merah replied.

"How long in Terran years?" Jehovah asked Lucifer quietly.
"Approximately four hundred and ninety years."

"Holy shit," Jehovah said in near disbelief. "I concur."

Captain's log: Stardate 13998.92. We have arrived at Terra. Elapsed time five hundred and forty-five years. We have made contact with the Archangels, who were left to observe the Terrans' progress when we went to attack Marduk. Our pacifist group has been enslaved by a military group who are now led by a leader named Ramses. We will use a former member of Ramses's upper echelon, a man named Moses, to convince Pharaoh Ramses to let my people go, rather than confront him as aliens or gods. I hope I'm making the right decision in trying to have these people solve their problems without our continued direct intervention.

s Moses stood outside of his tent and starred at the top of the nearby mountain, the sun sank slowly behind the mountaintop. Once the sun fell behind the great rock, darkness enveloped the mountain's base quickly, including Moses's tent. The stars filled every region of the night sky.

Moses settled his flock of sheep and was heading toward his tent when, out of the corner of his eye, he saw an object streaking across the night sky. As he watched, the object grew larger and turned toward the mountaintop. Flames shot from the bottom of the object as it slowed down and settled upon the top of the mountain. Moses headed toward the mountain to see what the strange object was.

It took him nearly three hours to reach the top, though he had no idea just how long. When he reached the summit, he was in awe of the sight before him. A large shiny, rectangular box floated silently above the ground. When he approached the box, a brilliant light blasted on from the bottom. Caught in the fiery red glow was a single shrub bathed in light.

"Moses," a thunderous voice boomed into the darkness, nearly deafening the terrified man who was down on one knee.

"Moses, this is Jehovah, god of your father and your father's father."

Moses remained on one knee and remained silent, fearful to look up.

"Moses," the voice continued after a moment. "I have a task for you."

Moses looked up with confusion. "Wha…what could the god of my fathers need of me?" Fear was thick in his voice.

"My people have been persecuted for too long."

"What is thy bidding, my master?"

"You will go to Pharaoh and tell him to let my people go."

"H…how can I convince Pharaoh? I am but one man. Pharaoh has armies. Our people are but slaves."

"Fear not, Moses. I will be with you. I will guide you." The thunderous voice boomed with a calming soothness. "When the sun rises, you will go to Pharaoh and demand the release of all of our people."

"Thy will be done," Moses said as he lowered his head.

At that moment, the powerful light went out, and the shiny box silently lifted away and sped off into the night sky. Moses looked up and, after a time, stood and made his way down the trail that led him to that spot.

On the shuttlecraft, Simeon sat with Lieutenant Aaron, the *Heaven*'s science technician and shuttle pilot. As the mountain got,smaller, the two sat quietly.

"I hope Moses is all right," Aaron commented. "Why wouldn't he be?"

"He was standing mighty close when you kicked on the marker light."

"It was all for effect."

"Yeah, but if you stand too close to one of those suckers, you can get a burn, and it makes your hair turn white for a few days."

"Bullshit," Simeon answered with a slight laugh.

"No, for real. I know from experience. My hair was white for five days, but I was a bit closer."

"Any permanent injuries?"

"No."

"Well, hopefully he will be okay."

"Yeah, we can only hope."

The two men circled the mountain as Moses descended, making sure he gets down safely. They sat silently while they watched Moses approached his tent and his family come out to meet him.

"I hope this works," Simeon said.

"Are you saying that you're doing this without any idea whether it would be successful?"

"It's not like I do this all the time, but I had an idea."

"You're risking Moses's life and the lives of all of his tribe on an idea?"

"Yep."

"That's balls."

"Yep."

"We'll set down on that ridge until sunrise," Aaron said as he pointed to an area west of the mountain. The shuttle silently set down and powered down for the night.

As Moses approached his tent, his wife and children came out to meet him.

His wife stood in shock and amazement as they see the patriarch. "Where have you been, father? What has happened to you?" the oldest of his sons asked.

"What do you mean?" Moses inquired. His wife walked up to him, face-to-face. She touched his hair.

"Your hair…it's as white as the finest Egyptian silk."

"And your skin, it is as red as fire." His son added.

Moses's expression became that of awe and disbelief. He stood motionless for a long time.

"What is it, father?"

"Yes, my husband, what is it?"

"I am truly blessed…for I have heard the voice of god."

"You heard god's voice?" his wife asked.

"I had a conversation with him," he said in near shock and disbelief of his own words. "He has tasked me with a mission."

"What is it god would have you do?" his wife asked.

"I am to see Pharaoh and demand the release of our people." His family looked at him with shock chiseled on their faces. "Pharaoh will never let our people go," his son said.

"He would sooner skin you alive along with a hundred of our tribe just to make a point."

"Yes, but god will be with me. I will fear no evil, not even Pharaoh." Moses looked to the sky. There was a faint glow of sunrise coming up over the hill.

"I will sleep for a few hours then be on my way." He looked at his wife. "My wife, prepare some food for my journey." He made his way into his tent and lay down.

The sun broke over the top of the ridge on the horizon. The rays shone right into Aaron's closed eyes. He woke with a moan of annoyance. He woke Simeon with a nudge to the shoulder. She responded with a backhand to his chest.

"What?" she asked as she shook the cobwebs from her head. "It's morning, and Moses just left. He will be out of scanner range in fifteen minutes."

"We'll leave in ten. I'm hitting the head then getting breakfast. You hungry?"

"Yeah. Whatever you're having is fine," he answered as she got up and headed to the back of the shuttle.

Simeon returned to her seat in about five minutes with breakfast for both. She gave Aaron his as she sat down. They ate quickly then went through the preflight checklist. Within minutes, the ship was airborne and homing in on Moses's position.

Moses walked to the top of the dune and fell to his knees in the sand. He shaded his eyes with his hand and focused his vision on the city gate about three kilometers away. He took a large drink of water from his sheepskin flask. He stood, took a deep breath, and started walking to the gates. As he walked down the slope of the dune, he looked into the late-afternoon sky.

"Okay, god…" he said as he walked. "I will be there soon. You said you would not leave me, so I'm counting on you not to let them skin me alive. Thank you."

On the shuttlecraft, Aaron and Simeon laughed at what he said, as they could hear him.

"I hope the implant doesn't malfunction," Aaron said.

"Not a chance. Just be ready to adjust the volume when someone goes to speak to him."

Moses approached the city gates and was immediately accosted by four guards. Within seconds, Moses had four spear tips at his throat. "What business do you have in the city, Hebrew?" the guard in command asked with a heavy tone of disgust in his voice. "I am here to see Pharaoh," Moses explained.

"Why should we let you in to see Pharaoh, Hebrew?"

"I have been sent here by god almighty, Jehovah, the one true living god, to seek the release of his people from bondage."

The guards started laughing, almost to the point of hysteria. "Your god has sent you to free his people!" the four men started laughing more.

Moses stood his ground firm and steadfast.

Behind him, over the peak of a nearby hill, a shiny metal box rose silently into the air. It rose about twenty meters and hovered. From the bottom center of the front, a glowing red beam of light shot toward the group. The beam passed by Moses and hit the guard standing to the left of the commanding officer. The man screams in agony as his body started to glow fluorescent red.

The man faded away into nothingness in front of the stunned onlookers.

The remaining three guards turned and ran screaming. By the time Moses turned, the ship settled behind the rise, not having been seen by anyone. Moses entered the city gates and headed toward the palace…and his destiny with Pharaoh Ramses II.

As Moses enters the court of Pharaoh, Ramses sat straighter in his seat. His face showed the confusion in his mind. *What does this Hebrew want with me?* Ramses thought to himself. "What nerve does this man have to do this?" He doesn't have long to wait for the answer.

"Moses," he said with a strong, arrogant voice. "To what do I have the honor of your presence?"

"Pharaoh Ramses, I have come here with a message."

"You have been ordered to let the children of Israel out of bondage." Moses's voice was strong and confident. The people of the court took notice. Pharaoh and those standing closest to him started to laugh. To Ramses, this was the funniest thing he's heard all day. They continued laughing for several minutes.

"Who has sent you to deliver this message?" he asked as his tone and expression change from comic disbelief to fierce outrage. "Who dares to challenge me, Ramses the second, god incarnate on earth?" his voice echoing through the palace in complete and utter contempt. "This message comes from the lord, god Jehovah…the one, true, living god!" Moses's voice boomed louder and fiercer than Ramses's. "And he has ordered you, saying, 'Let my people go so that they may worship me!"

Pharaoh's face suddenly shifted back to a calmer demeanor. "Moses?" he asked almost laughing. "Are you drunk?" He started laughing. "If it were anyone else but you standing before me, I would have them dissected alive!" he added, still giggling.

"Do not take my god lightly."

"Oh, I won't…I heard what you did at the gate. Very impressive trickery. How much did you pay my guard to run?"

"That was the power of my god."

"Moses, I have some advice for you." His tone more jovial. "Go home, tend to your flocks. Put this behind you."

"If you do not comply, terrible things will happen."

"Terrible things will happen?" He started laughing uncontrollably. "Do what you will, Moses, but be warned, my patience are thin.

If you make an idiot of yourself, I will have you put to death. Now leave here at once." Pharaoh motioned to the palace guards, and they approached Moses. He was escorted out.

"What can we do to convince this Pharaoh guy to let our people go?" Aaron asked. Simeon looked up from the computer screen after a few minutes.

"How would you convince them?" Simeon asked. "Blow shit up."

"Normally, yes, but not if you want to leave a lesson for the future."

"I don't get it."

"We could blow some shit up and that would be the end of it, for now. The next time a dispute needs to be settled in god's name and we are not here, what do you think would happen?"

"There would be no chance of peaceful resolution."

"Exactly."

"Then what is your plan?"

"Give me a minute." It was more like three or four minutes. "I think I have an idea," Simeon said.

"Enlighten me."

"A series of controlled natural disasters brought on by an angry god. A couple of those would make anyone surrender and believe."

"What is your plan?"

"If I introduce a toxin into the river that feeds the city, the computer can predict a series of outcomes. We can manipulate the timing of the events and warn Pharaoh of the coming events."

"A kind of 'Let them go or else' thing?"

"Yes, exactly." She inputs the data into the computer. "This will take a few minutes."

"What about Moses?"

"We'll catch up with him and fill him in when we're ready."

It took nearly ten minutes for the information to be displayed.

Simeon studied the view screen for another five minutes. "Got it!" Simeon shouted.

"Okay, tell me."

"If I introduce Hydrolyzne Thermolasyn into the river, it will turn the water bloodred. It will also kill all the fish. It will stay active in the water for two days and another five days to dissipate. It'll stink up a storm as well."

"What are the permanent effects?"

"None. after it dissipates all life will return to the river."

"What happens after that?"

"There will be an overabundance of reptiles and insects. We can maintain control of their growths. After the river, we can introduce various species upon the populace one at a time. That should do it."

"Hydrolyzne Thermolasyn is treatment for diterullium cyclopastic syndrome on Brantax eleven, isn't it?"

"Yes, yes it is."

"What effect will it have on the population?"

"They'll get very, very sick, but nothing permanent."

"What about our people?"

"There is a natural element here to counteract the effect. I'll introduce that to the water supplies within the Hebrew's domain before Moses introduces the poison into the river."

"How will Moses get the Hydrolyzne Thermolasyn into the water supply?"

"I've studied these people enough to notice their fascination with reptile, in particular…snakes."

"So what?"

"Gave me an idea."

"Enlighten me."

"I can build a staff that can mock a six foot, cybernetic python that we can control remotely." Her demeanor changed slightly but noticeably.

"What's the catch? There is always a catch."

"Two things…one, it'll only work in a two-meter diameter."

"And the second?"

"In order to eliminate a remote control unit, I need to build it to read brain waves."

"And the problem?"

"It has to be one of us."

"And let me guess," Aaron complained, "it has to be me."

"Yes."

"Great, I get to face certain death."

"Hey, I'm a woman. I'll get laughed at no matter what I do. You will fit in much better." She gave him a big cold smile. "Sorry, now let's find Moses."

"Okay," Aaron said as he pressed the lighted buttons on the control panel, and the shuttlecraft rose silently into the air.

As Moses walked along the quiet trail, passing the last person five full minutes before, he saw a shimmering object low in the sky in front of him. He watched and approached as it quietly descended to the ground behind a small hill. Moses ran toward the hill to see what the object was. He got over the hill and saw the metal box standing on three short skinny legs. Beside the box are two strangely dressed people, not dissimilar from himself. He approached the two strangers cautiously.

"Moses," Simeon said in a calm, soothing voice. "Who are you?" he asked.

"We are emissaries of the lord, god, Jehovah. God of your fathers and your fathers' fathers. We are here to help you free your people, for your people are our people."

"How can you help me?"

"We have the power to bring great and terrible plagues upon those keeping bondage without harm to your people," Simeon continued.

"You are beings of infinite power!" he said in awe as he dropped to one knee.

"No, we are not," Simeon explained. "But the god of your fathers, our master, is of infinite power. He will guide your journey to Pharaoh, and we will help you deal with him."

"My name is Aaron," the man said. "I will accompany you to Pharaoh and guide you."

"You will carry this staff, and when Pharaoh asked for proof of your god, Aaron will tell you what to do," Simeon told Moses as she handed him the long pole.

Aaron leaned toward Simeon and whispered, "How do we introduce the toxin?"

"The toxin is in a container at the bottom of the staff. Dip the end of the staff in the water, and it will release on its own."

"When you lift off, beam the implant out of Moses. We won't need to monitor him since I'll be with him."

"I must report to Jehovah," Simeon said to make an excuse to depart. She walked back into the shiny box and it flew away, to protect the chosen ones.

"You and I," Aaron explained, "are going to face Pharaoh first thing in the morning."

"What do we do in the meantime?"

"Sleep," Aaron said as he lay down on a grassy knoll ten feet away. "Okay." Moses said as he lay down a few feet away. The sun set quickly, and the night settled in, dark and thick. Sleep came quick to the two men.

The morning sun rose to find Aaron waking groggily and Moses up and cooking breakfast. Moses was all smiles.

"Good morning, my friend. Are you hungry?"

"Yes, I am."

"Rabbit is almost cooked. Come sit by the fire and have a flask of water."

"Why are you so happy? We will be seeing Pharaoh soon."

"With you here and god on our side, we can't lose."

"I sure hope so." The two finished their breakfast, cleaned up the area, and headed toward the city gates.

The two arrived at the gates in about twenty minutes. When the four guards on duty saw it was Moses, they stepped aside, way aside. The two passed through without incident. It's another five minutes to get to the palace. As the men started up the steps to the main gallery, a beep went off in Aaron's communicator earpiece. The beep was followed by Simeon's voice.

"The Hebrew's water supply is safe." He tapped his earpiece and transmitted a single signal of acknowledgement. They continued to the gallery.

Pharaoh Ramses sat upon his throne enjoying another morning of lavish luxury. Moses and Aaron entered the gallery at the far end and made their way hastily to the front of Ramses's throne. When Ramses saw the two men, his smile changed to a face of annoyance. After a minute, he forced his smile back on and stiffened in his seat.

"What can I do for you today, Moses?"

Moses handed the staff to Aaron, and dropped to one knee while spreading out his hands.

"Good morning, Ramses." He stood and looked into Ramses's eyes. "I am here to give you one more chance to do as the lord has demanded. Let my people go, and we will leave in peace."

"And what if I don't?"

"If you do not, the river Nile will be transformed into blood, unsuitable for drinking, bathing or farming. The choice is yours."

"Moses, like I told you yesterday, go back to your fields and tend to your flocks. You are starting to annoy me."

"So be it," Moses said in a louder, more commanding voice as he turned to Aaron and pointed to the river's edge at the left of Ramses's throne. Aaron walked to the edge of the landing and dipped the end of the staff in the water.

The chemical inside the end of the staff released into the river and quickly fanned out in all directions. The water turned a dark red color and, almost right away, started to stink a horrible stench. Within minutes, dead fish started to float to the surface. Pharaoh looked out at the river in shock and disbelief.

"Make it stop, Moses!" Pharaoh shouted in panic. "Make it like it was."

"Let my people go, and god will make things right."

Pharaoh fell back in his seat and, after a few minutes, hardened his face. He looked into Moses's eyes. "I can't let them go. You don't understand. I can't."

Three men came running into the gallery, winded, and panicked. They ran up to the throne and threw themselves to one knee. "Forgive us, Pharaoh, but you need to know," the man said as they sucked air into their strained lungs. "The river Nile has turned to blood. The fish are dying, and a foul smell has enveloped the land. But the Hebrew's water is not affected. Theirs is fine."

"I know this, you idiots!" he screamed. "Now leave here at once!" The two men ran out as Ramses turned to Moses. "Guards, kill them!" he ordered.

"If you kill me, god will never repair the river," Moses pleaded. "Your kingdom will surely perish." Ramses waved his guards off, and they stopped.

"Okay, Moses, return the river to normal, and I will release your people."

"No, Ramses, I will return in seven days," Moses said after speaking to Aaron for a moment. "If my people are ready to go, god will replenish your water supply."

"Don't leave us like this, Moses!"

"You need to see and feel the power of my god. Seven days, Pharaoh."

On the shuttle, with the temporal discriminators on, seven days went by in just over one minute, and again Moses and Aaron stood in front of Pharaoh.

When the two men walked in front of Ramses's throne, the Pharaoh made a visible effort to sit up straight. His lips were cracked, and his skin pale. His body was weakened from the onset of dehydration.

"Please, Moses," Pharaoh pleaded. "Tell your god to make the water clean again, and I shall grant your request. Please!"

Moses turned to Aaron and nodded his head. Aaron touched the end of the cane to the river, and the red color gave way to clear, blue, clean water. After several seconds of wondrous disbelief, the Pharaoh and his court jumped into the river Nile and splashed around laughing. As Moses and Aaron looked up and down the banks of the river, they saw thousands of people running into the water.

After about an hour, Ramses emerged from the river and headed back to his throne, his entourage in tow. He took his rightful seat with a renewed vigor.

He sat for several minute in silence staring between Moses and the river's edge, where his slaves were filling jars with freshwater. Finally he said, "Moses, after careful consideration, I have decided not to release your people. They will remain in bondage, and you will be punished." The guards approached the two men, so Aaron took the staff from Moses and threw it to the floor. With his concentration, the staff started to wiggle like a snake. The top end of the staff started emitting bolts of electricity. Everyone in the gallery ran and hid behind Pharaoh's throne.

Aaron's earpiece beeped, and he heard Simeon's voice in his head. "I've been listening, and sensors indicate there are plenty of reptiles and insects to raise holy hell on these people. The Hebrew people have been inoculated. They will be invisible to the bugs." Aaron tapped Moses's shoulder, and nodded toward the staff. As Moses bent down to pick the staff up, it became solid again.

"Behold, Pharaoh, the next plague to befall the people of Egypt," Moses said as he and Aaron walked away from Ramses. By the time the men get to the far side of the gallery, the buzzing sounds of millions of flies could be heard throughout the land. Moses looked around to see flies consume the gallery yard. Apart from the flies, Moses saw frogs by the thousands, locusts so thick they look like clouds filling the sky.

"Until tomorrow, Pharaoh. Until tomorrow." As they approached the gates of the city, they heard people screaming about lice over everyone's bodies. Moses started to laugh.

They stepped onto the shuttle, and in ten seconds, it was time to face Pharaoh again. When Moses and Aaron approached the throne, it has been a full day since they had been there.

"Are you ready to let my people go?" Moses shouted at Ramses. "Make this dreadful plague go away, and I will comply," Pharaoh said with a pitiful tone in his voice. A beep in his earpiece told Aaron that Simeon was ready for the next phase. He nodded to Moses, who lifted the staff above his head.

As he chanted a prayer, all the insects and reptiles disappeared in little blue shimmers of light. After about three hours, runners came in and whispered in Pharaoh's ears. He sat in contemplation for several long minutes. He sat up straight on his throne, and took a deep breath. The pitiful look on his face changed to arrogant anger. "My runners tell me all the insects and reptiles are gone. I have decided not to release our slaves and have the two of you put to death." As the guards approached Moses, he, once again, threw his staff to the floor, and with Aaron's help, it turned into a serpent spitting bolts of light around the room. Like the day before, everyone in Pharaoh's court ran and hid behind the huge stone throne that housed Ramses.

Moses picked up his staff, and he and Aaron head toward the end of the great gallery. As they approached the end of the gallery, Aaron's hand went to his ear for a moment. He then stopped and turned to Pharaoh.

"Ramses," Aaron shouted. "Be ready, the next plague will befall your people before the sun reaches its daily apex." Ramses's expression turned to concern, for he knew the apex would take place in just under an hour.

It took fifteen minutes for the two to reach the shuttlecraft, and Simeon was outside to greet them. She pulled a hypospray out of her medical bag and gave both of them a shot.

"What is that?" Aaron asked. "It's a hydrox compound."

"Isn't that for radiation poisoning?"

"Yes, all of our people have been inoculated."

"I see, isn't this a bit extreme?"

Moses just listened in confusion.

"Yes, but this Ramses is very stubborn, too stubborn." The mood became solemn as the three headed into the shuttle. The craft silently lifted into the air and headed above the palace. It hovered nearly a mile above the great building.

Pharaoh's court was bustling with activity. In the center of it all was Pharaoh's boisterous voice, booming laughter. Everyone around him were laughing with him. The center of his attention was still Moses.

"How mad is he to challenge the great Ramses?" he said, laughing so hard he had to hold his sides. After laughing for several minutes, he continued, "And one god! Ra will crush their god, and if not

Ra, then Baal will take care of it." Everyone in the gallery laughed along.

Laughter turned to shouts of screams from the center of the crowd. Pharaoh stood to see into the crowd and notice white hail-like stones falling from the sky. He noticed that when the stones hit an object, or a person, small explosions occur. Not enough to kill but enough to cause small open sores on the skin and appears to melt the brick floor of the gallery. People started running around in panic and pain.

"What kind of rain can do this?" Pharaoh screamed in anger as he looked to the sky. "My priests did not tell me of this!" Ramses looked at his head priest dead in the eyes. "Why are there no clouds in the sky? How can this be?"

The "rain" stopped after about five minutes. A few minutes after that, runners came in and ran up to Pharaoh.

Ramses stopped them in their tracks. He stared at each of the three. "Let me guess, it happened all around the city? And none of the Hebrew people are affected?" Anger foamed from his lips.

"Yes, Pharaoh," One runner said with the terror of what could happen hanging in his voice. Pharaoh lifted his eyes to the sky, shook a raised fist into the air and screamed, "Moses! Moses!"

The shuttle stayed afloat where it was for several more hours, sharing the same temporal realm as the beings on the surface. It set down, and Moses and Aaron approached the gates of the city. When they arrived at the usually crowded gates and city streets, they found nothing but devastation. People and animals alike were laying in the streets, most too weak to move, covered in welts, boils, and blisters. Some were vomiting while others were bleeding from the eyes, ears, and nose. Fingertips on some of these poor people were turning black with decay.

The two entered the gallery and headed up to the throne. All the people who once laughed at Moses and Aaron now lay on the floor, dying or wishing they were dead. Pharaoh was slumped in his throne, blood running from his eyes, ears, and nose. It took all of his strength to sit up in his seat.

"Will you now let my people go?" Moses shouted. "Moses, what have you done?" Pharaoh asked weakly. "Let my god's people go, and all will be made right."

"Okay, Moses," Pharaoh answered. "You win. Make this plague go away, and I will release your people." Contempt was heavy on his lips. Moses looked at Aaron, who nodded in acceptance. Moses lifted his staff over his head and began to chant. Shimmering silver light rained down over the land as far as the eye can see. A strange smell permeated the air.

"We will be back in two hours. Have all god's people ready to leave this place."

Pharaoh gave a weak wave of compliance and nodded his head.

Moses and Aaron left the gallery, and the city.

Two hours passed quickly, and the two men were back in front of Pharaoh and his court. Everyone had recovered, but their arrogant attitudes had been replaced by fear.

"Why are god's people not ready to leave here?"

"It has occurred to me, Moses," Pharaoh started, "as horrible as all your god's plagues have been, not one of my subjects has been killed. I see now that your god lacks teeth." Pharaoh stood slowly as he waved his hands. His guards approached the men cautiously, spears at the ready. The two looked at each other, and Aaron nodded. Moses looked back at Pharaoh.

"Guards!" Ramses shouted. "Kill them, slowly!" The guards stepped in closer but still cautious. Moses lifted his staff into the air, and the guards stepped back in apprehension.

"Pharaoh Ramses!" Moses now screamed above all other sounds. "If death is all you understand, then death is what you will know!" The guards moved in closer, but the two men vanished in a glow of fluorescent blue light and sparkles.

The gallery was silent as Ramses's face showed serious concern.

The silence lasted a long time.

The night came with dread to the people of Egypt. Pharaoh sat alone on his throne pondering what's to come. Fear swept over his being. He heard footsteps behind him and stiffened in his seat.

"Come to bed, my king," the woman said as she took his hand. "I guess you are right, wife." They headed off to their chambers.

Pharaoh's eyes opened quick, with a feeling of anxiety sweeping over him. His mind was racing because he didn't understand why he woke up. Then, after a second, he heard a woman's scream piercing the silence of the morning.

As his mind focused on what he just heard, the silence was pierced by another scream, from a different direction. He sat up quickly and tried to focus. Another, louder, scream pierced the cold morning air. As Ramses rose to his feet, he heard a scream from the palace. Then another scream caught his attention. This one came from the rooms of his children. He ran to the first door down the hall and swung it open wildly. The little body under the blanket stirred, but remained asleep. He closed the door and headed to the next one when the scream from his wife ripped through the air. It was coming from the room at the end of the hall. The room of his eldest son. He ran in to find his wife crying uncontrollably at the foot of the bed. On the bed was the cold blue body of his firstborn son, his open eyes staring at the sky, through the window. He walked to the bedside of his son. As he started weeping, his wife looked over at him. She forced the tears back and looked at her husband.

"I hope you are satisfied," she said through painfully emotional sobs. "Your stubbornness has cost me a son…and the kingdom its rightful heir."

She walked away slowly as the tears flooded back without control. Even as queen, she didn't hide her anguish as the servants came running in.

"Bring Moses to me," Ramses screamed angrily through his own tears as he spun around to face them. "NOW!" He turned back to the corpse of his son.

"Forgive me, my child. This is not what I intended for you." He kneeled beside the bed. "I will avenge you…but for now I must give in to the demands of Moses and his god." He stood and walked toward the door. He walked into the main gallery, heaviness in his legs making his walk slow and painful. His face showed the grief-stricken look of a father, not a Pharaoh, not a god. Everyone in the gallery stopped in their tracks when they saw Ramses enter. The room went silent.

Ramses walked to the throne and turned toward the crowd. All eyes were on him as he looked out across the sea of faces. After a long pause, he spoke, "Let it be known," he proclaimed in a loud, clear, but painful voice, "from this day forward, all Hebrews in bondage will be free."

Cheers exploded from the gallery. "Wait," Ramses continued as he raised his arms. "There will be one condition."

Moses and Aaron entered the gallery from the far side. "Moses." Ramses shouted as he pointed at Moses. "You will lead your people out of my kingdom! NOW!" Moses looked inquisitively at Pharaoh.

"Pack up and get out before the sun sets this day! Anyone left at sunset will be put to death. So let it be written, so let it be done!"

"By your command," Moses responded as he spread his arms and backed away a few steps. He straightened up and faced the nowfreed slaves.

"All of the children of the god of Abraham must assemble outside of the city gates. Spread the word," Moses shouted, and all of the freed slaves in the Pharaoh's gallery ran out to all points of the city and the kingdom. Moses and Aaron left the gallery and headed to the open area just outside the city gates.

Simeon swung the shuttlecraft above the Hebrew's section of the city and started to beam supplies and animals, strategically, so no one sees it happening.

She transported everything to an isolated area of the desert fifteen kilometers to the east of the city, on the shore of a large body of water, an inland sea.

As Moses and Aaron gathered the twenty-two thousand slaves from across the nation of Egypt, they are led by a hovering shiny box that silently glided through the air. They were led to the shore of the sea. It took a day and a half for all the people to arrive.

"Aaron," Simeon called into his earpiece, "sensors show approximately six hundred charioteers heading in your direction. Estimated time of intercept is three point five hours."

"Understood. Any idea how we get these people out of here? If the Egyptian charioteers get here, it will be a slaughter and, our mission will be over."

"I know, I know." After about fifteen minutes of silence, Simeon called, "Aaron! I've got it! But we've got to work fast!"

"Okay, then, what do we do?"

"Head south about three kilometers. There is a narrow bottleneck. I can use the tractor beam to part the sea enough for everyone to get across. Get it started now. I'll transport some of the animals and supplies to the other side and get into position."

"Copy that," Aaron replied and got everyone to start moving. Aaron filled Moses in on the plan and Moses led the group south along the seashore.

At the jetty three kilometers south, Moses stood at the edge of the water, on a bluff overlooking the sea, and the area now started to be filled with the refugees. The shiny box was floating over the water halfway to the opposite shore. It took nearly two and a half hours for Moses to get Aaron in his sight. As soon as Aaron saw that Moses noticed him, he called to Simeon and waved to Moses. Moses again threw his hands in the sky, with a firm grip on his staff, and started a chant.

The shiny box emitted a sparkling blue light that stretches the full width of the sea and fifty meters wide. The water separated like a zipper from one side to the other. The people started to walk cautiously between the forty-meter-tall walls of water. Moses led the crowds, and as they got to the other shore, he climbed a nearby bluff and looked out between the wet walls looking for Aaron.

"The charioteers are approaching. One point five kilometers until intercept," Simeon said to Aaron, who was just entering the trail between the water.

"We should be across in about thirty-five minutes."

"You don't have thirty-five minutes. They'll be on you in twenty."

"Wait for as long as you can, then close this thing up. See if you can close it from the other side first."

"It'll take a while to program the tractor beam."

"Then I suggest you get started."

Moses looked out across the field of faces looking for Aaron. It took five or so minutes for him to see the man who came over a rise about half a kilometer away. In the pale blue glow of the tractor beam, Aaron could see the darker shadows of the charioteers in the distant horizon.

"Can you close this thing up yet?"

"Yeah, but not all the charioteers are in the kill zone."

"No prob. Leave some survivors to return and tell Pharaoh what happened."

"Good idea. Activating." Simeon hit some controls, and the tractor beam started to shut down, and the valley between the walls of water started to fill up, trapping all but seven of the six hundred charioteers in the swirling currents of their watery graves. The seven surviving charioteers rode off in terror back to their Pharaoh.

Aaron made it to shore and, two minutes later, so did the water, crashing against the rocks below his feet. The shiny box led the way through the desert night with an intense spotlight lighting the way.

"Captain," said lieutenant Reuben, who was manning the communications console. "Message from Simeon, twenty-two thousand, seven hundred and fifty-seven people rescued, heading to prearranged coordinates."

Jehovah smiled for a second then turned to Lucifer. Lucifer turned and said, "We only need two million samples. If twenty thousand settle, we can have enough in twelve point five days."

"Excellent…Is the region ready for their arrival?"

"Terraforming will be complete in five hours." The captain turned to the communications officer. "Open a channel to the shuttlecraft."

"Channel open, sir," Reuben replied.

"Simeon here."

"Lieutenant, you have to keep those people safe but away from their designated home for another five hours."

"But sir, that's five years for them."

"Yes, we know. It's unavoidable. You have to keep them wondering in the region until we've finished terraforming their area."

"Understood, Captain. Shuttlecraft out."

"What are we supposed to do for five hours?" Aaron asked, having heard the conversation through his communicator's earpiece.

"You need to get clear so I can beam you up. Better five hours up here than five years down there," Simeon answered.

"I see your point. Give me five, and I'll call you back."

"Copy that."

The transporter cycle completed, and Aaron stepped away from the rear of the craft and sat by Simeon.

"Well," he started, "I'm gonna take a nap. What are you doing?"

"I'm going to write a book."

"Oh yeah, about what?"

"A religious guidebook, full of stories and songs about how to enjoy a peaceful coexistence," Simeon said with a touch of pride in her voice.

"Good luck with that," Aaron said as he slumped down into his seat and closed his eyes.

"Thanks," she said as she picked up a padd and began to work. The bridge ran smoothly and quietly for the past four and a half hours. Terraforming was winding up, and some of the technicians were returning to the ship. The damage control parties were finishing the repairs from the battle with Takel Ra.

"Captain," Reuben responded, "all stations reporting terraforming complete and all crews have returned to the ship and all equipment is accounted for."

"Great. Open a channel to the shuttlecraft."

"Channel open, sir."

"Simeon."

"Yes, sir."

"The area is secure. You can lead our flock to their chosen land."

"Aye, sir. On our way."

Whack!

Aaron woke up with a slap in the forehead from the back fist swung by Simeon.

"What the fuck!" he screamed as he flew around in his seat while she was laughing.

"Wake up, sleeping beauty. You've got to get back to the surface and get these buggers home."

He got up and walked to the transporter. In two seconds, he was standing on the surface. He walked around until he found Moses. The two conversed for several minutes, reuniting.

"I have been told by god," Aaron spoke to the leaders of the thirteen groups that have formed due to increased population, "that he has completed our land, and he will guide us to it now." The thirteen men started to speak among themselves.

"How long, does god say, it will take us to get there," the eldest leader asked.

"God said if we leave at the next full moon, which is in the day after tomorrow, it will take one full cycle of the moon to get there," Aaron answered.

The word spread across the settlement, and the packing began. On the first night of the full moon, the thirteen tribes of Israel, which means "god's chosen people" on H'Too Bar'kla, begun their trek to their promised land.

Captain's log: Stardate 14001.02. We have settled the Hebrews, as they call themselves, into a region of the area that should protect them from foreign invaders. We have twelve days to wait before we have our supply of genetic materials. We have started extracting what we need and predict completion of mission in fourteen days.

The day was rolling along smoothly, and the bridge crew were anticipating some well-deserved relaxation at the end of shift, in just over an hour. Lucifer was following the progress of the genetic material extraction, Jehovah was looking over daily reports while the rest of the bridge crew were performing various diagnostic tests on key bridge systems. Everything was uneventful.

Suddenly, the ship rocked violently. Before it had time to stabilize, the red alert Klaxon was sounding and personnel were taking their stations throughout the ship.

"What the fuck was that?" Jehovah screamed as he picked himself off the floor.

He turned to Lucifer who was keying in commands into his computer. Lieutenant Simeon was doing the same thing at her computer at the tactical station.

"Data is coming in, but some of the sensor arrays are off-line. Give me a minute," He answered without looking away from his monitor.

"Simeon, are you getting anything?"

"My sensors show two Nephillium cruisers, one aft, starboard, one aft, port, both vessels at one hundred thousand kilometers and closing."

"Confirmed," Lucifer interjected. "Both vessels moderately damaged but battle capable. The captain turned to lieutenant Kohath, at communications. He was busy channeling incoming messages from the different departments on the ship. It took a few seconds.

"Damage control parties report warp engines off-line, dorsal transporter emitters destroyed, aft phaser emitters damaged, and a hull breach on deck four, sections one through three."

"Helm, full stop then emergency reverse."

"Aye, sir" came from lieutenant Levi, as he hit the controls. "Tactical, lock forward phasers on starboard vessel, and fire when you have a shot."

"Aye, sir" came from Simeon, who, in an excited voice, continued, "sir, weapon's lock is non-responsive, having to switch to manual." In less than two seconds, the Nephillium cruisers were on the screen, being viewed from behind. Suddenly both ships broke away hard. Simeon fired but only caught the back end as it veered off to the left.

"Sorry, Captain," she said apologetically.

"No worries, Lieutenant. Try to restore computer control, but be prepared to fire. Helm, pursuit course, best speed, port vessel, engage."

Aye, sir" came from both.

As the *Heaven* banked to the right, the Nephillium cruiser came into view. It took a few seconds for the *Heaven* to come about completely and catch the cruiser.

"Fire as she comes to bear."

"Manual control only, sir."

"Understood, Simeon. Do your best."

"Aye, sir, just keep her steady."

As Simeon lined up her shot, the ship was rocked by an explosion.

"The other cruiser is aft. Shields holding."

"Maintain course, take that ship out." The ship rocked again as Simeon fired.

The phaser beam hit the ship just aft of center.

"Enemy shields at forty-five percent, our shields at seventy-three percent."

The ship rocked again, this time, minor explosions occurred at different bridge stations. "Correction, our shields at forty percent." Simeon fired the phasers again, and the beam hit the right engine. And after a few seconds of direct contact, the cruiser's engine exploded, and the ship went into an uncontrollable flat spin.

Another volley hit the *Heaven*, and the ship rocked as more systems short out on the bridge. A third volley hit. Simeon lined up the phaser emitters. A fourth volley hit. Simeon fired, and the Nephillium cruiser exploded. Another volley hit.

"Spin us around. I want to be face to face with this guy." The *Heaven* accelerated and turned sharply to the right. In the middle of the turn, the ship was hit and spun out of control. Simeon jettisoned six photon torpedoes just as the power conduit blew out, plunging the bridge into darkness. It took about three seconds before emergency power kicked in, and the bridge was bathed in red light.

The ship rocked lightly as two distant explosions echoed through the walls of the ship. Everyone held their collective breaths as they waited for more explosions while they get key systems back on line.

"Limited power on the scanners," Lucifer said loudly. "Partial short-range sensors showing a debris field, ten thousand kilometers. No other ships in the area."

"Did we get them?" Jehovah asked aloud. "Apparently so, Captain," Lucifer answered.

"Confirmed," Simeon jumped in. "Tactical display shows no vessels in the area, just a large debris field."

"Damage control report, now," Jehovah shouted. Kohath sent the order out to all departments. Reports started to come in right away.

"It's not good news, Captain," Kohath started. "Main energizer hit. We're on battery power. Life support down. Warp drive off-line. Transporters off-line. Thrusters off-line. We are adrift."

"Lucifer, how long before we are operational?"

"Depends on what you consider operational. To get all systems back online, we're looking at three months."

Jehovah gave him a hard look. "That's what we need to get home. We can push it to two months, maybe. But guaranteed we are not moving under our own power for at least forty-five days."

Captain's log: Stardate 14009.01. It has been fifty days since our battle with the Nephillium. Life support, thrusters, warp drive, and partial transporters back online. Luckily, the spacefold drive wasn't damaged, but without the main energizer, we cannot produce enough power to get home nor can we use the warp drive. Estimated repair time is fifteen days. We are heading back to Terra. Arrival time is five days.

"Entering standard orbit," Lieutenant Levi told Jehovah. "Finally. Lucifer, what's going on down there?"

"It appears we've been gone for nearly thirteen hundred years."

"Wow, that sucks, our people better be okay. Can you determine their status?"

"Not now, there is still no form of electronic communications. We need to contact our ground team."

"Can you raise Professor Cronus at Olympus Station?"

"Channel open, sir."

"Cronus here."

"Jehovah here, professor. Have you been monitoring what's been happening?"

"Yes, Captain, and we've been collecting the genetic material that we need."

"Lucifer and I are coming down."

"We'll be standing by. Out." The channel went silent. "Simeon, you're with us."

The three moved into the turbolift and headed to Olympus Station.

Captain's log: Supplemental. After meeting with Professors Uranus and Cronus, as well as Lieutenant Simeon and Lucifer, we have learned hard facts and make hard decisions. The current world power, the "Romans," have subjugated most of the inhabited region, our people included. These Romans are brutal in their control and relentless in their subjugation. We have reluctantly agreed to present, to all the people, a messiah to guide these people to coexist peacefully. I pray we are doing the right thing.

"We have found a suitable candidate," Simeon told Jehovah, along with the other officers in the briefing room, all seven of them. "She is fourteen years old, and her family lineage is one of the purist back to Eve."

"Is she still a virgin?"

"Since that is the most important thing—duhh—that's the first thing we checked," She answered, not hiding the sarcasm.

"My apologies," Jehovah said. "No disrespect intended. I'm just nervous about this whole thing. I've never participated in this kind of project."

"No worries, Captain. I understand."

"Thanks. Please continue with the briefing."

"Ensign Michaels is speaking to her now. He will convince her that she will give birth to the son of god."

"What good is that going to do?" asked Commander Anak, chief medical officer.

"It is our intention to bring the infant aboard ship for schooling and training after which he will be reintroduced to his people. We are confident that he will be embraced as the messiah that our people have been praying about since before their captivity by Ramses."

"Why do you think he will be embraced?" Anak continued. "He will be endowed with abilities, provided by us, that will make him superior in every way."

"What types of abilities are you talking about?" Ensign Malcham, senior ship's biologist, asked.

"We are using modified DNA from the captain, and he will be physically perfect and in perfect physical condition, with an IQ of around one-eighty, slightly taller than average, he will also be implanted with some electronic components that will allow the computer to interface with his brain."

"What good is that?" Anak said with an accent of confusion. "We want him to be the son of god, so he needs to be able to perform some of what these people would consider miracles. The implants that we give him will allow the computer to assess the situation and initiate the proper protocols to do whatever he thinks should be done. The computer can easily do this as fast as it takes to keep up with the temporal deviation, unless you want to stay here for twenty years."

"When do we get started?"

"As soon as Michaels gets ba—"

Beep, beep, the communicator chimes rang.

"Sorry for the interruption," said the disembodied voice on the other end of the speaker. "You want to be informed when Michaels got back. Well, he's back."

"Gets back," Simeon finished. "Time to get this show on the road. Remember, every ten seconds is one day. I will beam down and implant the girl right now."

"You heard her," Jehovah said as he stood. "Let's get this done."

They all got up and move with a singular purpose.

Forty-five minutes later, the virgin, Mary, was giving birth at an inn in a small town. Ensign Michaels was on the surface. He approached three shepherds tending their flocks. He disengaged his phase discriminator and proceeded to scare the hell out of the shepherds. After their initial shock wore off, he told them that the savior of mankind has been born. He told them of a light in the sky and how it is a beacon to the baby.

Several kilometers away, Ensign Gabriel was doing the same thing with three men practiced in the art of education and influence.

Aboard the *Heaven*, an incandescent satellite was placed in a low geosynchronous orbit above the inn.

It took several hours for the two groups from the two most diverse classes of men to come together at the little inn. Mary had given birth several hours earlier, and the child was already bigger than the average baby with a skin tone several shades lighter than the populace.

The men came in and knelt before the baby repeating similar stories to Mary and her husband, Joseph, the story of how an angel appeared to them. And for a minute, it looked like the newborn baby understood what they were saying and smiled.

Two days later, Mary woke to find her baby, named Jesus, missing, and the archangel Michaels by her bed.

"Your child," Michaels told her, "will be brought back to you on the twelfth year of his life. By this time, he will be able to prove to all men that he is in fact the son of god." Mary nodded in agreement as she fell to her knees, and Michaels vanished in an array of blue light.

In sick bay, there was a bustle of activity as the baby was put into an isolation tube. The tube was designed for long-term use even though for the child inside, forty minutes will be twelve years. The isolation tube is in a force field allowing the flow of Terran time to proceed uninterrupted. Outside of the force field, it is the flow of

Heaven time, protected by the temporal discriminators. The child inside was connected to all these probes and wires, and everybody wanted a look.

The wired connections to the computer were allowing the child to learn at an incredibly accelerated rate. After forty minutes, a twelve-year-old child was greeted by uniformed men and women who promptly whisked him away to the transporter room and beamed him down to a waiting mother.

Captain Jehovah sat in his chair watching the deeds of Jesus. Right from the beginning of his teachings, Jesus was known as a prophet and a healer. As hours passed by on the bridge, years passed by on the surface.

Jesus was now thirty-two years old and was faced with a serious dilemma, a dilemma that no one on the *Heaven* had anticipated. Jesus, instead of being accepted and embraced, was being persecuted by the very people he was sent to assist and defend. Simeon was trying to figure out how to turn the situation around.

"Captain, there is no other way," Simeon said apologetically. "There has to be."

"I wish there was, sir. I don't see any other way. It has to happen. But we can spin this."

"What do you mean 'spin'? They're going to kill Jesus for nothing, and you say we can't interfere."

"Not until after he is dead."

"What are you talking about?"

"This is what I'm trying to say, sir. We can save him."

"What's your plan?"

"He has to endure the brutality of execution. When he dies he will be entombed. Once that happens, we can beam into the tomb and repair all his injuries. To the locals, it will appear that he has risen from the dead. That will set the cornerstone of a religious upheaval."

"How much time do we have?"

"Minutes."

"Then get moving," Jehovah said as he returned his attention to the view screen. Simeon got on the turbolift and headed to the transporter room. On the view screen unfolded the drama—Jesus's execution. It was done the way of the times, but for Jesus, the brutality was unmatched.

First, there were the beatings. After the beatings were the whippings, over every inch of his body. A crown of thorns was forced onto his head, in honor of Jehovah. This caused the captain to weep openly on the bridge, as well as most of the other bridge officers. The sun set and rose again in seconds.

The beatings started again, reopening the wounds that started healing. Jesus was forced to carry a large wooden beam across his shoulders as he was led through the narrow streets of the city. He was led to a hill outside of the city. His wrists were nailed to the beam, and the beam was secured to a vertical post. His ankles were the nailed to the support. This angered Jehovah.

As Jesus died, Jehovah ordered a barrage of torpedoes to be airburst above the execution site. This airburst caused the ground to rumble and the skies to grow dark for hours. His body was taken down and sealed in a tomb.

"Jehovah to transporter room," the captain said into the communications panel on his chair. "Simeon, you're on. Do it."

Simeon and Lieutenant Nazay, the senior nurse, beamed into the sealed tomb. They activated their temporal discriminator and proceed to heal Jesus. Simeon used a dermal regenerator to heal the whip marks and bruises from the beatings. Nazay applied a cortical stimulator to repair the damaged portions of the brain and replaced his heart. The whole procedure took about three minutes, the Terran days, to complete. Jesus woke with only the holes in his ankles and wrists and the spear hole in his side left unhealed. Simeon used a portable tractor beam generator to move the rock from the tomb entrance. As the huge stone rolled away from the entrance, the two women beamed back to the ship.

Sarah, a cousin of Jesus, was sitting outside of the tomb, under a large tree. She was crying because she missed the funeral, and she sat alone thinking about her late cousin. The still and the silence were broken as the huge rock sealing the tomb began to vibrate. It slowly started to roll open, and out of the tomb came a brilliant blue sparkling light. A slight high-pitched hum was heard coming from the tomb.

The rock was completely out of the way as the light and sound faded, and standing in the darkness was Jesus—alive. Sarah screamed and was heard by Joseph, the owner of the land and the tomb. He arrived to see Jesus standing outside of the tomb.

In the days that followed, Jesus met with his disciples and apostles. He showed all of them that he had, in fact, conquered death. A religion was born. A religion based on peace and love.

"It will be one point five days before we have all the genetic material we need," Lucifer informed Jehovah. He continued looking at his monitor for almost a minute when, someone spoke, "Captain, I'm picking up an anomalous reading."

"Explain."

"Give me a minute." He looked up at Jehovah. "I'm reading Nephillium life signs."

"What!" the captain said with surprise. "How many?"

After a few seconds, the voice answered, "Reading twenty-one Nephilliums on the surface."

"Can we beam them?"

"What the fuck!" Lucifer cut off the captain. "What now?" he asked wearily.

"I just registered a Nephillium merging with a Terran."

"What do you mean 'merging'?"

"A Nephillium walked up to a Terran, there was an energy spike, then only a Nephillium–Wait! Amazing! They are separate again. Analyzing."

"Well, what's up?"

"I believe the Nephillium are using their phase discriminators to enter and manipulate the Terran bodies that they merge with."

"How do we stop them?" It took nearly a minute before he answered.

"I must address all of our personnel, on the ship and on the surface, in five minutes."

"About what?"

"I'll explain to all at once. Trust me, Captain."

"Okay, five minutes it is." Lucifer turned his attention back to the monitor.

"Attention, crew. This is first officer Lucifer. Twenty-two Nephilliums survived our battles and are on the surface. Using their technology, they can merge and essentially 'possess' Terrans. The only way to destroy them is close proximity detection and elimination. Our mission will be complete in one day. Therefore, I have decided to stay behind and hunt them down before they destroy the Terrans. We are the reason the Terrans are being killed, and it is our responsibility to protect them. I am asking for nine volunteers to stay behind with me, for one year, to hunt them. Lucifer out."

In a second, Lieutenant Kohath, at communications, said, "Comm lines are jammed, Captain. Seems there will be no shortage of volunteers."

Captain's log: Stardate 14079.63. All the genetic material we need is now aboard ship. Repairs are complete, and we can return home anytime. The one issue remaining is the Nephilliums on the planet. Ten of my people, Lieutenant Commander Lucifer; Lieutenant Simeon; Archangel Ensign Michaels; Archangel Ensign Gabriel; Lieutenant Nazay, medic; Lieutenant Kohath; Lieutenant Hercules; Ensign Aeolus; Ensign Eris; and Ensign Hecate have volunteered to remain behind to destroy them and protect the Terrans. There is just one thing left to do.

"Helm, set a course to orbit this star system at one million kilometers from the edge of the temporal distortion on all planes."

"Aye, sir. Course and speed laid in" came from lieutenant Levi. "Tactical, drop the six marker buoys at even intervals to cover the entire spherical orbit of the system. I don't want one square meter of space that will allow entry into this system without hearing my warning."

"Yes, sir. Coordinates locked in and buoys ready to go" came from Lieutenant Korah.

It took ninety-five minutes to drop the six buoys at the proper coordinates. After dropping the buoys, the *Heaven* turned and headed away from the star system. As it streaked away, the spacefold drive was engaged, and the ship vanished in a flash of light.

Left behind were six buoys that repeat the same ominous warning over and over again: "To all those who approach this system, heed my warning. Beware the third planet. The inhabitants of this world kill their own kind for sport, out of anger or jealousy, and for material wealth. They are clever yet conniving. They are violent and unpredictable. For this, I can only offer my sincerest apologies. Captain Jehovah. USS *Heaven*. United Planetary Alliance. Out."

ABOUT THE AUTHOR

Russ Chevalier was born in Woonsocket, RI in 1963... Graduated from Lincoln High School in Lincoln, RI in 1981... Served in the US Army and the US Air Force in the early 1980's...Played in the band, Ego Trip, in the late 80's early 90's... Worked a variety of jobs, including factory work, truck driver, mover, private investigator and fire suppression equipment service tech... Married wife, Donna, in 1993... Daughter, Jasmine, born in 2000, while living in St. Petersburg, Fl... Diagnosed with ALS in 2012... Retired in 2014... Continuing to write next novel and write and record third album.

www.ingramcontent.com/pod-product-compliance
Lightning Source LLC
Chambersburg PA
CBHW040526170726
48295CB00012B/356